BETRAY THE LIE

SYDNEY RYE MYSTERIES
BOOK 11

EMILY KIMELMAN

Heading illustration: Autumn Whitehurst
Cover Design: Christian Bentulan
Formatting: Jamie Davis

I am a red man. If the Great Spirit had desired me to be a white man He would have made me so in the first place. He put in your heart certain wishes and plans. In my heart he put other and different desires. Each man is good in His sight. It is not necessary for eagles to be crows.
-Sitting Bull

Betrayal does so many different things to people.
-Trai Byers

CHAPTER ONE

Sydney

I PRESS OUT AND AWAY, the rollerblades zipping under me.

The Atlantic Ocean glitters to my left, aqua blue and shimmering gold. This winding concrete path in Miami Beach is the perfect place to rollerblade. *The most perfect.*

Music pounds in my headphones, the beat driving me faster.

My dog, Blue, and two of his puppies, Nila and Frank, run beside me. Blue to my left, the younger dogs to my right. They are all on loose leashes, their strides long and steady.

I used to jog—loved it. But when in Rome...rollerblade.

My trainer, Merl, showed up with a pair of the ridiculous footwear a few months ago, and I laughed, which I hadn't been doing much. "Funny enough," I told him. "This is kind of my worst nightmare."

He waggled his eyebrows and grinned his gap-toothed smile. "What? You're too cool to rollerblade?"

"I had hoped so."

"Just try them. You're going to love it."

And, as so often happened, Merl was right. I love rollerblading. So, I added it to the list of changes.

Old me: Named Joy Humbolt, foul-mouthed, quasi-alcoholic, pot-smoking dog walker.

Newer me: Named Sydney Rye, foul-mouthed, quasi-alcoholic, hash-smoking vigilante.

Newest me: Hallucinating, blacking out, foul-mouthed, teetotaling, non-smoking rollerblader.

Life is weird... and kind of wonderful.

EK

"CARRYING A GIRL/ Across the river;/ The hazy moon." Robert glances up from the book of Haiku verse. "That's like us."

"Is it?" I ask with a smile.

Blue shifts on the couch next to me, pressing more weight against my side. Nila and Frank lay together, their limbs intertwined, on the marble floor.

The open sliding glass doors let in a gentle, humid breeze, scented with salty ocean. Waves slap softly against the bulwark, their constant, ever-changing rhythm the only music.

Robert is half in shadow, his green glass shaded reading lamp throwing a pale yellow circle across his lap and chest. A small, leather-bound book lays open in one of his long-fingered, elegant hands.

The last wisps of the sunset, just the palest, most powdery blues and darkest hues of purple, light up the sky and filter through the wall of glass, casting shadows around the living room.

Robert's phone, lying on the end table next to him, vibrates, sending a low hum through the quiet, peaceful room. He glances at the screen and then answers it.

"Yes, Brock." Brock is his head of home security, a thick, muscled, ex-military man responsible for the safety and impenetrability of this mansion on Star Island—a refuge for the extremely wealthy in Biscayne Bay, just east of downtown Miami. "I see."

Robert's gaze meets mine, his blue-green eyes narrowing. The fine lines around them deepen as he listens. In his fifties, with dark hair silvering at the temples, Robert is an imposing presence. It's not just that he's over six feet tall and well-muscled. Or that he moves with the elegance and speed of a killer, either. There is an aura of power that surrounds Robert Maxim—wafts from him—and demands to be acknowledged.

He closes the book of poems and places it on his side table next to a cut crystal glass of sparkling water.

Blue, Nila, and Frank lift their heads, collars jangling. The puppies look to their father for direction. Eight months old, with gigantic paws, soft features, and keen instincts, they are almost as tall as Blue.

A mutt I adopted back when I lived in New York—a lifetime ago— Blue is the height of a Great Dane with the long, elegant snout of a collie, the thick coat of a wolf, and the markings of a Siberian husky, with one blue eye and one brown. Blue is trained to protect and his offspring are learning… Nila better than Frank.

Frank is a dumb dog—which I love about him. The guy is almost too sweet for the job. Whenever Merl, a dog expert, tries to get him to attack, Frank turns it into a game. Nila, on the other hand, is ruthless, smart, and quick.

She takes after her mother, an all-white Kangal mastiff who is fierce, loyal, and dangerous. Nila's eyes are an intense ice blue and Frank has his father's mismatched eyes, and his markings. With gigantic paws that make him clumsy at times, Frank is likely to be even bigger than Blue… so huge.

The puppies' mother is back in Syria. My mind wanders there for a moment, returning to the cave where I almost died. To the woman who saved my life…the scent of smoke fills my nostrils and Rida's smiling face appears before me. *Almond-shaped, dark brown eyes lit with intelligence and the fever of revolution; a narrow, scarred chin; and her smile: grief and hope tangled across one curled lip.*

Robert hangs up the phone, and Blue leaps off the couch, pulling me back into the room, back to the present. The puppies scramble to their feet, facing the door.

Robert stands, slipping the phone into his pocket, and crosses to me. He reaches out a hand—the shirt-sleeve rolled up, exposing a strong forearm dusted in dark hair. "Time to go," he says. I twine my fingers with his, and Robert pulls me from the couch, holding me tight as we begin to move.

A heavy fist pounds on the front door, echoing through the large house. My soft-soled sneakers are almost silent on the marble as we begin to jog. The dogs' nails click along with us.

"Homeland Security. Open up!" A man yells, his voice muffled by the large house. Robert presses a button, and a bookshelf slides away, revealing a doorway.

The loud crash of a battering ram striking the front door echoes as Maxim punches a code into the keypad next to the elevator. My heartbeat remains even. *I am not afraid.*

EK

Declan

FIVE YEARS. I've been waiting five years for this moment. And now here I am, standing behind my men, controlling them with the microphone at my mouth. Sydney Rye, aka Joy Humbolt, will not escape. I've got the warrant. I've got the manpower. We are on US territory.

I will defeat her.

The pounding of Fermont's fist against the tall wooden door echoes inside Robert Maxim's Star Island mansion. From the road, all you can see are white walls fronted with lush tropical gardens, but on the ocean side it's all glass.

The guy lives quite the life.

He offered me a job, years ago—tried to lure me away from the New York police force right as I made Detective. I thought I'd go. Figured I'd make a killing.

But then...Joy Humbolt. She upended my life. Instead of being the easy, fast, fun fuck I wanted her to be, she turned out to be a goddamn assassin. She humiliated me....made me into a fool.

After murdering her brother's killer in New York, she went on the run, but her act of vengeance—those few bullets sunk into a man's chest —spawned a movement. Joyful Justice, a vigilante network that started

4

as an online forum, soon mutated into an international fighting force causing havoc around the world. *Taking justice into their own hands and making headlines doing it.*

Robert Maxim protected her all these years. *Fuck that.* I'm bringing them both down, then I'll destroy the rest of Joyful Justice, one member at a time. But I need to stay calm now, in this moment of victory.

No one answers the door, so I call for the battering ram. The team moves in seamless formation. The ram appears, and the men swing it back and smash into the mahogany doors. Once...twice...on the third time, the big frame lets go and the door swings in. My men pour forth: black, armored warriors here to win the day.

I follow in their wake, my weapon up, the weight of my body armor making me sweat in the warm night.

I doubt Robert will try to fight his way out of the house. He's too slick for that.

It took me five judges to find one who would write the warrant, but I found one. *I always win.*

EK

Sydney

The doors to the hidden elevator open just as a voice behind us yells, "Freeze. Now!" Glancing back, I see three men in the living room, their weapons raised, the matte black of their helmets absorbing the last rays of the sunset.

With the elevator doors open, on the precipice of escape, Robert and I freeze, our bodies stilling. *The calm before the storm.*

Blue growls, and Frank gives off a deep bark of excitement. Nila presses against my leg, waiting for a command.

"Turn around slowly," the man orders.

Robert releases my hand, and we both turn to face the armed intruders, joined now by two more. Their radios crackle. Bodies hunched around their weapons, the heavy armor under their uniforms putting a sheen on their skin, they keep their rifles aimed at our chests.

A strong gust of wind puffs through the open glass doors, bringing the briny scent of the sea. I take a deep breath. *I love that smell.*

My hands are up—Robert's, too. But we are not surrendering. That's not what Robert and I do.

Declan Doyle pauses at the top of the four steps leading down into the living room. His brown eyes land on mine. A smile, predatory and satisfied, leaps into his gaze—the look of a wolf who's crept into the center of a flock of sheep. Declan thinks he's about to feast.

Poor Declan Doyle—so wrong, so often.

A hint of sympathy curls in my stomach, considering what it must be like to pursue someone so desperately, to believe in one moment you've captured them, only to lose them again in the next.

Parting is such sweet sorrow...for one of us anyway.

"Sydney," Declan says.

I nod. "Declan, how are you?"

He starts down the steps. "Better than you."

"Perhaps, but I have been well recently. How has your recovery been?"

His face darkens, and his hand brushes against his side where I shot him. "I'm fine."

"Hello, Declan," Robert says. "Making more terrible career choices, I see."

Declan glances at Robert for only a moment before returning his attention to me. "I wouldn't take career advice from him," Declan says to me. "Could land you in jail." He grins. "Oh right, you're going there anyway."

Robert huffs a laugh but does not speak.

Declan frowns, and then, looking down at Blue, a smile crosses his face. "It's a shame," he says. "If those dogs don't come easy, they will be put down."

"Declan," I say. "Do you really need to threaten my dogs? Aren't you bigger than that?"

"Besides," Robert says, shrugging. "I've never seen threatening Blue go well. For anyone. Ever."

Declan looks over at Robert. "Well, Robert Maxim, things are changing."

Robert smiles, slow and scary, like he knows so much more than anyone else in the room…hell, anyone else in the world. "The more things change, the more they stay the same." Robert says it quietly, almost humbly…minus the glee in his gaze.

"Not this time, Robert," Declan says, his own smug smile pulling at his lips.

A sigh escapes me as the two men's egos clash. *The ego is to be transcended, not bargained with or defeated.*

Declan turns on his heel. "Cuff and ready them for transport," he says to one of his men as he heads back out to the hall.

Sympathy wells in me for one more moment as I watch his broad back leave the room. *He won't even be here to witness his defeat.*

EK

Declan

"We got them sir, we got them both," I say to my superior over the secure sat phone, not even trying to keep the shit-eating grin off my face.

"You've taken Robert Maxim into custody?"

"That's right."

"Are you insane?" His voice is low, quiet…deadly.

"I've got a warrant."

"You've got a problem. Or maybe it's a death wish."

Gunshots echo in the living room. *Fuck.* I rip open the door. Sydney Rye stands in the center of the room, her back pressed against Robert Maxim's, her three dogs calm and close. Robert and Sydney have pistols, and, helpless, frozen like a goddamn statue, I watch as Sydney shoots the only man left standing in the room—Officer Taylor Winston, father of two, highly decorated soldier, my personal pick to lead this raid. *I got him killed.*

Sydney's gray gaze lands on me, her pistol tracking with it.

I jump back and to the side, hiding behind the second door, pulling my weapon.

My phone is on the floor, the line still open. But my superior isn't talking. *He knows what's happening.*

Gun up, I step to the doorway and glance in quickly. Robert and Sydney are gone. Cautiously, I move into the large space. The secret door we found them trying to escape through is still open. I approach with caution, stepping over the bodies of my fallen men. *Sydney will pay for this.*

My heart hammers and sweat slicks my palms, but I'm steady. Ready for whatever lies beyond that door. *I can't let them get away.*

The rev of an engine outside spins me around. Through the glass window I see a speedboat flying away from the shore, its white, frothy wake glittering in the moonlight.

Running through the open doors out onto the patio, I can just make out two human figures…and three dogs.

Shit.

Moaning draws my attention back into the room, to the men on the floor. What the hell? I step back into the house, one of the sheer curtains billowing around me and clinging to my shirt. I push it away, my gaze scanning the men. *There is no blood.*

Winston rolls onto his side and begins to retch. I cross to him, dropping to my knees, and help to hold him up. There is a spent projectile syringe on the floor. My gaze rakes the room. The rest of the men are stirring.

They're not dead. They were drugged.

Relief swells in my chest, and tears prick at my eyes, but I quench my emotions quickly.

This is still a shitshow, and I'm going to have to answer for it. Using the radio on my shoulder, I call for medical help. The medics are on standby and rush into the room moments later. I leave my men in their expert care and retrieve my phone from the hallway.

With numb fingers, I call my superior back. "You are relieved of your command. Return to Washington for a debriefing. Now," he barks then hangs up. I close my eyes and lean against the wall, anger and shame creating a dangerous cocktail in my gut. My hands fist, and I can't help but turn quickly and jab the wall hard enough that I dent the drywall. *Fuck.*

Forcing myself to take deep breaths, I walk out of the house, down the front steps, and through the garden, back out to the road where vehicles, their lights spinning, throw red, blue, and white around the quiet street. Two paramedics bring Winston out on a stretcher. "How is he?" I ask as they load him into one of the waiting ambulances.

"We won't know until we find out what he's been shot with, but vital signs are normalizing."

"He's going to be okay?"

"I'm right here, boss," Winston says, the ghost of a smile on his face.

My lips purse, and I nod but can't bring myself to say more. *I won't apologize. And I won't give up.* Sydney Rye and Robert Maxim will pay.

CHAPTER TWO

Dan

I SHOULD GO TO BED. But I don't. Instead, I switch screens, giving in to my obsession. *What you don't know can't hurt you.* What a lie. It's the things we don't see coming that get us. *We must remain vigilant.*

A knock at my door pulls my attention from the screen. George, one of my best coders, stands on the other side of the tinted glass holding a cup of coffee. *Is it morning already?*

"Come in," I say, running a hand through my hair. It's getting long, almost to my shoulders.

"Morning, Boss," George says as he enters. I nod. "Ready to go?"

He's talking about paddleboarding. *I don't want to.* But I stand up and stretch. "Sure." I give him a smile—one of my *I'm relaxed and easygoing* smiles. The kind I've perfected.

Taking the coffee, I sip it as we head down the spiral stairs leading to the main floor of the command center. Consoles with individual monitors all face a wall of screens where surveillance video, maps, and other information display. There are three teams working—all reconnaissance missions. *Nothing out of the ordinary.*

I nod to my teams as we pass, and they all nod back.

In the elevator, George asks me about a computer script he's working on. I answer in a haze, my mind still back on my screen. *Watching her.*

"I've got to run up to my room and change real fast," I tell him.

"Sure, sure. I'll meet you at the beach."

Back in my suite of rooms, I take off the jeans, worn at the knees, and T-shirt I've been wearing for...I'm not sure how long. I throw on some board shorts and a rash guard, slipping back into my flip-flops. Pulling my hair into a bun at the back of my head, I tuck it under a billed cap.

My eyes are becoming more sensitive to the light. *I'm getting older.*

What would my mother think if she saw me now? I owe her a phone call, another set of lies. She thinks I'm living in Thailand, working for a start-up. She's proud of me. I have her phone tapped, so I know she brags to her friends. But I also listen in on her Alexa so I know that she is lonely—talking to the cats and crying softly some nights. *The sound breaks my fucking heart.*

I should visit her.

But it's dangerous for both of us.

My flip-flops slap against the bottom of my feet, echoing in the empty hallway as I head back to the elevator. A door clicks open in front of me, and Tom, Anita's husband, steps out. Spotting me, Tom gives me a smile. "Morning," he says, his voice scratchy, like I'm the first person he's spoken to today.

Anita sleeps in now. She used to be up at dawn, pacing, worrying, *hurting.* I give Tom a smile—he deserves it; he makes Anita smile. *He's the reason she sleeps.*

"Going for a paddle?" he asks.

"Yup, want to join me?"

He shakes his head, brown curls flopping. "Thanks, though."

We walk toward the elevators together. Tom and I are almost the same height but very different men. *He doesn't like my relationship with Anita.* He'd never admit it, but I know he's jealous I was there for her, that *I'm* the one she turned to after being attacked. She didn't even call him, never reached out. Tom had to chase her down. *Anita is worth every effort.*

At least he doesn't try to make small talk.

"Which floor?" I ask as we get on the elevator.

"Headed to the cafeteria," he answers. It's on the second floor. The structure we live and work in is housed inside an inactive volcano. Originally built by a paranoid billionaire—he planned to weather Armageddon on this isolated island in the Pacific when *shit hit the fan* but died before he got the chance.

The command center for Joyful Justice—the vigilante network I helped found—is five floors underground with housing for more than 100 workers above. We have a state-of-the-art fitness center, a cafeteria, medical facilities, and a shopping center where people can buy groceries, clothing, and other supplies.

The staff includes computer experts like me, strategists like Anita, and tactical experts. Tom is an odd man out; he used to be an international human rights attorney but followed Anita here after they reunited in London. I refuse to let him take on any responsibilities since he's not an official member of Joyful Justice. There is too much at risk. My research into his background and connections remains ongoing.

So, for now, Tom reads books on the beach, works out, and brings Anita coffee.

The lights in the elevator flicker. *That's strange.* It jerks to a stop, throwing Tom and I off balance. We look at each other, his forest green gaze meeting mine for just a moment. *He is hiding something.* The lights go out, leaving us in total darkness. "What's going on?" Tom asks.

This should be impossible. We produce our own solar and wind power. Our batteries have enough stored electricity to last days. Could it be a fire? But there are no alarms.

"Dan?" Tom's voice has an edge to it, as if he's frightened. I pull out my phone and activate the flashlight app. "What's going on?"

My phone can't pick up the Wi-Fi.

That's when my heart begins to thud in my ears. I cast my light onto the ceiling, illuminating the hatch. *Stay calm.*

First, I pull the stop on the elevator. If the power comes back on, I want us to be stable.

Then I turn to Tom. "Give me a leg up," I say.

Tom nods, bending over and cupping his hands. I slip off my flip-flops and, gripping my phone between my teeth, push off him to raise myself high enough to open the door in the ceiling. The scent of dust and oil pours over me as I grip the edge and haul myself onto the roof of the elevator.

The emergency lights, orange and spaced at each floor, illuminate the dark walls and grease-smeared elevator structure. The doors, painted gray-blue that open to the 6th level, are half hidden by the elevator. But the restrictor release is exposed, meaning we can open them.

There are footsteps running on the other side. A shout, the words muffled.

"Hey!" I yell but get no response. A distant rumble and everything shakes. Dust rains down around me, itching my eyes and tickling my nose.

"What's going on?" Tom yells, his voice high.

"We need to get out of here." I turn back to the hatch, lower to my knees, and reach down. Tom grabs my forearm and jumps, his free hand grasping the edge of the opening. I haul him up onto the elevator roof with me.

Another impact and more dust sprinkles down around us—floating gently in my flashlight beam.

We wait for it to pass, and then without needing to communicate, approach the doors leading to the 6th floor.

When the elevator is within its landing zone, the hoist-way door-release roller contacts the restrictor vane, opening the door. Depressing the restrictor vane by hand will also release the outer doors and get us out of here. Of course, if the power goes back on, it will send a lot of electricity through anyone touching it—possibly enough to kill.

"Press that," I say to Tom, pointing at the release with the flashlight on my phone. He reaches for it—totally trusting. A twinge of guilt turns my stomach, but I let him do it. *I am responsible for the people on this island. I can't die right now.*

Tom presses on the release, and the doors slide open. The floor is a few feet below us. Emergency lights in the hallway catch thin swirls of smoke. The scent joins the musty air in the elevator shaft. I leap down into the hall and Tom follows.

Suddenly, the piercing wail of an alarm sounds, echoing in the empty chamber. But it's not the fire alarm. *We are under attack.*

EK

Lenox

SHE STANDS in the lamp light, her black dress shimmering in the yellow glow. Petra reaches up to remove an earring—a sparkling five-carat sapphire surrounded by a crown of diamonds. I know the designer. Introduced Petra to him in Prague years ago. She thanked me with kisses and moans and cash.

Now I sit in the leather armchair in the corner of her room, my legs spread, one hand wrapped around a snifter full of cognac. The caramel burn of it layers my tongue, the perfect accompaniment to watching Petra place the heavy adornment onto her dressing table. Her nails, painted blood red, stand out against her pale skin. She's lost weight since I last saw her.

The stress of another failed marriage.

Her thin fingers toy with the second earring, taking longer to remove it, her bright green gaze finding mine. She gives me a sultry smile, the red of her lipstick smeared from when I kissed her in the car. She loves that— being wanted so badly I can't wait to get her somewhere private, but then taking my time—my sweet, expensive time—once I do.

The fine lines around her mouth only make Petra more beautiful. She's had work done, like almost all my clients, but has retained some of her natural aging. I like that. A woman who knows how to face time, who isn't afraid to let her years show in subtle, elegant ways.

"I enjoy the way you watch me," she says, her Czech accent still thick even after all her years of speaking English.

I nod but do not smile. "Take off your shoes," I say. They are black patent leather heels, and while they give shape to her calves, I want her natural, bare to me. *Just Petra.*

The smile fades from her lips, and an almost distraught hunger enters her gaze. Here is a woman who has so much control, so much power, and to be in someone else's—in the power of a trusted employee and friend—that is pure erotic pleasure for her. *It allows her release.* Petra pays me to pretend she is weak.

She slips out of the high heels, stepping her stocking-clad feet onto the thick carpeting of her bedroom. The space is masculine: dark wood and brown leather, an oriental rug in golds and greens. The bed, a four-poster that would be comfortable in a medieval Scottish castle, is covered in black sheets and a silver wolf fur blanket.

Petra could probably kill a wolf. With her background, she probably has.

"Can you reach your zipper?" I ask.

Petra shakes her head, pupils dilating. *Is that a lie?* Petra lives alone these days. Who pulled up her zipper? One of her security men, a maid? Pity swells in my chest for just a moment as I imagine Petra's life, where such an intimate act must be performed by a paid attendant.

"Come," I say. She shivers, a smile pulling at those smeared lips again. She crosses the room to me, her hips swaying, the gold bracelet on her wrist catching the low light and shining.

"Turn around." She does as I say. Leaning forward, I reach for her zipper. Petra is barely over five feet tall, so I can grip the hold between my thumb and forefinger without getting up. She stands perfectly still as I slowly drag it down, each tooth releasing in a satisfying click.

Loose now, the black silk garment slips off her shoulders, and she is left standing in front of me wearing only her bra, panties, garter, and stockings.

I sip my cognac and sit back, just watching her. Watching the goose bumps break out on her skin. I'll take my time. That's what she pays me for—slow, strong seduction.

HOURS LATER, Petra sleeps, her breathing even, her mascara smudged under her long lashes. I watch her, the light of the moon sneaking in through the sheer curtains, gracing her petite curves, turning her into a statue—a cold symbol instead of a living woman.

One of my first clients, Petra showed me this larger world. This world where I could be more than just a bumpster—more than just a whore. *A master.*

Growing up, I had two career choices: become a thief like my father or a prostitute like my mother. I chose my mother's path, preferring to provide value rather than steal it. I've always wanted to make the world fair. To make all the sums come out.

My mother taught me math, reading...she borrowed books from the library at the resorts where she plied her trade to teach me. European tourists found her irresistible, and they felt the same about me once I reached a certain age. But my mother protected me, wouldn't let me work as a bumpster—the term used by tourists to describe the young African men they bought—until I turned fifteen. "I give you everything you need," she told me. "You can wait to sell the body I made until I'm ready for you to do it."

I loved my mother. Respected her. And almost always did as she asked.

Sadness sweeps over me as her face fills my mind's eye—the same honey brown eyes as mine, same dark skin, same smile. The way she died wasn't right. It wasn't fair.

But the world isn't. That's what my father always said...when he was around. He came by a couple of times a year. My mother always let him in, and she always kicked him out again. When his drinking ramped up, and the beatings became so frequent she could barely work, my mother would make him leave; she didn't let him kill her. Her murderer was a stranger. A trick. A john.

Her body washed up on the beach, her clothing ripped, neck broken, eyes gone...eaten by some creature of the sea or sky.

She left our apartment that night like every other, gave me a kiss as always, her perfume lingering long after the sound of her heels on the steps had faded. But her memory will never fade. My love for her will never dissipate. No creature, no man or woman, can take her away from me. Not really. Not in the ways that matter.

She raised me to be me. To be Lenox Gold. She raised me so that now I can fight to make the world fair.

I brush a kiss on Petra's cheek, and she smiles in her sleep. Climbing out of the bed, I pull on my boxer briefs. Leaving the room, I jog down the wide, sweeping staircase to the office off the den. Petra is my oldest client, a close friend. But her business interests are seeping into my world. Into the world of Joyful Justice.

And now, the scales must be balanced.

CHAPTER THREE

Dan

IT HAS to be an inside job. There is no way law enforcement could get here without me knowing. *Impossible.*

I turn to Tom. He's pale, his eyes wide and lips tight. I move quickly, fisting his thin T-shirt and slamming him up against the wall. "What did you do?" I demand, my voice a low rumble.

"Me?" he stammers. "I, what? I'm..."

I lean my face closer to his. "You're the new element."

"But...what? No."

His eyes are holding mine. *Confusion, innocence.* "I can't be the only new person here."

He's right. But I'm not going to tell him that. "You're coming with me," I say, pulling him off the wall and releasing his shirt. "Go, to the stairs." He starts to walk, his steps unsteady. "Run!" He breaks into a jog.

"I swear, Dan, I have nothing to do with this," he yells over the alarm.

"Shut up."

He does. The lights come back on as we push into the emergency stairwell. Tom turns to me. "Which way?"

"You go to Anita." He nods, relief washing over his face, and starts up the steps two at a time. He loves her. But would he betray her?

We so often betray the ones we love…often when we don't even mean to.

I wait for Tom to disappear then check my phone—the Wi-Fi is still out.

Shit. I dash back out through the door and to the left, where the emergency cabinet for this floor is located. When I arrive, there are already two members of the security team grabbing weapons.

"What's going on?" Tanya raises her voice to be heard over the still-wailing alarm as she straps a pistol to her hip. A former sex slave turned vigilante, Tanya has worked with Joyful Justice for years. I know I can trust her. I monitor all communication that comes and goes from the island. I am fastidious about checking people out before they arrive—I'm all up in their business, in their family. How could this happen?

Tom is the only person here I didn't invite. But I checked him out too…the alarm stops screaming. "Our security system has been breached," I answer. "But I won't know how until I get to my computer." I grip my phone, willing the Wi-Fi to return. "I'm going to head down to the command center. There is a battery room at the end of this hall. I think that's where the smoke is coming from." The smoke is thin and tinted with the scent of hot plastic. "Check it out, please."

She nods, pulling a radio from the utility closet and handing it to me. I test it and hear the harsh crackle of communication. "Thanks, let me know what you find."

"Good luck," she says, her voice heavy with a lifetime of bad breaks. *She expects the worst.*

"You, too." I turn and run back toward the stairs. Tanya and her team will secure this floor. There are teams assigned to every section of the compound. *We are not vulnerable.*

My steps echo in the concrete stairwell, and I'm huffing for breath by the time I get down to the command center. I put my ten-digit code into the keypad and enter.

The scent of plastic and ozone envelops me in a comforting cloud. *I'm in my element.* Striding quickly into the main room, I scan the desks.

The computers are on; the large screen is showing surveillance footage from around the compound. A feed from the backup battery room on the sixth floor shows a cloud of smoke, but also figures moving through the gloom, wearing fire gear and working to extinguish the off-screen blaze.

My second in command, Mitchel, is standing at the back wall, talking quietly into his headset. A little shorter than me, with bright blue eyes and sun-streaked brown hair, Mitchel is a brilliant hacker whose reputation started when he was ten and broke into his school's system to cancel exams.

The three teams I left here thirty minutes ago are bent over their consoles, hard at work.

Mitchel looks up and meets my gaze, relief crossing his features as he starts to move in my direction. We paddleboard together most days, and he moves with the assured elegance of an athlete. "Get that contained," he's saying into his microphone, "and then check on servers in room seven. I'm seeing high temperatures there I do not like."

"Catch me up," I say, still walking, headed for the center of the room so I can see the entire screen and everyone working. Mitchel falls into step with me.

"Someone set off an explosive in Battery Room C. They put the cameras on a ten minute loop, but I've got Rachel working on it now." I nod. Rachel is good at uncovering what people try to hide. "We've also lost Wi-Fi to the compound."

"I noticed."

Mitchel nods, his mouth drawn down into a frown. "This is an attack."

"Yes, but what are they trying to do?" I ask, my gaze raking the main screen as I stop at the top of the center aisle. On screen, I can see the most sensitive areas of the compound—all our server rooms, the weapons caches, our generators and solar fields, the wind turbine, and the most important egress points. "This is minor. We'll recover quickly. They must be trying to distract us."

"I've got Melody on watch; she's scanning all our systems for a breach."

"Good." I turn back to him. "You did really well. I was stuck on an elevator."

A smile tugs at his lips. "Stuck on an elevator with no Wi-Fi. You must have gone almost insane."

I shrug, giving him a half smile. "I survived. But I'm worried, Mitchel. This is strange. Obviously an inside job." My gaze scans the room again, looking for answers and finding none. "There will have to be a full investigation. First, let's make sure everything is secure."

"Yes, sir." Mitchel follows me as I head to a console and pick up a headset. My voice travels to everyone in the command center. "Okay, folks. What's going on?"

Their answers start coming in as my eyes stay on the screen, monitoring the video feeds, temperature readings, and system alerts—taking in all data points. With enough data, we can figure this out. With enough data, we can change the world.

EK

Lenox

THE OFFICE WINDOWS open to the gardens, formal and rigid, with tightly cropped topiaries and white gravel that sparkles in the moonlight. Beyond the gardens the forest hunkers, a dark, shaggy wall against a star-draped sky.

Petra's desk, made of thick, glossy, marbled wood, is clean—not even hinting at the wildly passionate woman who does her work here. I sit in Petra's seat, the leather slippery and cold against my bare skin. Her perfume permeates the space, a blend of jasmine and rose with just a hint of sandalwood. Petra's scent, like her life, is feminine with a shadow of masculinity.

It's all sex.

I run my hand over the forest green blotter at the center of the desk, feeling indentations from her pen. My hand traces the invisible lines, and I close my eyes. It's just a jumble. Too many words written over each other. Most of it is in Czech, I figure—the language of Petra's homeland. Though it's been many decades since she lived there. This estate, a castle really, in the Romanian countryside has been her base for the last five years. The air is fresh, the water clean, and the government unconcerned with her activities or the source of her wealth.

Opening my eyes, I pull out the top drawer to my right and find checkbooks, packs of matches from a local restaurant in the village nearby where we had dinner tonight, pens, and stationery. I sort through the sparse contents finding nothing out of place. Nothing of interest.

The next drawer down is equally mundane—paperclips, a stapler, a silver letter opener with Petra's initials engraved into it, blank envelopes, and a calculator. The file drawer is locked. I can't force it with the letter opener so leave it to explore the other drawers before searching for the key.

The rest of the desk proves to be as boring as the first few drawers. I push back the chair and look under the desk, expecting to find the key for the file drawer secured there but am disappointed. Turning to the bookshelves, I scan them, hoping to discover a false volume in which a key might be stashed.

The books are leather bound with gold lettering—English, French, Russian and Czech dominate, but I see a few Spanish volumes as well. Petra and I spoke French and English to each other when we first met. My mother made sure I knew the languages of my clients. "Speak to a person in their language, and they will feel safe with you, trust you, and eventually even love you. Once they love you," she smiled, her eyes glittering, "they will give you whatever you want."

She was right about that and so many other things.

I trace my fingers over the volumes, pausing randomly to pull them forward, to test they are real. A mother of pearl box, its ghostly white surface gleaming in the darkness, catches my eye. It's small enough to fit in my palm and sits on top of several books, pushed to the back of the shelf. I reach in and take it out. It's heavy for its size, and when I open it I find a gold key, large and old-fashioned—something from a fairy tale—sitting on a cushion of velvet.

Removing the key from its plush nest, I weigh it in my palm. *What a pleasant object.* But far too large for the filing drawer.

A sound in the hall makes me pause. Footsteps are approaching. I quickly return the key and its box to their place. Taking down a French book of poetry, I head into the attached den where I settle into a chair by the window and turn on the reading light.

Petra enters the room as I flip through the pages. She's pulled on a black silk robe but not cleaned up her face. Mascara darkens under her eyes, and the remnants of her lipstick accentuate the puffiness of her lips. "What are you doing?" she asks, her voice gravelly.

I hold up the book. "Reading." Her eyes narrow with suspicion and then scan my chest, taking in my near nudity. "Sorry if you missed me." Her lips part as her gaze reaches my crotch. "Come," I say, laying the book aside and waving her to me. She follows my command, dropping to her knees in front of me.

I cup her cheek and lean forward to kiss her. She moans, one petite hand running up my arms and circling my neck. I pull her onto my lap, cradling her as I devour her mouth.

Petra twists quickly, and her lips leave mine as a cold blade presses up against my inner thigh. "What were you doing down here, Lenox?" she asks again, her voice clear now, eyes burning into mine, as the knife in her fist moves slowly closer to my manhood.

Adrenaline floods my veins as I stare at her. *A minx in rabbit fur.*

"Reading," I say again, my voice low, my hands gripping her waist. I could push her off me, but I'd risk getting cut.

"Liar," she says, the blade pressing closer.

"I should have tied you up," I say, dropping my voice down to a dangerous purr. Petra bares her teeth. Her robe has fallen open, and I lean down slowly to kiss her collarbone. She shivers under me, the press of the blade softening. I pull the tie of her robe free as I lave her neck, and then slowly cover her hand with mine, pulling her wrist forward and the knife away from my flesh.

She lets me, giving no resistance now, opening to me like a flower blooms for the sun. My fingers sink into the silky tresses at the base of her neck, and I take full control. *She is mine now.*

The knife drops almost silently to the carpeting, and I shift her so that she straddles me, her robe spread, her legs around my waist. The hand that held her knife now reaches for me, loosening me from my boxers and guiding toward her center.

But I stop her, my large palm engulfing her. "Not yet," I say. "I want you to beg."

She whimpers against my lips, her body quivering. Petra needs so much, has so much, and yet can't ever get enough. A curse or a gift, hard to say, this insatiable devotion to moving forward, going faster, getting what she wants.

"Please." Her voice comes out a soft whisper, and I smile under her. Petra's hair falls around us, tickling against my bare skin, sending shivers of desire racing through me.

I enjoy the sweet sensation of delay. The moments when a train is hovering at the entrance to a station, the rev of a plane's engines before it takes flight, the scent of a woman before she releases around me.

My lips grace hers, softly, barely...then her chin, the small point of it...her jaw—elegant, sharp, delicious. Petra's head falls back, tendrils of hair reaching my hand where it grips her lower back, curling around to hold her ass. To stop her from moving how she wants. To maintain my control.

My lips find her collarbone again, nipping at its length. I push her back, bending her so that her breasts face the ceiling, her head in my one hand, ass in the other, laid out in front of me—any straight man's fantasy, and my profession.

The lamplight glows against her skin, gets lost in the darkness of her nipples. "Please," she says, again, louder, her body quivering with desire, with unmet passion.

"Say my name," I command, my voice rough against her nipple. I pull it between my teeth, and she cries out in that sweet tone of pain and pleasure.

"Lenox. Please, Lenox, fuck me." Petra's voice has gone all throaty, all desperate. But I know she can beg more. She can threaten and cajole. I won't take her until she is a bundle of need, a desperate creature ready to tear me apart.

My foot brushes against the knife, and it sends a thrill up my leg right to my crotch. A hushed moan escapes me at its cool touch, at the danger this woman in my arms presents. God, her power is sexy.

"Dammit, Lenox!" Now she's getting mad. I love making her angry. "Fuck me, or you're fired."

I bite harder, hurting her now, so that she almost struggles to get away, but I grip her harder through the silk robe, digging my fingers in as a warning and a promise. *I will take you the way you want. The way you need.*

"Now!" she screams, the banshee released, the desperation undoing her so she wriggles and fights to close the distance.

"Now?" I ask, letting my tongue grace her skin as I speak.

She makes a strangled sound, can't even form words anymore. And that is my moment. That is the final push of the jet, the rumble of the steam engine, the moment I love. Slowly I pull her onto me.

She's starving and melting, and I bury my face in her chest. Petra arches over me, wrapping her arms around my neck, her mouth finding my earlobe and pulling it between her teeth.

"Yes, Lenox. Oh, yes," she purrs.

I keep one toe on the blade of the knife, reminding me of the danger that rides me, that begs for me, that needs me...and that, perhaps, I need in return.

CHAPTER FOUR

Sydney

ROBERT SPEAKS QUIETLY into the phone, but I can still hear him. We are moored off Key Biscayne; he's lounging in the captain's chair while I sit on the back bench of the speed boat. It's a beautiful antique—glossy wood and white leather. Her name is MY WAY.

And right now, that's what Robert Maxim is getting: *his way.*

He's actually berating someone about the raid—someone who has much more power than Declan Doyle. Maybe a politician or a director at Homeland Security. For all I know, he's on the phone with the head of the CIA.

It doesn't matter.

He's going to fix this. We'll be home before dawn, and the place will be spotless. As if none of it ever happened.

Home.

When did Miami begin to feel this way? When I began to take getting better seriously? When I took my care into my own hands. Three months ago...

"I'M NOT WORKING with Dale anymore," I yell at Robert as I storm into his office, Blue by my side.

Robert looks up at me, his gaze flat. "He's the best."

"He's a creep." I'm standing right in front of Robert's big, glass-topped desk now, lightning sizzling in the corner of my vision, thunder pounding in my ears.

A smile pulls at Robert's lips as he sits back into his chair. His hands come to the armrests, and he looks down at his lap. "How do you know?"

"Puh-leez." I drop into one of the two chairs that face Robert's desk, and Blue settles by my side, resting his chin on my knee. This room is all modern furniture--crisp lines, cold metal, hard glass, and pale earth tones. *Has his decorator ever heard of a freaking accent pillow?* "A creep that big I can spot a mile away. Guy is creepy."

Robert's smile grows larger. "I suppose you're right," he nods. "So, how would you like to continue your treatment?"

"Dale made really clear what's wrong with my brain but didn't have any good ideas how to fix it." I tick off on my hand. "Hallucinations, blackouts, depression...I've been Googling..." Humor lights Robert's blue-green gaze, and I narrow my eyes. "Don't laugh," I warn.

"At you, Sydney? Never."

"Hmmph...well...what do you know about Ketamine?" I chew on my lower lip, surprised by how much I care about Robert's opinion.

His brows raise, and he steeples his finger like the evil villain he plays on the international stage. "It's an anesthetic—used on the battle-field, on children and the elderly—as well as other patients with compromised respiratory systems—because it does not affect breathing."

"Yeah...it was also a party drug." I shrug.

"You want to rave your problems away?" He smiles, teasing me. But we both know my problems are no joke.

I shake my head and reach out for Blue, petting one of his velvety ears. He sighs in appreciation. "I read that it has some amazing results for people with mood disorders and other issues...including suicidal thoughts." I force myself to meet Robert's gaze. He's sitting very still, the sun streaming in the windows behind him catching the silver at his temples and making it sparkle. "Apparently, it regrows...your...brain."

Robert frowns.

"I don't really understand the science." I watched a few YouTube videos and read some interviews with people who'd gone through the infusion process, but I didn't really *get* it. But I don't know how the internet works either, and that doesn't stop me from surfing it. "The point is, I want to try it."

"Okay, do you have a doctor in mind?"

"His name is Dr. Munkin. He has a clinic downtown."

Robert leans forward and pulls his silver laptop in front of him, opens the sleek computer, and begins to type. "I'll have him checked out."

"Thanks." I get up to leave. "Sydney," Robert says, stopping me. "There is something else we need to discuss."

I turn back to him. He looks up from the computer. "I spoke with Dan this afternoon." I nod, my throat tight with anxiety. *What now?* "He is concerned that Homeland Security is closing in on us. Declan Doyle is making himself a nuisance. You know he's been assigned to your mother's case."

I don't want to talk about that. Lightning sizzles across my vision, and I close my eyes, willing it away; but the bright beam of electricity dances behind my closed lids and thunder crashes so loudly I feel its vibrations.

"Dan wants us to leave Miami," Robert continues, his deep voice pulling me out of my hallucination. "I told him it's not an issue. My contacts have assured me I'm safe. And you are under my protection."

"Okay..."

"I thought you had a right to know his thoughts, though."

"He couldn't tell me himself?" I ask, cocking a hip, the familiar spark of anger giving me strength.

Robert sits back in his chair, steepling his fingers again. "He said he tried calling you, but you didn't pick up."

I nod, looking down at Blue, my righteous indignation fading in the stark light of the truth. *I am willfully ignorant.* "Yeah, right."

"Why didn't you answer his call?"

"I can't deal with anything right now, Robert," I answer, my voice low, my gaze still on Blue.

"That's fine. I'm happy to care for you. But please, don't act like I'm trying to keep things from you." I raise my eyes to Robert. *He has a point.* I try to apologize, but the words just won't come. Instead, I straighten my spine and glare at him, trying to kindle that sweet rage keeping me alive. Robert smiles. "Confrontational even at the very edge of madness." He shakes his head, an amused smile playing over his mouth.

"Let me know what you find out about Dr. Munkin," I say.

He grins. "Yes, ma'am."

EK

DR. MUNKIN IS in his mid-seventies, wearing thick glasses, a salmon-colored button down shirt and khakis. He's pale, unlike the majority of Miamians, and gives me a warm smile as he walks into the room.

"Hello, Ms. Rye, how are you feeling today?" I force a smile onto my face, but that just makes him frown, his eyes softening with concern. Dr. Munkin sits on a wheeled stool and scoots over to where I wait on a lounge chair. There is a TV in the room, an IV stand, and soft music whispers from unseen speakers. "Tell me what's going on."

I take a deep breath and let it out slowly, reaching for Blue, who inches closer, pressing his entire weight against my thigh, grounding me. "Well…this is all confidential, right?"

He nods, looking grave. I get the sense this guy takes his Hippocratic Oath seriously. The clinic is open 24 hours a day, seven days a week. *They save lives here.* Save people from the demons inside their heads.

"I guess I should start at the beginning."

"We have plenty of time."

I stifle a laugh and he nods, his brows pulled into a furrow of concern, encouraging me to "let it out" with his gaze.

"It all started about five years ago, when my brother was murdered."

"I'm sorry to hear that." He does sound sorry but not shocked—he is used to traumatized people.

"So…" I look down at Blue; he's staring up at me with his

mismatched eyes. "I tried to kill his murderer." I don't look up, but I hear a sharp intake of breath. "The police weren't going to do anything about it. The guy was very powerful, and I just couldn't have him walking around, living his life, when my brother was gone. So, I *tried* to kill him, but I was too late--the guy had enemies far fiercer than me, and when I got to him, he was already dead. But, those fiercer enemies, they were also smarter than me." I look up for a moment and find the doctor's eyes wide, his mouth formed into a small o. "So they framed me. And I fled the country."

The doctor nods, letting me know he's with me, even though he looks a little like he just saw a pigeon get hit by a bus—something shocking and gruesome but not related to him.

I take in another deep breath and sink my hand into Blue's ruff, massaging him. "I started working as a private investigator after that— so fast forward a few years, and I'm working a case in Miami—my brother's ex-fiancé actually. Ex...is that the right term?" Hugh's face crosses my mind—his wide smile and bowl haircut. The way his eyes light up when he talks about cooking. The way he made my brother laugh so hard James would bend over and slap his knee, his face going red and tears leaking from his eyes. A bolt of lightning sizzles, and I blink against the bright ray. Of course, that doesn't help—the lightning in my mind cannot be escaped.

I shake my head, trying to clear it. The doctor waits patiently. "My brother's ex...Hugh, he was accused of murder, so I came here to clear his name and ended up getting doused with a highly potent strain of Datura." The doctor nods, he knows the stuff—The Devil's Breath is a powerful hallucinogen that leaves its victims trapped in a nightmare while their bodies become totally pliant. It's mostly used to rob people. While under a Datura spell, victims will empty their bank accounts, lead their burglars to all their prized possessions...they will do anything anyone asks. "I was lost in the Everglades for several days during a big storm." I bring my hand up and swirl it near my head. "And the lightning and thunder kinda stuck with me." I try another smile and get that same sad frown in return. *He won't pretend it's funny with me.*

"How long were you in the Datura haze?" he asks.

"A few weeks." I turn my gaze back down to Blue. "My dog, Blue, he rescued me, kept me alive in the Everglades, and brought me to safety. Then my friends took me to a private hospital and looked after me. But I can't seem to get rid of this lightning and thunder. I know what's real. But it's still annoying."

He nods. "Are those the only residual effects?"

I chew on my lip for a moment. *Should I tell him the rest?* "It's okay," he says, "you can trust me."

I release another sigh. "Well…a couple of months back I almost died."

He grunts. "May I ask, was it suicide?"

"Sort of. See, this assassin, he tried to kill me, and I couldn't just let him, but I also was kinda ready to go." I stroke Blue between his eyes, running my finger out to his wet, black nose. "But Blue really wanted me to stay. I was bleeding a lot, and this woman found me." I look up at the doctor. "She was a surgeon and saved my life, but I don't remember the months I spent with her recovering. I…" *How do I put this?* "I kind of convinced her to say she was a prophet from God and start a…a kind of…well," I take in another deep breath. *Just get it out.* "A revolution. You've heard of the Her Prophet?"

"Of course." By now anyone who listened to the news had heard of the burka-clad woman hiding in the wilds between Syria and Iraq, claiming to be a messenger from God, telling women to rise up and force men to accept and acknowledge their value. *To let the wolf out.* I look down at Blue again. His eyes are closed, long dark lashes spread against white fur. *He sees the whole world in black and white.*

Thunder rumbles so loudly I have to close my eyes and let it rage over me. I'm not sure how long I stay like that, but when I open my eyes, the doctor is still sitting in front of me, his gaze holding mine. "Anything else?"

"My mom got shot. She almost died." I shake my head. "I have not seen her…we have issues." He gives me a warm smile, like he knows about Mommy issues. He waits and I go on, weirdly desperate to fill the silence. *I know that trick, and yet I'm falling into it.*

"I'm in love with someone who doesn't even know I exist." He cocks his head, this one seeming out of context with the rest of my saga. I swallow and look down at my hands. *Clean and healed.* The hands of a civilian. Not the calloused, wounded weapons of a warrior. Not right now.

"His name..." I can't say it out loud. *Mulberry.* I blink away tears. "He was injured, badly. Because he went looking for me. Lost part of his leg, lost a lot of blood. Almost died." I look up at Dr. Munkin again, and he's giving me that same soft, understanding smile. *Like this isn't freaky. Like I'm just another hurting person.* "He has amnesia and doesn't remember me. And—" Sucking in a deep breath, I sit up taller, strength seeping into me as I force myself to speak. "He's happy now. Not remembering— it's better."

Dr. Munkin purses his lips but does not argue with me. "I think I can help you," he says.

"Really?"

"Yes, really."

I send up a prayer to a God I don't believe in...*don't let Dr. Munkin be full of shit.*

EK

"SYDNEY," Robert's voice pulls me from my memories back onto the gently bobbing boat. "Should we grab dinner before heading back?"

"Sure," I say, giving him a smile. "Where do you want to go?"

"You still haven't gone to see Hugh, right?"

"No," I answer quietly.

Robert sighs. Hugh's restaurant is his favorite in Miami. "Fine, Saphina's then?" Robert turns the engine over, and I help him bring up the anchor—I drive the winch as he maneuvers the lithe boat.

We take off across the bay, headed for Saphina's, the casual French bistro Robert likes almost as much as Hugh's restaurant; *James.*

If I go to see Hugh then Miami *will* be home, and I won't ever want to leave. I watch Robert's hair twisting and fluttering in the wind and know I should leave. *And soon.*

It's dangerous to get too comfortable. People die when I'm happy.

CHAPTER FIVE

Dan

I'M SITTING in my office, looking out at the command center, still buzzing with energy and purpose. I've checked our system repeatedly and found no breaches...not even an attempt.

Maybe they are waiting until we calm down, until we think we've averted a crisis. Or maybe their plan went wrong somewhere. Maybe they hurt themselves in the explosion.

I pick up my radio. "Sick bay, come in."

"This is sick bay." A female voice I recognize as one of our nurses, Camilla, answers.

"This is Dan. Tell me, what kind of injuries do you have up there?"

"Nothing serious, a few cuts and bruises from falling in the dark. And George burned himself on hot coffee."

"Hot coffee?"

"Yeah, all over his hands, knocked the pot over."

"Where?"

"Where? His hands."

"No, which pot of coffee? In his room, the cafeteria?"

"I'm not sure."

"I'll be right up. Don't tell him I asked."

"Yes, sir." Her voice comes out unsure...almost frightened.

George. He was supposed to meet me at the beach. Could he possibly have gone to Battery Room C and set off a device in an attempt to distract us, with plans of infiltrating our servers, but then hurt himself and had to abort his mission?

My mind rebels at the idea. *George is loyal.* He has worked with me since early on. He looks up to me. I'm his freaking mentor.

I sit back in my chair and close my eyes, letting my mind go blank for a moment. Too many thoughts are pushing at me; I'll never see clearly with so much clutter.

Several deep breaths later, I open my eyes then stand and begin to pace. If it was George, then someone has something over him. And I've got to find out what. I wrestle with the rage and hurt that is trying to rear up and control me. This is not the time to indulge in personal grievances. I have an entire compound, seventy-two people, and an international justice operation to protect. *My feelings don't matter.*

I jog down the spiral staircase and stop by Mitchel's console.

"I'm just going up to check on George. He burned his hands on some coffee in the dark. Hold down the fort here."

Mitchel nods, his expression grave. "Rachel should have something soon from that video." His knee is bouncing with anxiety under his desk.

If it was George, there won't be anything to see. *He's one of the best. I trained him.*

Mitchel turns back to his screen, sun lines around his eyes standing out in the glow of his computer. When I met him, he didn't have any wrinkles. *Time takes its toll on all of us.*

The infirmary is on the fifth floor, too far for the steps. As I get into the elevator I take a deep breath and close my eyes again, letting my mind go blank as I'm carried skyward.

I find George in one of the private rooms, his hands bandaged in white gauze. "Hey," I say. He turns his head slowly and meets my gaze with eyes fuzzy from the pain meds.

"Hi," he says back, tension pulling at his mouth.

"How are you?" I ask, taking a seat next to his bedside.

George looks down at his hands. "I've been better."

"What happened?"

"Spilled some hot coffee." His voice is low. *George is lying.*

"Where? In the lobby?"

He clears his throat, still staring at his hands. "In my room. I ran up there to grab something—some sunscreen—and remembered my pot was still on. The power went out as I reached for it, and I'm not totally sure what happened next."

"But you managed to burn both your hands?" He just nods. Anger sizzles in me. *He's lying.* My hands itch to grab his chin, to force his gaze to meet mine.

Why not?

I give in to the instinct, standing up and reaching for him, digging my fingers into his jaw and making him look at me. "Don't lie to me," I hiss.

His glazed eyes focus, then blur with tears, but he does not speak.

"George," I lean close to his face. "Tell me what you did...*now*."

He hiccups a sob. "I can't," he whispers.

I rear back, staring down into his face—at the man I've trained, mentored...trusted. *Fuck.*

"I'm so sorry, Dan." Tears begin to stream down his face, and his body shakes. "They have my sister. They're going to kill her. I failed, and now they are going to kill her." He breaks down, his voice gone, his body shuddering under the pressure of his sobs.

"Who has her?" I ask, keeping very still, refusing to react emotionally.

He doesn't answer; he's sobbing uncontrollably. Sympathy and anger war in my chest. I let go of his face and sit back down, clenching my fists. "Tell me who has her. We will save her."

He shakes his head. "It's too late."

"George," I clench my jaw. "It's never too late, talk to me."

"I'm so sorry."

I bite my tongue to keep myself from railing at him. "George," I keep my voice low. "Tell me everything."

He nods and swipes at his running nose with his bandaged hand. I grab a tissue from the box next to his bed and pass it to him. He can barely hold it as he wipes at his eyes. George won't look at me, and that's fine. I don't think I can stand to meet his gaze right now.

He betrayed me.

"My sister, she's only sixteen." I nod. *I know that.* George is from Texas. His parents are both Mexican immigrants, but he and his sister were born in San Antonio. He's ten years older than her—he has a savings account for her college fund.

The picture George showed me from her quinceañera last year comes into my mind's eye. Young-looking for her age, she was dressed in a white gown, poofy and bedazzled, grinning at the camera from between her parents and George.

"What happened to your sister, George?"

"She called four nights ago." I knew that. But I didn't listen in on the call. *We need to change some policies.* "She is being held—I don't know where. But she said if I didn't destroy our servers and cut off power they'd kill her. At first they wanted to know the location of the island."

"But you don't know that."

George shakes his head, his face red with shame and eyes still welling with tears. "But I would have told them, Dan. I'd do anything for her."

"I know, George."

"They said if I told anyone they'd kill her."

"How would they know if you told anyone?"

His eyes widen, and he shakes his head. "I don't know."

I stand up so fast the stool I'm sitting on falls over. *Shit.* George isn't the only mole.

My eyes scan the empty room. *No one can hear us in here.*

"George." My voice is quiet. "Shut up." He sniffles and looks up at me, his breath coming is sharp pulls. "No one can know you've told me." He nods. "But I need every detail."

"I'll tell you everything."

I pick up the stool and sit back down next to him, gathering my patience. *I will remain calm and steady...I will figure this out and defeat my betrayers.*

ℲҞ

Lenox

IN THE MORNING, Petra wants to go riding. The stable is grand. Original to the property, it's built of stone and wood, scented of hay and leather. A smile brightens Petra's face as we step into the aisle between the horse stalls.

Velvety noses and majestic heads pop over the stall doors, and a black Friesian, at least seventeen hands tall, whinnies to her. She grins and waves to him. He stomps in anticipation. "Tarzan," she coos. "I'll be right there." I wait as she steps into the tack room and grabs a handful of treats from a bin by the entryway.

Petra passes a few to me. "You'll ride Jane," she says, pointing across the aisle to a gypsy horse—just as tall as Tarzan, with the black and white markings her breed is known for. She is working the latch to her stall with her lips, trying to escape. "I figured you'd want a mare," Petra laughs, stepping up to Tarzan, who lowers his giant head and pushes it into her chest.

Jane snorts and bobs her head, eyes narrowing at me. *You think you can ride me?* I approach her stall, hand extended, two of the oat treats on my palm.

Petra taught me to ride. *A true gentleman can handle a horse.*

Jane sniffs my hand, her breath warming and whiskers tickling my skin. Her lips fumble over my palm as she takes the treats. Crunching them down in two bites she raises her gaze to mine. *More?*

I smile gently, reaching out to pet her nose. She lets me, even leans in a little. A groom appears at the far end of the barn and, seeing Petra, hurries over. He speaks to her in rapid Romanian. She answers, and he hurries to the tack room, calling to another groom who comes into the barn at a jog.

Through the open barn door I can see the kennels on the other side

39

of the yard. Two German Shepherds pace behind a tall chain link fence and muffled barking from inside the handsome brick structure reaches us. "What do you use the dogs for?" I ask.

Petra comes to stand next to me, following my gaze. A handler is entering the side door and the dogs head inside, presumably for break-fast. "Protection," Petra says simply, walking back to her horse.

"Ah," I say. "Is there a lot of crime out here?"

"Enough," Petra answers quietly, clearly wanting the conversation to end. A sick feeling stirs in my gut as I stare at the kennels. *Something doesn't feel right.*

Our horses are tacked quickly, and we mount, heading across the giant lawn at a walk. Both horses have long strides and gentle mouths. They keep their necks curled, step their feet high, and carry themselves regally—as if they are the beasts of a queen, not one of the most powerful pimps in the world.

Petra's organization is a web of human trafficking that spans the planet. Though ruthless and powerful, she always struck me as ethical... which has a different meaning in my world than others. Many people think exchanging sex for money is immoral. But it's not. If both parties are consenting adults, and the transaction is equitable, then selling one's body is a perfectly reasonable way to make a living. And buying a body to pleasure oneself is far preferable to more coercive courses of action.

However, recent intel about a scheme to move Isis sex slaves out of their territory and into other markets suggests Petra may be involved. I hate to believe it.

"How is business?" Petra asks as we move deeper into the woods. We ride side by side, entering the forest where light plays between the leaves and sparkles on the dew-covered ground.

"Good. You know I don't work much anymore."

She smiles, glancing over at me, then back to the path. "Only for very special clients, I'm sure."

"It's true," I say. "I have not taken on a new client in years."

"You have many men working for you though."

I nod, reaching forward to pet Jane's neck. "Yes, you taught me well."

"Still no women, though?" she asks.

I nod. "That's right." My business is selling men to women. I understand it and prefer it because of my firsthand knowledge.

"It pleases me that you still come to me," Petra says.

"I am forever grateful for your guidance." I turn to look at her, and she is watching me.

Petra nods, her eyes holding mine. *She is suspicious.* "Is that why you called?"

I hold her gaze, keeping the lies that flow from my lips from entering my eyes. "I heard about your marriage and wanted to check on you. Why are you questioning me?" I do not let any accusation tinge my words—only innocent curiosity.

Petra turns away from me, staring over Tarzan's head at the path before us. "These are dangerous times, Lenox." She pauses, pulling her lower lip between her teeth. "Do you have any trouble with Joyful Justice?" Her eyes flick back to me, and I smile at her.

"Joyful Justice? The vigilantes? Why would I have any trouble with them?"

Her brow furrows. "Lenox, do not be so blind. They are against what we do."

"Are they? I know very little about them."

Her fingers tighten on the reins, and Tarzan snorts in complaint. Petra loosens her grip but her jaw is still clenched and body stiff with tension. "Maybe they do not mind you selling men. But women selling themselves..." She snorts. "It's not allowed."

"You've had trouble with them? How unfortunate."

"No," she shakes her head. "Not me, but associates have told me."

"I see. And you trust these associates are...being respectful."

She nods aggressively. "Of course. Lenox, you know how I operate."

"I do. You taught me well."

She smiles and her shoulders relax a little. "You've picked up a few of your own tricks along the way." Her gaze travels down my body, and she laughs, the last of her tension leaving.

"Yes," I agree, smiling at her. "Of course, but you showed me how to make this business work for me, rather than me for it."

Petra nods but does not respond. We continue in silence, the sounds of the forest a symphony around us. My gaze scans the woods. The first signs of spring are unfurling. Sprouts of green push up through the dark soil, buds wait on branches, coiled in their hard shells, preparing to explode into summer. My eyes catch on a stone archway, some kind of old building.

"What is that?" I ask, pointing to it.

"An old cell, a dungeon I think, from when this was a real castle."

Petra is frowning, peering through the woods at the half hidden stone structure. Patched in moss with a wooden door, the dungeon blends into the forest, looking as though it has not been used in decades. But then the sun glints off something shiny. I narrow my gaze. *The dead bolt is new.*

A shiver runs over me, and I keep my face averted, knowing that my expression of horror cannot be contained or covered up. *Petra is keeping someone in that cell.*

EK

Dan

EIGHT HOURS after the initial attack, and I still have almost nothing. I'm pouring over the communication in and out of the island, but while we record every transaction, we don't keep the content of the conversation. *That is going to change.*

My fingers shake as I scroll to the next page of calls, my eyes blurring. It's been about twenty-eight hours since I last slept.

A knock on my door brings my head up. Anita, holding two steaming coffee cups, her hair loose and falling like a sheet of black silk over one shoulder, is framed in the glass. She's wearing a bright green, thigh-length tunic and a pair of dark jeans. Her bare lips raise into a smile as I stare at her.

She looks well-rested, even with the lines of concern around her eyes.

I swivel my chair around and wave Anita in. Using her hip, she pushes open the door. "How are you doing?" she asks, crossing the office and extending one of the mugs.

I can smell it's chai, not coffee. Anita makes an amazing cup of chai: strong black tea, cardamon, cinnamon, and a heavy pour of whole milk. *The milk comes in tetra packs. It does not need to be refrigerated until opened. Our last shipment arrived six weeks ago; another will come next week.* The company name and our contact there flashes through my brain, falls under brief suspicion, and then fades. *We helped bring his mother's murderer to justice. He has no family left. Besides, he's not here enough to monitor George's behavior.*

I take the proffered mug. "Thanks, I'm okay."

Anita sits down in one of the other office chairs and spins back and forth on her toes, cupping her own mug. "When's the last time you slept?" She says it with curiosity rather than reproach, but I can't stop the hairs on the back of my neck rising like hackles. *Leave me alone so I can figure this out.*

"I'm fine," I say, my voice harder than I mean it to be.

She frowns, her dark, sculpted brows conferencing. "Dan." There is sympathy in her voice. *Understanding.* She holds my gaze, her beautiful, almond-shaped brown eyes not letting me turn away. "You need to take care of yourself in order to take care of the rest of us." I open my mouth to respond, but she leans forward and continues, cutting me off. "I understand how hard this is for you. But you have to let others help. And you have to sleep. Oh—" She gives me a smile. "And eat."

I turn away from her and back to my computer, scrolling through the list of calls again. "Anita, someone close to me is watching. I can't trust anyone." I told Anita about George—she's the only person I totally trust here.

"What about me? Can you trust me? Can you trust the rest of the Joyful Justice Council? When are you going to tell them?"

I grit my teeth and continue to scroll. I am not ready for them to know yet. *Don't want to admit my failure.*

"Dan." Her voice is lower now. "Tom told me what you did."

I turn to her quickly, anger sharpening my vision. "Tom? The guy you brought here without any background checks? And then suddenly we have an attack. You don't find that at all suspicious?"

Her cheeks brighten with color. "Without any background checks? He is my husband."

"That doesn't mean I trust him." My hands are shaking again, and I turn back to the computer before she sees it. The mug of chai sits untasted next to my elbow.

"Either let me help you, or I'll call the council myself." Her voice is steely. She's taken all pretense out and left behind only her bold, iron will.

"I need more time. I want to have something to tell them, a possible solution." I keep scrolling through the communications, the black lines of text dancing in front of my exhausted eyes. *There is nothing out of the ordinary here.*

But then again, a call from George's family isn't out of the ordinary either. I sit back into my chair with a weary sigh and look at Anita. *I'm being unfair.* But so is she. My suspicions about Tom are warranted. She knows that.

"I'm sorry," I say. "I shouldn't have spoken to you like that, but I am suspicious of Tom. I expect you can understand that."

She nods. "I do. And I wasn't going to reprimand you for accusing him." She takes a sip of her chai, her eyes turning thoughtful. "I was just going to suggest there might be a better way to investigate this."

"Like what?"

I turn fully toward her, picking up the cup and breathing in its spicy, sweet scent before taking a sip.

"First, I want you to get some rest. You need to sleep. To be clear-headed."

My eyes jump to hers. "Anita, you know I can go long stretches without sleep."

"From what I can tell, you've been up for over twenty-four hours, Dan." Her voice is cold. *Calculated.* She's been watching me.

"That's possible," I hedge. "But, I often go long stretches without sleep. And I *need* to figure this out."

"I know how you get, Dan, the way you get sucked into your work and ignore the clock, but this is too much even for you. Nothing has happened since the attack. George appears to be the only one."

"Impossible. George may be the only compromised person who had the know-how to mess with our systems—to hack into the main servers. But he's certainly not the only person working against us. There must be at least one other person, someone reporting to whoever took George's sister."

"But then they don't have any power to hurt us."

"I'm sure they're just waiting. Waiting for me to go to sleep so they can attack again." The anxiety of the situation builds anew in my chest. *I don't have time for this. I need to keep searching.* I swivel back to my computer, putting the chai down away from my keyboard.

My gaze latches onto a call; George's parents' line, two hours before the attack...*I have to ask him about it.* I make a note in the text document I have open with all suspicious activity and set a hyperlink to the record. *There are only four other calls on the list, and they are all long shots.*

"Fine," Anita says, shifting closer to me, her elbow brushing mine. "If you won't rest, at least let me help you."

I glance over at her but don't respond. She frowns at me, her eyes darkening. "I'll call the council right now," she threatens.

"Fine," I say. "I'm checking everyone's communications. Seeing what kind of calls have been going in and out recently. You can start checking emails. I doubt anyone would be stupid enough to put this in writing, which is why I'm checking calls first. But it can't hurt."

"How do I check emails?" Anita asks. I point to one of my other computers, and we scoot toward it together. Typing in my password, I bring up my system for tracking the email accounts of everyone who lives on the island. "Start at the top. Check George's," I swallow and force myself to continue. "Mitchel's. And then move down." Anita is looking at me, but I can't hold her gaze. *Yes, we are checking those closest to me first.* "I'd look at the last ten days. See if you can find anything. We can go back further after that, but George got the call about his sister four days ago, so ten days is a good start."

Anita nods, her eyes riveted to the screen.

I scoot back over to my console to continue my work. As I hear the clicking of Anita's keyboard, my shoulders begin to relax. I should have asked for her help earlier. I do trust Anita. And just because she has Tom here now doesn't mean we can't work together in the way we used to. Really, he changes nothing.

Unless he's helping orchestrate this attack. In which case, everything will change.

CHAPTER SIX

Declan

My superior, Donald Phelps, slams his hands down onto the almost empty desk with a loud slap. *It's the third time he's done that since this meeting began.* Breathing heavily, his clean-shaven face glistening with sweat, jowls quivering from the impact of his palms against the desk, Director Phelps glares at me with his beady eyes—so dark brown they are almost black. *Very rat-like.* "He's a drunk, and you know it."

My jaw clenches, and I don't respond. Just hold his gaze. Phelps grabs at the only file on the desktop and shakes it at me, the manila folder crumpling in his meaty grip. "You went through four other judges. Then show up at Justice Minerette's house at ten o'clock at night like this is some kind of emergency!"

The manila folder gets mashed a little more before being smashed onto the desk again. "Then!" Phelps pauses to take a big breath, inflating his wide chest and standing to his full height. "Not only do you fail to apprehend Maxim and Rye, they actually knock out your men. And!" Another lungful of air, his face going a little purple around the edges. "I've got Senator Daniels breathing down my neck about how this was an illegal act." He grabs the file again, shaking it. "Do you know how far up my ass he wants to shove this bullshit warrant? Do you know how much of a field day Maxim's lawyers will have with this? What the fuck were you thinking?"

I'm guessing that's a rhetorical question since it's the third time he's asked, but this time he just stands there, his frown so deep the wrinkles could hold a pencil. I clear my throat, and he raises his brows. "Take your time son, I've got all day." His Texas accent is dripping with sarcasm.

I shift in my seat, sitting forward a little. "Well sir, I was thinking those two have gotten away with their crimes for too long and ought to pay for them. Joyful Justice is a dangerous criminal organization, and we need to do something about it."

He shakes his head, snarling, and leans back onto his heels, lording over me. "You're on administrative leave." His voice goes low and almost sad—he sounds tired. "No pay. I'm gonna fire your ass as soon as I figure out how."

Like I need your money.

I move to stand and he clears his throat, the color of his face normalizing. "One more thing before you slink off into whatever hole you climbed out of." I raise my gaze to his. "I want you to go over your findings about the April Madden shooting with Officer Consuela Sanchez." He shakes his head, making a sound of disgust. "Remember, the case you were sent to Miami to work on?"

I almost remind him April Madden is Sydney Rye aka Joy Humbolt's mother, so the cases are connected, but I don't. "Consuela Sanchez, sir?"

"Do you know her?" he asks.

I shake my head. "Her, sir?" I raise my brows, trying to drop the hint without having to say it. *A woman on that case is a bad idea. Especially a woman of color.*

"What?" He's starting to smile, hoping to find a sexist racist in front of him. Hoping I'll say something else that will sink me deeper into the shit, as if there is someplace lower to go after that fucking debacle.

"I'm sure she is very capable, but Men's Rights Activists, specifically the Incels, are an all-male, mostly white group—they hate women. It's why Jack Robertson shot April Madden." *Duh.*

"I know that!" His voice raises again, the bluster coming back into his tone. "I read the reports you sent. Involuntarily celibates." His eyes break from mine for a moment to glance at the gold ring shining on his wedding finger. "Poor bastards." He shakes his head, his eyes returning to me.

Phelps and I both know my work on the Madden case was exemplary. Not an i left undotted or a t left uncrossed. *I'm good at what I do.* He clears his throat. "According to your reports, the community is online."

"Mostly, sir. But they have meet-ups. That's where I gathered a lot of my intel." His gaze travels over my thick hair, muscled chest, and down to my gold watch. The Incels consider me a "chad." A guy who can pick up women easily. *They have no idea.* "Using a confidential informant," I clarify. "But I did the interrogations." The Incels respect chads. They *hate* women.

With her allegiance to the "Her" prophet, and the crusade to free women from oppression, April Madden is the Incels' worst nightmare. And she was an easy target. The Incels believe women oppress men, using their sexual wiles to control and manipulate us. *Dumbasses.*

"Sanchez is an excellent agent." Phelps nods to himself. "Give her everything you've got."

I don't argue further. The fact is, my CI isn't going to talk to a woman. I turn to leave and am almost at the door when he barks my name again.

"Doyle." I turn back to him. He's leaning over his desk, fists resting on the wood. "Don't go back to Miami. Leave Rye and Maxim alone."

"Yes, sir."

"I mean it," he growls.

"I always take you at your word, sir."

His eyes narrow and he nods once, turning to his chair, and I leave the office. Phelps's secretary, Debra Armer, gives me a sympathetic smile. She must have heard the yelling. I offer a sheepish, bad boy grin in return that brings a touch of pink to the woman's cheeks. I tip an imaginary hat to Debra and head down the hall—a disgraced man in his tailored suit under order to leave my quarry alone.

Like that's going to happen. I almost laugh but hold it together as I wait for the elevator. Once I've briefed Sanchez, I'll be back in Miami within hours. *Maxim and Rye will pay for their crimes.*

EK

THE NIGHT COMES ON FAST—THE crisp warmth of the bright fall day giving way to the chill darkness of evening—as I sit in a beer garden near the Capitol.

The bar's backyard, smelling of dried leaves and car exhaust, provides a respite from the busy streets—a place to wait until my meeting with Sanchez, then onto a midnight flight back to Miami. *To continue my work.*

The space, empty when I arrive, fills with the same speed that the sun retreats. People in dark, government-regulation suits mingle under the strung lights, their beers clenched in white-knuckled fists, laughs strained until the first drink soothes their nerves, loosening their fingers and deepening their guffaws.

Settled into a dim corner, sipping seltzer, I check my phone repeatedly, waiting for the minutes to tick by. Keeping my eyes cast down to avoid attention, I almost make it to the appointed time without a single interruption save the waitress's occasional visits to refresh my sparkling water.

I've only got another fifteen to go when a giggle brings my attention from the condensation dripping off my glass to the woman standing in front of my small table. A young, attractive brunette, wearing just enough make-up to appear professional without tipping over into harlot, stands before me. Her cheeks are flushed with either drink or nerves—when I meet her hazel eyes, she bites her bottom lip in a moment of hesitance before speaking. "Hi." Her full lips spread into an inviting and friendly smile I can't help but return. *It's just instinct.*

Shifting to sit up from the slouch I've eased into while waiting, I raise one brow at her, letting a sparkle come into my gaze. Her cheeks brighten further. "Hi," I say back.

She glances over her shoulder, pushing silky mahogany hair behind her ear. My gaze follows—three young women huddle together, all holding glasses of white wine. They gesture encouragingly to her, and she blushes even harder as she turns back to me.

"I'm Declan," I say. "Do you want to join me?" I gesture to the empty chair at my table. She slides into it without a word, her almost-full wine glass settling in next to my seltzer.

"I'm Jane." Her voice is high, and I detect an accent, something Southern maybe.

"Nice to meet you, Jane." I lean forward, my eyes glancing at my phone for a moment before returning to hers. *I have ten minutes.*

Jane sips her wine. "I just saw you sitting over here all alone and..." I give her a warm, soft smile. "You looked like you could use some company." Definitely Southern...Georgia, probably.

"That's awfully nice of you, Jane." She drops her gaze when I use her name, the blush pinking her cheeks, turning them almost red...*almost.*

My phone pings with a reminder that I need to leave in seven minutes to make it the three blocks to my meeting.

The waitress passes, catching my eye, and I gesture to Jane's drink and then for the check. She nods. "I'm sorry," I say to Jane. "But I have to leave. I have a meeting that should take about an hour. Will you still be around? I'd love to finish our conversation." *Get you into bed and relieve some of my pent up frustration.*

Jane's mouth opens in surprise, and I lean my forearms onto the table, making my biceps bulge and inching closer to her. Jane's hands flutter for a moment around her wine, unsure of what to say. "Give me your number," I suggest, my voice low and thrumming. "And I'll call you when I'm finished."

The waitress returns with the check and a full glass of wine for Jane—who looks up at the waitress, almost for help. But the older woman is already moving on to the next customer.

Pulling the bill over, I glance at the total before dropping a twenty onto the tray. *That's a 50% tip.* A little nectar to help lure my hummingbird...

"How about this?" I say, beginning to stand. "I'll give you *my* number. And if you want to see me later, call." I'm hovering over her now, and Jane watches as I slip into my tailored suit jacket. Her gaze strays to my tapered waist, and I control the surge of victory that pulses through me as I extract a card from my wallet.

Laying it next to her glass of wine, I lean forward, so my shadow falls across her, and the space between us is suddenly narrow and intimate. She sucks in a breath, her eyes dilating. "I hope you call," I say.

She pulls that lower lip back under her teeth and nods just slightly. My fingers brush against hers in a brief goodbye, and I turn from the table. Her friends are all watching, and as my gaze lands on them they quickly turn away, pretending to be looking at the ground, or the sky... anywhere but me.

I tip an imaginary hat at them as I pass, and they giggle in appreciation.

EK

OFFICER CONSUELA SANCHEZ does not strike me as a giggler. I'm guessing she is the kind of woman who laughs rarely and only in intimate settings. She's got soft, sexy curves draped in a nice, though off the rack, navy suit. Her black hair, pulled tight to her scalp and twisted into a merciless bun, glimmers under the florescent bulbs.

Take off the glasses, unwind the hair, remove the suit, and you've got a hot piece of ass. But here, under these lights, in this cramped office, with the scent of old coffee and carpet cleaner thick in the air, she's a ball breaker. A woman in a man's world who's learned how to move, speak, and think in a way that keeps us at bay. And yet...when she smiles at me, her chocolate brown eyes soft behind those lenses, I want to help her. *Take care of her.*

Instincts again.

"Thanks for taking the time to see me." She comes out from behind her desk, extending a well-manicured hand.

Consuela Sanchez is petite, probably only about 5 feet 3 inches. A full foot taller and twice her width, I'm so much bigger and stronger it's kind of amazing we are the same species. I take her hand, almost engulfing it in mine.

Sanchez's grip is firm, and she holds my gaze. "No problem, Ms.

Sanchez," I say as she lets go and steps back, gesturing to a wooden chair facing her desk. It creaks as I sit down.

"I'm impressed by your work." She takes her seat and looks to her computer screen. The blue glow turns her skin pale and sickly. *I'd like to see her in the sun.*

"Thank you."

She sits back in her chair and it wheezes. "You want coffee, water, anything?"

I shake my head and give her a professional smile. "I'm fine." She nods, just watching me. "So," I say, raising my brows. *You called me here.* "How can I help?" Her eyes narrow in thought—as if she's assessing me. "I'm not sure what I can add—everything is in my reports."

"I'm old school," she says. "My father worked a beat for thirty years, and he always taught me to go to the source, not the report. To talk to people."

"Sounds like he was a good cop."

"You were a cop in New York, right?"

She knows the answer to that. I give her a half smile. "That's true."

"Seems to me"—she gestures at her computer—"that you're good at talking to people. Getting information. It's amazing the details you got out of some of these guys. Why do you think they shared so much with you?"

"They want to be me." I keep my voice even, making sure it's not a brag.

Her brows shoot up. "Be you?"

"Good looking, articulate, at ease. Not an outcast."

She smiles. "You get laid."

"That's how they see me. And that's very important to them."

"It's important to most men." She says it with an amused smile and doesn't break eye contact.

I laugh—she's funny. And bold. "Yeah, I guess it is. Most women too, probably."

She shrugs. "Probably." She gives a little laugh—it's like a tinkling bell in a fog, and I want to dive into the mist to find it. *Damn instincts.*

"There is one question I don't feel got answered." She leans forward, slipping off her jacket to reveal a short-sleeved silk blouse. It's buttoned close to her neck, with a rounded collar. Her arms are toned but still soft, like she eats what she wants within reason and hits the gym, too. *Disciplined but not neurotic.* Draping the jacket on the back of her chair, she continues. "Where did the money come from?"

"The money?"

She twists back around, facing me again. "Yeah, where did Jack Robertson get the money to buy that nice a weapon? Then he catches a flight, last minute, that cost over $400." She frowns, ticking off on her fingers. "The taxi to the hotel, the room at the hotel, his meals." My shoulders tense with each item. "It adds up fast. That's a lot of money for a guy working at a fast-food joint."

"The money was crowdsourced. That's in my report." There is a hint of annoyance in my tone, and I force a smile onto my face.

"But who gave him the money?" She's staring at me like it's obvious.

"Like I said, he crowdsourced it. All the donations were in cryptocurrency. The site he used doesn't track its users. It's been shut down."

"And popped up again," Sanchez says, her frown deepening. "Nothing ever truly dies on the dark web."

"Maybe not, but we couldn't trace any of the donations."

"So, then, the question remains. Where did it come from?"

"My guess is other members of the community." *It seems pretty obvious to me.*

"We don't even know how many people donated. Right?"

"No." I cross my legs, fidgeting in the hard wooden chair. *How much longer is this going to take?* "But the community is tight. They are active and"—I gesture at her computer and my report on it—"fired up. They don't have anything to spend their money on but video games and rent. Half of them probably are living in their parents' basements."

"What if it was just one source?"

"I'm not sure what you mean." I take a deep breath and release it slowly, calming myself.

Sanchez leans back, her eyes going narrow again. "What if instead of the money coming from all these individual guys...what if there was just one source?"

"Like what? One rich Incel?"

"No." She shakes her head. "What if they've banded together with other criminal groups and are hiding it really well?"

"Banded together? I'm not sure what you mean."

"What if the Incels and others are working together on criminal enterprises and raising funds to fuel terrorism?" She says it quietly, but I can tell this theory is her baby. *Am I the first person she's told?*

"I don't think there is any evidence of that." Sanchez purses her lips and leans forward, resting her forearms on the desk in front of the keyboard, eyes narrowing again in that way she has. *Sanchez is trying to decide if she can trust me.* Curiosity stirs in my gut. "What?" I ask. "You have evidence?"

"You know Billy Ray Titus?"

"He's a very active Men's Rights activist. Speaks around the world to Men's Rights groups." Titus is a weasel of a man in his early forties, with a hatred for women and a gift for gab that combine into one stirring speaker. He gives talks at conferences and gatherings—nothing big but always absurd.

"Take a look at this." Sanchez moves her mouse and clicks a few times before turning the monitor to me. On the screen is a surveillance photo: Billy Ray Titus, his ponytail fluttering in a breeze coming off the water behind him. He's talking to a man I don't recognize—tall guy, with blond hair and broad shoulders, wearing a leather jacket and looking like a thug. There are a few men on either side of them. I recognize a lanky redhead next to Billy Ray as an active Incel member: Nathan Jenkins, a known associate of Billy's with adult acne and a permanent wrinkle to his face, as though he's just smelled something bad. *Easy to see why the guy can't get laid.*

"That's Ian McCain, do you know him?" Sanchez says, pointing to the thug talking to Billy Ray.

I shake my head, keeping my eyes on the screen. "Should I?"

"He's an Irish national. Runs a sex-trafficking business with his two brothers. They've recently started dealing in Isis slaves."

My chest tightens as I stare at the image, suddenly recognizing the railing at their elbows and body of water beyond it. They are in Istanbul,

Turkey, standing on the promenade above the Bosporus. "You think Billy Ray is involved in some way?" I ask, turning to her.

"Billy was in Istanbul for a conference when this photo was taken. Ian is often there—he has brothels all over the world."

"Who took the photo?" I ask. Sanchez shakes her head without making eye contact, reaching for her mouse again. *She's got sources.* "So you think that Billy Ray is dealing in war slaves to fund his movement?"

Sanchez nods. "Something like that."

I ease back into the chair, glancing at my watch. *Jane should be calling soon.* "I don't know. That's a big escalation." I look back up at Sanchez, giving her a smile. "He strikes me as a man of big words but...dealing in female war slaves? That's no joke."

"I don't think Billy is dealing himself. I think he's partnered with Ian and his brothers."

"What are the McCain brothers getting out of it, though?"

"Customers." She points to the screen, which displays a photo of Billy Ray entering a building, talking on the phone. "That's an auction."

"I thought you said he wasn't dealing."

"He made no purchases. But he sat next to Ian on his phone the whole time."

"So, he's hooking up Incels with Isis sex slaves. That's your theory." She shrugs, sitting back in her chair, trying to look casual, but there is a muscle twitching in her jaw. "And he used the money from Ian's organization to try to kill April Madden." She doesn't comment. Just narrows her eyes. "The shooter acted alone but with the support of his community." *Those were my findings.* "There have been two other acts of terror attributed to Incel members." I tick off a finger. "John Stanhope in Toronto killed two women and a man with his van." I hold up a second finger. "And Mark Espie, in California, shot six people at a Victoria's Secret. In both cases they left manifestos, but there was absolutely no evidence of a terrorist network. Just single white males with mental health issues."

Sanchez gives a brief nod. "I know. But what if Jack Robertson was hired, trained, and funded by Billy Ray Titus?"

"Hey," I say, throwing up my hands. "It's your case now. You can do what you want with it. But I didn't find any evidence of that."

She nods slowly, watching me. "Well, thanks for your time."

My phone vibrates, and I stand to leave, slipping it out of my pocket. "Sorry I couldn't be more help," I say, reaching out to offer my hand.

Sanchez doesn't stand. "Can I ask just one more thing?" I glance down at my phone and see it's a local number. *Probably Jane.* "How long were you fucking Joy Humbolt before she killed the mayor of New York?"

My eyes jump to Sanchez. *Oh, fuck me.* Her eyes are narrow and bright. *She thinks she's got me.*

I hold up my phone. "Sorry, I've got to go."

"Sit down." Her voice is suddenly deep and commanding. I almost do it—*instincts*— but manage to stay upright.

"Excuse me?"

"Sit down. We are not done here." She leans forward, slowly rising. "I want to know everything you know about what happened in Syria last year."

I cock my head. "That's all classified."

"Were you fucking Sydney Rye while there?"

I give her a tight-lipped smile, looking down at her. *I am bigger and stronger.* "I don't know where you get your information, but I'm not at liberty to talk about my assignment in Syria. Phelps told me to catch you up on the April Madden case. I've done that. So I'm gonna go."

"You don't see a link? April Madden was *in* Syria. That's where she was radicalized."

A sigh escapes as my phone goes silent. *I missed Jane's call.* "What's your clearance?" I ask.

Sanchez turns to her computer again, bending over the keyboard. A tendril of hair escapes from her bun, curling around her face. She points to the screen. *My report on Mission Impersota is there. She's already read my findings.*

"Please," she says. "Sit."

I sigh, returning to my seat. *I'm not going to get to see Jane tonight.* "You've read the report."

"A bold idea," Sanchez says, settling into her own chair.

"Not mine."

"I never met Director Leventhal. Did you enjoy working with her?"

Mary Leventhal, my superior on Mission Impersota, came up with the idea of using Sydney Rye's status as a hero to the Kurdish Peshmerga all-female fighting forces, to help us defeat Isis in the Iraqi-Syrian badlands. "She died honorably," I say.

Sanchez smiles, knowing that I've given her nothing. "You knew Sydney Rye aka Joy Humbolt in New York." I nod, keeping my mouth shut. "No one thought the fact you'd dated the accused was a conflict of interest?" I don't react, just sit there. Sanchez sits forward, picking up a pen and tumbling it over her fingers, looking off into the distance as if she's deep in thought. "Did Director Leventhal know your history?" Her eyes land on me.

"I'm sure that would be in her notes."

"Have you seen them?"

"No." *I don't have clearance for that.*

"Did you know April Madden before this case? Did you meet her in Syria?"

"No."

"Have you seen the video of Sydney at the battle of Surama?"

"Yes." It went viral only weeks after the battle. Caught by Isis cameras and released by an unknown source, it shows Sydney Rye, Blue, and an entire pack of Kangal Mastiffs by her side, wreaking havoc and terrifying Isis soldiers.

"Do you believe?"

I raise my brows. "That she's a miracle woman brought back from the dead by a prophet from God, sent to free women from the oppression of men?" Sanchez nods, and I can't help the hiccup of a laugh that escapes. "Uh—no. Do you?" I ask.

She shakes her head. "Do you think Sydney believes it?"

"No." I shift in my seat, crossing my legs again. "She's not a believer."

"You know her intimately."

"I know if her mom believes it, she's not going to." I smirk. *Mommy issues.*

Sanchez gives a quiet laugh. "Sounds like me and my mother." She begins to play with the pen again. "What do you think of April Madden's movement?"

"Pretty harmless here, but a lot of violence sprung up in Syria and Iraq attributed to followers of the Her Prophet."

"There was a suicide bombing in Saudi Arabia just last week that is being linked to the movement."

"Right, but April Madden is not preaching violence."

"Though the original prophet does."

"It's not necessary here. We don't live under Sharia law. This country protects women's rights."

Sanchez lets out a huff of a laugh. "Right. It's very different here."

"What? You don't think so?"

She shakes her head, sitting back in her chair. "No, it is. Very different. So, you don't expect to see any violence from Her Prophet followers on our shores?"

"I've not been tasked with analyzing that risk."

"What does your gut say?"

"We have a lot more to fear from the Incels."

"Yes," Sanchez says. "But what if April Madden and her followers find out what they are up to? What if Joyful Justice finds out? What do you think will happen then?"

My heart picks up its pace. "It could be a bloodbath."

She nods, her eyes bright. *I've gotten her point.* "What are your plans for your leave?" she asks, abruptly changing the subject.

"Rest and relaxation," I say.

She leans forward, her chair creaking in protest. "Well, if you think of anything or"—she raises her brow—"make any connections, please let me know."

I give her a tight-lipped smile. "Sure." I go to stand, and she follows me to the door.

"Have a safe trip home," Sanchez says as I step into the hall. "Enjoy your time off."

"Good luck with the case."

She shrugs. "It's not luck, Declan; it's hard work and being at the right place at the right time." She cocks her head. "Something you seem to be awfully good at."

She reaches out her hand again, and we shake. I keep a relaxed smile on my face until I'm at the elevator and then allow my lips to be pulled down into a deep frown—the heft of our conversation weighing on me.

If the Incels are organized and allied with sex traffickers, and if followers of the Her Prophet find out, we could have a literal war of the sexes on our hands instead of a figurative one.

CHAPTER SEVEN

Sydney

I DUCK under Merl's jab and shift left, going in for an uppercut, which he dodges, bringing his fist around for a body blow I spin away from, separating us by several feet. We bounce on the balls of our feet, smiling at each other.

Merl's shoulder-length dark curls are pulled back into a tight bun, and his brown eyes, with their ridiculously long and thick lashes, watch me closely as we circle each other. The toned muscles of his shoulders glisten with sweat and his red gloves shine in the fluorescent lights.

We are training in Robert Maxim's gym—a warehouse not far from his house that has everything an army would want for staying in shape.

Our dogs wait for us outside the ring, sitting in a row—all six of them watching us intently. Merl has three Doberman Pinschers: his bitch, Lucy, a whip smart, quick, and dangerous beast; the largest dog, Michael; then Chula, the youngest—a son of his first Doberman, Thunder, who passed away a few years ago.

My three mutts lounge next to the sleek black beasts, looking almost fluffy in comparison. Frank's tongue is hanging out like the goofball he is, and I smirk as I catch a glimpse of him. He scoots forward and lets out a soft whine. *Can I come play?*

Merl laughs, showing off his gap-toothed smile.

"Do you think he'll ever get it?" I ask.

Merl shrugs. "Maybe. I think in the heat of battle he'd realize there are good guys and bad guys. Right now he's just too used to comfort. How did he do last night?" Merl asks, referencing the Homeland Security raid.

I give him a half smile and a shrug. "Good. Frank stayed close but never got aggressive. At least he didn't slobber all over Declan, trying to get a kiss." Merl gives me another grin. My lips press together, and I drop my gaze for a moment to the sweat-stained mat. "I like that Frank's never been in any real danger. I wish I could have done the same for Blue." My gaze jumps back to Merl's when I see his feet shift with intention. But his eyes are soft, listening. "I don't want Frank to ever be in danger. Nila either."

Merl shakes his head and gives a soft laugh, bouncing on his toes so the curls escaping from his bun dance around his shoulders. "Are you going back into one of your 'I'm going to go live on the beach and not fight for justice anymore' phases?"

I frown. "I'm not saying that. I know that wouldn't work for me."

"Ah, growth." Merl laughs. "I do love it."

I jab with my right fist and he steps back, maneuvering out of my reach and lashing out with his back leg, forcing me onto the ropes. He steps forward and into me, pummeling my middle with several swift punches before jumping back and grinning. I spin away from him, recovering easily—he didn't even try to hurt me.

This is just a friendly spar, a little action to keep us both in shape. "How is Mo-Ping?" I ask, inquiring about Merl's girlfriend. She left last week to visit friends in New York. Mo-Ping is a member of Falun Gong, a persecuted religious and martial art organization outlawed in China. Merl and I freed her from imprisonment last year, and this is the first time the two have been apart for any length of time.

"She's good. Having fun visiting her friends, but of course, there is a sadness to it with so many of their fellow Falun Gong members gone."

Either in prison or murdered. Merl frowns and loses his concentration for a moment. I jab, and he steps easily out of my range, returning his focus to me again.

"You must miss her," I say.

"Not so much that you're going to land one."

I laugh and shrug a shoulder. "You never know...I might get lucky."

"Have you gone to see Hugh yet?" Merl asks, jolting me out of my focused zone for a moment. *The bastard.*

"No," I mumble.

"What's holding you back?"

"What makes you so nosy?"

He touches his nose with a glove and grins. "I care about you." I don't answer, just frown. "And Hugh does, too. Why haven't you gone to see him?

"Well—" I stop mid-sentence and strike out with my front leg. My foot grazes Merl's chin then lands on the mat, and I spin on it, striking out with my back leg and getting him right in the gut. Merl oomphs out a lungful of air and spins away. I prance back to my corner on the balls of my feet. *That's one way to avoid a conversation. Ha!*

"Don't look so satisfied," he says, grabbing a water bottle and taking a long sip. "I'm not letting this go." *Shit.* "I want to see him, and I'm not interested in lying about your whereabouts." I grab my own water and take a long slug, not looking at Merl. "Look." He drops his voice into something conciliatory. "Go see him tonight. Or I'm going to. And I won't lie. I'll tell him you're avoiding him. And that will hurt him."

"Fine," I bark.

"Hey, don't get pissy with me. He's a good friend. You love him. You're going to have fun."

That's what I'm afraid of...

EK

I COME in through the back door of the kitchen. The heat and speed of the place envelop me before I've even stepped fully into the small space. Hugh is at the center of the swirling vortex, his head bent over a pan, his white chef's jacket crisp and starched. I stay by the door, just watching him.

He's so graceful—grabbing plates and checking them before they go out, speaking softly to his sous chefs, moving through the cramped space as if it were a grand dance hall. His eyes are lit with humor and joy as his mop of dirty blond hair swings and bounces, giving him an almost Muppet-like quality. *If Muppets could be handsome and sexy, as well as goofy and fun.*

My heart fills, watching him, just drinking him in. Hugh's happiness is infectious. He looks up suddenly, his gaze riveting on me, his eyes going wide, and then a grin breaks over his face like a wave crashing onto the shore. In four long strides he's in front of me, and then I'm in his arms, wrapped up in his warmth and comfort.

Tears spring to my eyes as I take in the scent of him: roasting tomatoes, onions in butter...home. "Joy," he says, his voice tight with emotion. "It's so good to see you."

"Good to see you, too," I say, finally getting it together enough to wrap my arms around him and hug back. "It's been too long."

"Isn't that usually my line?" Hugh says, stepping back but keeping his hands on my shoulders. He looks down at me, examining my face, his gaze running over the fading scars around my left eye, the hint of color in my cheeks from my recent roller blading, and the tan line on my shoulders from sunbathing by the pool. "You look good," he says.

"You sound surprised."

He laughs and squeezes my arms. "I just mean, you look relaxed." His eyes narrow. "Peaceful."

"I've been working on that."

"I want to hear all about it. Can you hang out? I've got to finish dinner service." Hugh turns, looking back into his kitchen. "Let me make you something to eat."

"I'm good. I don't wanna be a bother. I can come back."

"Don't be ridiculous. I'm not letting you out of my sight." He laughs. "I better text Santiago. He'll be pissed if I don't let him know you're here."

"I'm glad to hear you two are still together," I say, meaning it. *Hugh deserves to be happy.*

Hugh blushes, his eyes returning to mine, and an almost embarrassed smile taking over his face. "Yeah, me too."

"What?" I ask, cocking my head.

"Santiago will kill me if I tell you before he gets here."

"What!" I slap him on the shoulder.

Hugh spins away from me back into his kitchen, laughing—the sound as robust and full as the scents floating through the room. "Take a seat over there." He points to a tiny table with two chairs pushed into a corner. "Santiago will be here soon enough."

I navigate through the tight kitchen, feeling Blue's absence keenly. *He should be right behind my left leg.* But showing up in Hugh's kitchen in the middle of the dinner rush is rude enough without bringing a giant hairy mutt with me.

I sit at the table and watch Hugh melt back into the madness. He puts a pan on a burner and drops a dollop of butter into it before pulling out his phone and shooting off a quick text.

By the time Hugh is serving me a gorgeous plate of mushroom risotto, Santiago bursts through the kitchen door. "Sydney Rye!" he yells, crossing the space and pulling me out of my seat into a tight embrace. I squeeze him back, his affection and warmth so damn welcome I can barely take it. "You have been gone too long!"

"I missed you."

Santiago releases me and laughs. "Not so much that you came to visit though, huh?" I shrug, my cheeks heating. "Don't worry about it, we know you're busy." He winks at me—Hugh and Santiago know I'm a founding member of Joyful Justice, but they have no idea what I've been up to for the past year...and I have no plans to tell them.

A waiter arrives with a glass of red wine for Santiago, and he notices my plate of food. "Sit, eat," he commands, moving to the other side of the table and taking the empty chair. He is a big man, broad-shouldered but slim, with radiant black hair pushed off his brow—it looks wet, like he just got out of the shower—and his golden complexion shines under the harsh lighting. He's gorgeous and smart and fun, and I really do enjoy his company. Watching Hugh move on from James is painful and yet healing. Life does go on. I'll never have another brother, and Hugh will never have another first love, but we can both find happiness and joy none the less.

"Hugh says you guys have some news," I say.

"He managed not to spill the beans, huh?"

"Tell me already! I'm dying over here."

Santiago laughs, the sound bold and somehow brave, as if his happiness is a testament to his character and cannot be laid at the feet of any circumstance. "Let's wait until Hugh gets off work, okay?"

I narrow my eyes and frown, but the magical buttery scent of the risotto draws my attention. "Eat!" Santiago points at the bowl.

So I do, slipping into the pleasure of sustenance, of nourishment... and of a taste that is just so close to home it brings tears to my eyes and warmth to my chest.

I'm so lucky.

"I heard about your mom," Santiago says, turning the rice in my mouth to sand. "I'm sorry."

I cough and take a sip of my wine to wash the food down. "Thanks, but I'm sure Hugh told you, we're not close."

"Not even after all the work she's done to spread the message of the Her Prophet? I would have thought you two reconciled."

I shake my head. "Some things cannot be forgiven." My voice comes out strange, low...almost like that old thunder.

"Amen, girl, amen. How is Mulberry?" Santiago asks after another founding member of Joyful Justice...the man who helped me escape New York. The man I love. The man who doesn't remember me.

Another painful question. I smile weakly. "He's doing well."

Santiago cocks his head, clearly not believing me. "Really," I say, forcing myself to believe my own words. "He got back together with his ex-wife. They are really happy. Mulberry is living a normal, good life."

Santiago's eyes narrow. "And that's making him happy?" he asks, skepticism dripping off each word.

I nod. "Sure, of course. He's not in mortal danger anymore. Is in—" I have to swallow before I can continue. "He's in love. Happy. I'm happy for him."

Santiago spins his wine glass stem, eyeing me across the table. But he doesn't contradict me. And I don't share any more details. I don't tell Santiago that Mulberry lost much of his memory, and part of his left leg. That he's living a safe, normal life that's one big, fat lie. That I want him to be safe and happy so badly I can't dwell on any of that. So instead, I turn to my food. And I eat it.

I start a second glass of wine while Hugh finishes up dinner service. Once it's winding down and only the pastry chef is still moving at speed, Hugh comes to our table. "So," I say, feeling pretty buzzed. It's the first time I've had more than one drink in a few months, and the wine is going straight to my head. "What is going on with you two?"

Hugh and Santiago look at each other sharing a silent communication. Then Hugh turns to me, his gaze bright and yet tinged with a hint of worry. "What?" I say, anxiety brewing in my chest, fueled by the wine and that crinkle around Hugh's eyes.

"We're getting married." He says it quietly, a happy hush over his words.

My voice freezes in my throat, and I open and close my mouth a few times like a fish struggling to find water. "That's so great." I cough and have to take another sip of wine before continuing. "That's really...I'm so happy for you two." My gaze bounces between them—they are radiating happiness, and their hands find each other on the table, like water molecules, drawn together by nature. *They belong together.*

"You should have the wedding at my place," I say, the words spilling out before I can stop them.

"Your place?" Hugh asks. "You're in Miami?"

I nod, looking up at him. "It's gorgeous. On Star Island."

His eyes narrow. "Wait, are you staying with Robert Maxim?"

"Yeah, I am."

"What?" Santiago's voice rises. "That guy?"

"Yeah," I hold his gaze. "He's changed actually." Santiago's eyebrows are up at his hairline. "I swear." A laugh escapes me. "And his house is ridiculous. Come by tomorrow for drinks. You'll see what I mean."

The two men turn to each other and share another silent communication that makes my heart ache. It's Hugh who answers me. "We'd love to come for drinks."

I smile, something inside me loosening. *I can help give them a beautiful wedding. I can be a part of this.*

Reaching for my wine I fight back tears. I'm not sad. I swear. I just can't seem to swallow the lump in my throat. Because…James is gone. And Hugh is marrying someone else. And people *do* change. And life does go on.

But sometimes I just don't want it to.

CHAPTER EIGHT

Declan

I'm in a small rental boat. I've got a fishing pole, and I'm watching Robert Maxim's mansion. This is a free country, and I've got a right to be out here. But he doesn't have a right to do whatever he wants, to just live his life like he hasn't destroyed thousands of others. Like he hasn't *killed.*

The sun beats down—I'm getting seared under its rays. It reflects back from the water, catching in my eyes, bronzing my skin...it's all good, though. I can handle the heat.

Sun glints off the glass walls of Robert's mansion. My heart skips a beat as one of the doors opens. A figure, wearing a long white dress that swishes around her slim legs and a wide brimmed hat, steps out, followed by a giant dog. *Sydney Rye and Blue.*

She leans up against the rail and looks out to the horizon. Her attention is drawn back toward the house, and Robert appears, holding a phone. He passes it to her. She takes the handset and turns back to the horizon.

But she doesn't see me. She's not afraid of me. *She should be.*

Sydney stands straighter and turns back to Robert. Blue presses up against her side, his head as tall as her hip, his gaze on her face. She speaks to Robert, and they all move indoors.

I settle back into my seat. The sun drifts below Miami's jazzy modern skyline, and the sky blushes pink. I wait until darkness settles and electric lights glow to life all along the shore before starting up my engine and heading back.

After returning the boat to the rental place, I throw my fishing rod and cooler in the back of my rental car and head back to my apartment, a sterile, short-term place with a balcony and views of a bay. The water shimmers under the moonlight as I drink a beer on my couch, sitting in the dark.

A plan is slowly formulating. Its emerging picture reminds me of watercolor painting. My mother used to paint gardens and seashores, places we visited. Often, my siblings and I would be added to the picture: tiny splotches of fast-moving arms and legs in a great big world of swirling colors—blossoms and waves undulating around us.

My phone rings, pulling me out of the memories. *It's my mom.* "I was just thinking about you," I say as a greeting.

"That's sweet. How are you?"

"Great," I lie.

"You know I worry."

"Yes Ma, I know." A silence stretches between us. She hated that I got shot. Hell, I hated it too, but she hated it worse. "I'm okay, I promise." She sighs, and I hear the clinking of ice against glass as she takes a sip of something. "How's Dad?"

"You know him, keeping busy." He retired over a decade ago but still serves on several boards and stays active. Once a rich and powerful man, always a rich and powerful man. "Are you liking Miami?"

"I am. The weather's great."

She laughs, low and throaty. "It's miserable here. Gray and cold... maybe I could come visit?"

I sit up, adrenaline flashing through me. "Not a great time. I'm working a lot."

"Well, you should take a break."

If only she knew.

"That's not how cases work, Mom."

"I know, I know. The bad guys never take vacations."

"Well, they do." I laugh. "But that's the best time to sneak into their mansions and gather evidence."

She laughs again, and more ice clinks. "When will you come visit, then?"

"When I close this case."

"Do you think it will be soon?"

I stand and pace to the wall of windows, looking out at the bay— boats bob in gentle waves. "I'm not sure. But I hope so."

"Good." The glass thunks onto wood. She's probably in her study, surrounded by leather-bound books, the windows frosted, a fire roaring in the hearth. My chest aches at the image I've built in my mind, and a part of me wants to just lay my head down in her lap and cry. She never judged me for not going into the family business—for turning down an easy life in exchange for the danger and difficulty of law enforcement— but it didn't make her happy or proud.

She wanted me safe above all else.

"Have you met any nice women?"

I close my eyes and rest my forehead against the glass. "I'm working too much for that."

"Your sister is pregnant again."

"That's great," I force enthusiasm into my voice.

"That makes six children." There is judgment in her voice. *What kind of people have so many children?* "All girls so far."

"Maybe this one will be a boy."

"Well, you know I don't get involved."

A smile pulls at my lips. "No, of course not." I open my eyes and stare out at the moon. "I should go."

She sighs. "Okay, I love you, honey. Call me soon. You know I worry."

"Yes, Mom, I know you do. I love you, too."

I hang up first and turn back to the sterile living room, pushing my family out of my mind. There is no room for them now. Once I corner Sydney and Robert, then I can spend time with my mother, find a wife, do all that normal shit. But not yet. Not now.

CHAPTER NINE

Sydney

"YOU'RE sure Robert can't hear us?" is the first thing Dan says. He and Anita are sitting next to each other at Dan's desk on the island, video conferencing into the meeting, their image split with Lenox's on a large monitor. This is a meeting of the Joyful Justice council, the governing body of our organization.

"Yes." Merl answers Dan's question. He's sitting next to me, both of us in rolling chairs. We're in the office space we've rented in downtown Miami under the name "Dog Trainers Inc.," which helps explain all our freaking dogs, who are curled up around the room, sleeping lightly as they wait for our next move.

Across from us, floor to ceiling tinted windows face another tall, shining office building—we can usually see office workers buzzing around, living their ordinary lives. It's late now, so there are only a few brightened windows, a few hunched figures typing at desks. We headed straight here after Dan called the secure line at Robert's house, but it took a while to get everything set up.

"You did a sweep before the call?" Dan asks.

Merl nods. "Yes."

We used the bug detection device Dan ordered for us when we set up the office months ago and scanned the entire suite and the hallways just before streaming in.

"Okay," Dan relents, his face grave. The usually fine lines around his mouth and eyes are deep grooves.

"What's going on?" Lenox asks. He's sitting in a thick armchair covered in burgundy and gold paisley fabric, his laptop on his lap so that we're looking up at him. He's wearing headphones and a stern expression.

Dan called this meeting, saying it was an emergency. Lenox is on assignment, and it's a risk for him to call in now—it could blow his cover and jeopardize his mission.

Dan sighs and runs a hand through his sandy blond, sun-streaked hair. "We were attacked." Both Merl and I shift forward at the same time, our elbows landing on the glass-topped table. The island is in the middle of nowhere. How could they be attacked?

"It was an inside job. George Gonzales. Only minor injuries..." Dan looks as if the words hurt him. Anita is chewing on her lip, her hands on the desk, gripping it, as if she's fighting back an urge to reach out and touch Dan's shoulder—to comfort him in some way.

"I'm sorry," Merl says.

Dan's pale green gaze burns through the computer screen. "No, I'm sorry. I never should have trusted him. We should trust no one." The words send a shiver over me. Dan has always been cautious but also optimistic. *Something has changed with him.* "But he's not the only one," Dan continues, running his hand through his hair again. "George got a call that his sister, Elsa, was being held captive. And that if he didn't infiltrate our security system and find out the location of the island, she'd be killed."

Great effort has gone into keeping the location of our island base a secret from all but the trusted few. Wi-Fi access for anything beyond email is highly restricted, and no one is allowed a device with GPS.

Lenox is frowning, listening intently, his dark eyes unreadable.

"She's only sixteen, and I knew she was a weak spot for him. I should have listened in on his call. Or at least had it traced. Dammit."

"This isn't your fault," Merl says quietly.

"Of course it is," Dan grits his teeth. "But that doesn't even matter. Because there is someone else working for our enemies. Elsa told George that if he tipped anyone—me for example—they'd kill her."

"So, someone else close to you must be compromised," Lenox reasons.

"Yes." Dan nods, casting his eyes down to his desk top.

"Any idea who?" I ask.

He shakes his head, a long strand of hair falling forward only to be forcefully pushed back behind his ear. "I'm going through call logs and emails but have not found anything yet. I'm not sure who else to trust, so right now it's just Anita and me going through everything."

"It's a slow process," Anita says, her dark eyes staying on Dan. She looks concerned, sucking her lip between her teeth and biting down as she watches him fidget.

Merl is nodding next to me. "How can we help speed up the process?" he asks.

"I don't think you can," Dan says. "I'm not opening access to my files to anyone right now, and you wouldn't even know what to look for...who everyone is." He sighs again, and the sound feels almost like a weight draping around my shoulders. Dan used to be so carefree. So fun and laid back. Now he's wound tighter than a Tea Party Republican at a pride parade—exhausted from the energy it takes to hide so many secrets.

A twinge of guilt tightens my fists, but I force myself to let it go. *I did not make Dan pursue justice at any cost. He wants this as much as I do.*

"Is there anything we can do here?" I ask. "Obviously, we need to figure out who is threatening our people. Have you spoken to George's parents? Found out any details of how their daughter was taken?"

Dan shakes his head. "I'm keeping it super quiet at this point. I have not told anyone we know. Their phones are probably bugged."

"That's smart," Lenox says.

"Where are the parents?" I ask.

"In Texas," Dan says. "Outside of Dallas. I'm sure they are being watched. I don't want to get his sister killed." Dan nods, as if to himself.

"Me either," I say. "But we need to talk to them. See if we can figure out what happened."

"Their phones are probably monitored. Along with any smart devices they have in their home." Dan sips from a mug, his eyes losing focus as he works on the problem.

"Do they have any dogs?" Merl asks.

"Yes, a mutt named Bradley. Part Shepherd, part Rottie."

Merl nods, a frown pulling at his lips. "Do they go to dog runs?"

"I don't know," Dan answers, his eyes focusing onto the screen again.

"What if I pretended to be a truancy officer or something?" I ask. "She must have missed a few days of school by now."

Merl shakes his head. "If parents are calling in and saying the kid is sick then you wouldn't have officials showing up. Not for a while."

"I think we need surveillance on them," I say. "We need more information. I can run into the mother at the dog run or something."

"What's the neighborhood like?" Merl asks Dan.

"Suburban. Working class. Mostly Hispanic."

Merl turns to me. "You'll stick out like a sore thumb."

"We can't use any of our operatives," Dan says. "We don't know who's compromised. If they can get to George, they can get to anyone."

Anita nods. "I've been on the sister's social media accounts. My best guess is they took her seven days ago. George got the call five days ago. Not sure why they waited so long."

"Maybe they were transporting her somewhere," Lenox says.

"But wouldn't you start your threats right away?" I ask.

Lenox shrugs. "I wouldn't kidnap a young girl to begin with."

"What if she escaped?" Merl asks. "Maybe they didn't have her for a few days."

"I like that possibility," I say, picturing a teenage girl outwitting international criminals...even if only for a short time.

"I checked her parents' phone records," Dan says. "They got a call the first day from a blocked number. So I think they knew from the get go but probably have no idea this is about their son. They must be holding off on calling the police because of threats they received."

"Any parents would be sick about this," I say, my mind wandering to my mother. *Would she have even noticed if I'd disappeared when I was sixteen? Probably not.*

Lenox shifts in his seat and glances over his shoulder. *We need to wrap this up.* "What do you suggest?" Merl asks.

Dan runs a hand through his hair again. "I really wish we had Mulberry on this." I stiffen at Mulberry's name, and Merl glances at me. I give a small shake of my head to let him know I'm okay. "He's the best investigator we've got."

"Should we ask Robert?" Merl suggests.

Dan raises his gaze to him. "I don't trust him."

"I do," I say, my voice quiet.

Dan lets out a long breath. "I think it's better to keep this in as tight a circle as possible until we figure out who else has been threatened."

"I may be able to help," Lenox says, his voice quiet. "Give me some time to do some investigating." He glances over his shoulder again. "It may be that Petra and the McCain brothers are behind this."

"Really?" Dan asks, leaning forward.

"Petra mentioned they planned to take on Joyful Justice. And I suspect she is keeping someone locked up on the property. Let me see what I can find out. I'll contact you soon."

"Okay." Dan's voice is weary. "We've shut down communications to the island while we work our way through older messages, but you can still reach Anita and me."

"What should I do?" I ask.

"Not tell Robert," Dan snaps.

It feels like a slap—I open my mouth to respond but realize Dan is exhausted. His eyes are red-rimmed, his skin gray. Anita is looking at him with concern.

"Fine," I say, mimicking his posture. "I'll keep my mouth shut if you promise to get some sleep."

Anita turns to me, relief in her eyes. Dan's face shutters. "I'm fine."

"And I'm the queen of England," I say, my voice edged with anger. "I know you can go a long-ass time without sleep, but I want you well-rested. Take a fucking nap, you asshole."

Dan can't help the smile that creeps onto his lips. "Fine," he says.

Anita is nodding. "Watch him," I say to her. "You know he will try to take a tablet or something."

Anita smiles. "Yes, ma'am," she answers, her voice laced with humor.

We disconnect, and I stare out the window at the sparse office workers in their lit-up boxes. *There but for the grace of God go I.*

EK

Lenox

I CLOSE the laptop and slip the headphones off, storing them in my bag along with the secure mobile hot spot. A knock on the door jerks my head up.

"Yes?"

The door opens on well-oiled hinges, and Petra steps into the guest bedroom I've been using, her fingers never leaving the handle. "You're up early."

I smile, feeling tension behind my eyes. "Yes, working. Did I disturb you?"

She shakes her head. "I'm used to sleeping alone."

The words tug at my heart. *I'm used to sleeping alone, too.* I have to bite my tongue to keep from asking what she is doing. *Why has she become a slave trader?*

"Should I come back to bed then?" I run my eyes over her body, clad in a rose-colored silk negligee, her matching robe hanging open.

She shakes her head, loose waves of hair dancing around her shoulders. "No, let's get up. I want breakfast. We need to talk." Petra turns and pads down the hall, leaving me alone. A sick feeling stirs in my stomach. *Does she know?*

I dress in exercise clothing—easy to run and fight in, if it comes to that. My gold chain bounces against my neck as I jog down the steps and my phone thunks against my thigh. Dan's words float through my mind. *They kidnapped George's sister...*

Right now, Joyful Justice has over sixty research operations in motion—which is the first stage of opening a mission. After a complaint about the exploitation of a vulnerable group is registered with Joyful Justice, we investigate the legitimacy of the claim. If the complaint is deemed valid, and our help is warranted, we create a packet detailing the activities that must be stopped to avoid retribution. This happens in about 20% of cases.

We deliver the packet with a warning and timeline. Depending on the activities of the accused, they have anywhere from 30 to 90 days to change their behavior before we move into active mission status.

In that time, we train and prepare for the eventual takedown while continuing to monitor activity. In most cases, the original complaint comes from someone with inside knowledge, who Joyful Justice then trains to take part in the mission—either as a leader, member of a team, or lone wolf, using their access to attack sensitive areas. We believe in empowering the abused to cleanse their victim status and lift them up to become avengers.

If the accused complies with our demands, then no further action is taken, though monitoring is continued for an appropriate length of time. The initial complainant typically leads the surveillance and is responsible for the follow up reports given to the council.

As of right now, twenty-three missions are in what we call the "Wait and See" stage—our demands have been made, and the accused has promised to reform. Ten missions are on the cusp of "active"—the accused refused our demands or violated them, and our team is preparing to go in and force compliance.

The McCain brothers' sex-trafficking ring uses Petra's smuggling services to move women around the world. They also share intel and co-own sixteen brothels. The brothers received a packet six weeks ago and immediately refused to comply. Petra's knowledge of this development seems inevitable, but I'm here to make sure our suspicions regarding her are correct.

The McCain brothers, Ian, Michael and Murphy, were originally brought to our attention by a young Yazidi woman who escaped after being bought at an Isis auction in Saudi Arabia. She identified Ian, the oldest brother, as the man who purchased her. I went to Saudi Arabia and attended an auction, where I recorded Ian buying more girls.

I then followed him and the women he bought to an airport, where Ian used one of Petra's connections to move them out of the country by private plane. Did Petra know these women were unwilling victims of war? I hope not. But can't be sure…yet.

And now the McCains appear to have struck back by kidnapping George's sister to gain leverage over Joyful Justice. I know this is a long-shot, but could Petra be part of that plot and, if so, could that girl be imprisoned behind that shiny new lock on the door of that old dungeon? Only one way to find out.

Petra sits in her breakfast room—the morning sun bathing her in warm, dewy light. A handsome wrought-iron frame sealed with panes of glass makes up the walls and ceiling, through which the wide, mani-cured yard shimmers almost silver, still wet from the night. Beyond, the wild, untamed forest hunkers dark and foreboding, the sun not strong or high enough to breach its denseness.

A piece of wheat toast with a thin layer of butter and jam sits by Petra's elbow, and an elegant china cup brimming with coffee is raised to her bare lips.

She sips the coffee, its mocha color contrasting with the pale cream of her own skin, then replaces the cup on the saucer with a tinkling sound. Her gaze lifts to mine, and she smiles, slow and sultry. "How did you sleep?" she asks, eyes still heavy from her own night's rest.

I sit down across from her. "Very well, and you?"

She leans back into the chair, its glossy wood and pale blue satin upholstery making her eyes that much greener. *The green of greed.*

"I was thinking quite a bit." Lacing her fingers together, she rests them across her flat stomach, keeping her bright gaze focused on me, as if I'm a subject to study rather than a lover come for coffee. "I want to ask you something, but I'm nervous."

"Nervous?" My smile feels tight and my heart thumps harder. Cocking my head, I force the muscles around my mouth to relax, wrestle my heart into a steady rhythm, and take a slow, deep breath. "Why be nervous?" I ask, leaning forward, weaving innocent curiosity into my voice and gaze. "We are old friends. You can ask me anything."

She leans forward, mimicking my posture, and sips from her coffee again. Her gaze drifts to the table. "Things are changing rapidly in our business. Joyful Justice is a thorn in our side."

My chest tightened, and I reach for the coffee carafe to pour myself a cup. I hold my tongue, letting her speak, knowing that my silence is more powerful than any response. *Will she admit to having the girl?*

"I want you to help me."

The coffee comes out black and fragrant, filling the cup quickly. I replace the carafe and pick up the cream, pouring it into the dark brew so that it blooms into a pale brown.

"I know that you work rarely now, and have a solid recruitment policy for the men in your employ. That you are an honest and good man."

My eyes rise to hers, hearing truth in her voice. Petra has a high opinion of me. *As I used to of her.*

My gut twists. Is she about to confess to me that she is dealing in war slaves? Helping to move them around the world. Not only have these young women suffered the abuse and losses of war—seen their fathers and brothers murdered, their sisters and mothers raped—but now, because of Petra's greed and willful blindness, they face a lifetime of rape and servitude. *No.* My jaw tightens as my resolve hardens against my old friend, against the bonds we have built over the last fifteen years.

Petra freed me, in her way. But I cannot sit idly by if she is enslaving others.

"Will you help me take down Joyful Justice?" she asks, her eyes finding mine. Petra's green eyes are round, pleading. She looks almost frightened. *Is it an act? Or is she more entwined with the McCain brothers than we knew?*

She has not received a package but maybe she should…

I sit back in my chair, taking the china cup with me, dropping my gaze to hood my eyes with thoughtful shadows—hiding my contempt. "I do not feel that is my fight."

Petra leans forward quickly, her speed a reminder of how dangerous she really is—all of the fear is gone from her gaze and in its place the feral determination of a cornered animal sparks into life. "Don't you see? They will come for you too. We must unite in order to defeat them."

I sip the coffee, rich caramel and dark chocolate. I take a measured breath, and her shoulders slowly relax as we stare at each other. "Petra, you say that you believe me to be an honest man. That you admire me. And yet, you want me to defend practices that are against my nature, against what I believe to be a good way of doing business. A good way of living. Joyful Justice, from my understanding, is only attacking those who are breaking what I consider to be a reasonable moral code. There is no fight here for me."

Petra's hand reaches out for me. I'm sitting too far back for her to touch, so I extend my hand, twining my fingers with hers, showing her that she is not my enemy. That we are still friends. Still peers. Still lovers. *But I will not fight by her side this time.*

"Then do it for me," Petra says, her voice low and throaty. Almost begging, but also commanding.

I do owe her. She is reminding me—calling on our history. Claiming a debt I never agreed to but owe nonetheless.

"Can you prove to me that Joyful Justice's accusations aren't true about your business partners? The McCain brothers are not among my contacts. I do not work with them."

Her brow furrows, and she sits back, her hand releasing mine in a jerk. "You don't trust me?"

I keep my expression flat and my eyes on hers. "I trust you, Petra. I don't trust the McCain brothers. Their reputation is not clean."

"I know them. I've known them for years."

I suck my lower lip between my teeth and worry it, as though I'm being torn here, as if I can't decide whether to help her or not.

"Risking my business, my customers and the men who work for me, is a big request. Will you share more information with me?"

Petra's eyes darken. "I understand that I am asking a lot, but this will do you good in the end. We must take down Joyful Justice if we want to continue to live our lives."

I don't respond, sipping my coffee instead. *She ignored my question.*

Petra turns to her toast and crunches on it. Silence fills the breakfast nook. Moments later, her maid appears with a plate of eggs and bacon for me. She knows me well. Has she guessed I've betrayed her? Or does she believe I will join her?

CHAPTER TEN

Dan

I WAKE up to the sound of silence. There is nothing in my room—not even the soft hum of my computers. I shut them down, to finally get some sleep.

Anita insisted.

The memory of her sitting on my bed, long shimmering hair draped over one shoulder, flashes across my closed eyes. "If you don't sleep, Dan, I'll have to kill you," an indulgent smile playing on her lips as she tucks in the sheets around me.

How long did I sleep? I reach over for my phone, but its screen is dark. I close my eyes again as it reboots. *There is so much to do…*

My phone vibrates, letting me know it's back online.

I slept four hours.

Better than nothing.

I climb out of bed and pull back the curtains. It's dawn; the sun sits at the waterline, shimmering off the restless ocean and reflecting off the few clouds in sprays of pink, peach, and orange.

All communication between the island and the outside world is shut down—except for Anita and me, who still have access. It's a small protection and gives me a little room to breathe. *But we are not safe.*

All missions are on hold, until I can figure out what's going on.

Leaving the window, I head into the sitting room of my three-room suite, turning on my computers and starting the coffee maker before hitting up the bathroom.

The florescent lights flicker on, and I grab my toothbrush. Glancing at my reflection, I pause, struck by how old I look. There are crinkle lines around my eyes that weren't there last year, flashes of silver in the blond stubble lining my jaw, and a slight slump to my shoulders. I straighten, forcing myself to stand tall so I can see the outline of my muscles under my shirt. *I'm still strong. Maybe stronger than ever.*

I hold my own gaze—bloodshot, pale green eyes stare back at me. Shaking my head, I turn on the tap and brush my teeth, keeping my eyes on my phone, flicking through my apps, checking for messages and alerts. *All is quiet.*

I'll head down to the command center soon, but there are some personal things I want to do first. Some tension-relieving work.

A cup of coffee in hand and my passwords entered, I settle in across from my computer at the desk I keep by the living room window. First, I check on my mother. It's evening in New Jersey, just about dinner time.

Her Alexa streams play across my screen, the sound waves moving up and down in spurts and starts. She's watching TV. Or at least has it on. It seems she always does. That's not unusual, using a device as a friend.

My mother has three Alexa units. I gave them to her. The one in the kitchen captures the clatter of dishes. *She's making dinner.*

"Hello, honey," she says in the sing-songy voice she uses for the cats. "You want some?" she asks.

A heavy hand squeezes my heart, and I turn off the sound, closing my eyes for a moment. I spend so much time trying to make the world a better place, and yet what can I do for my mother? I'm sacrificing her for some illusion of greater good.

I shake my head, trying to clear my thoughts.

This is not the time to question my life. It is a time to find out who is trying to destroy it.

Opening my eyes, I sip my coffee and change screens. Black and white CCTV footage fills my monitor. I have six cameras in Mulberry's apartment. He and his ex-wife, Sandy, moved in together soon after he recovered from his injury, and I keep track of him. For his own good and ours. If his memories come back, we need to know. If one of our enemies goes after him, we need to know.

Sandy is sitting at the dining room table. Her blonde head rests in her hands. At her elbow, a half-empty wine bottle sits next to her full glass. Her shoulders are shaking. She's crying.

What happened?

I pull up the recorded files, switching from the live stream, and begin to watch the day in reverse. Sandy backing up into the kitchen, pouring the wine back into the bottle, and closing it. I check the time stamp as she walks backward out the door—she got home from work at her normal time. But Mulberry wasn't there. Strange, but not alarming enough to explain the crying.

Time continues to rewind.

The house sits empty all day, where is Mulberry?

He's usually in and out. Heading to physical therapy, to the local café. He lives this incredibly awesome normal life where he works out and goes to the library and reads the paper. Last time I spoke to him he mentioned they might be getting a cat. *A cat.*

Not knowing who he was, what he fought for, gives him a special kind of freedom. A part of me envies him while another pities his memory-deprived existence.

But maybe he woke up.

The day passes in reverse and morning comes, and there he is, storming into the house backward, a duffel in his hand, his shoulders braced. *He left.* The footage keeps going, and he strides to his bedroom, ripping clothing out of the duffle, his jaw set into a hard line.

Where is Sandy?

She runs out of the bathroom, face in her hands, sobbing. *She ran in there crying. They had a fight.*

She is begging him. And he is speaking quietly, his movements so hard—every line of his body stiff—as firm as his prosthetic leg. Time keeps reversing, and then I see him wake up. I see his eyes pop open that morning.

I pause the footage, zooming in. The image is grainy and hard to make out, but it seems like he...remembered.

I let time proceed at its normal pace and in the traditional direction —forward—Mulberry sits up and looks around the room, as if seeing it for the first time. His gaze landing on Sandy, who sleeps peacefully next to him.

Mulberry puts his elbows on his knees and his head in his hands. His shoulders shake for a moment as if he is crying.

God, it must all have come back to him.

We knew this was a possibility. Perhaps even an inevitability.

My hand is gripping the mouse. I'm on the edge of my seat.

There's a knock at the door, pulling my attention from Mulberry's shaking form to the front door of my suite.

I click over to a blank screen and put the computer to sleep before standing. Checking the video monitor by the door, I see it's Anita. She looks relaxed, her hair shiny with wetness, like she just got out of the shower. Opening the door, I smile at her.

"I hope I didn't wake you," she says in that accent of hers—the cool confines of a British boarding school mixed with the evocative lilt of a childhood in India.

I shake my head. "Been up for a bit. Come on in. You want coffee or anything?"

She nods and enters, the scent of her mint and rosemary shampoo coming with her.

"Anything going on I need to know about?" I ask, crossing the living room to the coffeemaker.

"I want to reopen communication. People are getting antsy."

"You know that's far too dangerous." I refresh my cup and then turn to her, asking with a raised brow if she wants the same. She nods.

I pour her a coffee, adding sugar and cream just the way she likes.

BETRAY THE LIE

Anita sits on my couch, and I bring her the mug, sitting down next to her.

"It's not fair to punish everyone."

"Anita, you're being unrealistic, and you know it." I sip my coffee, watching her. She's not making eye contact. *Something else is going on here.*

"What is it?" I ask her.

She cocks her head, eyes narrowing. "By putting everyone under suspicion, by saying no one can talk to their family or friends, we are making them all into suspects. And when you start to make everyone a suspect, you risk the possibility of turning them all into enemies. Besides, don't you think if we open the lines then maybe we can catch something? A call coming in? Something?"

I sip my coffee, watching her. She holds my gaze, her large brown eyes wide and sincere. "So you're suggesting we let them believe we trust them, while in reality turning them all into suspects?"

She blushes and turns away.

"Let's give it a few more hours. See if anything turns up on the scans of our systems. If no one tries to breach anything then I'll open communication to phone calls only."

Anita smiles. "All right, that works. Want help listening in?"

"I'll need it."

"Great." She puts her cup down on the coffee table and moves to stand.

"One more thing," I say and she turns back to me. "I think Mulberry remembered."

Her jaw loosens in surprise, and she drops back into the couch. "My God, what makes you think that?"

I'm not going to tell her about the surveillance. She doesn't need to know.

"I have my reasons."

She shakes her head, a smile on her lips. *She knows my ways.* "I'm going to call Sandy," I say, "and see if I can confirm it."

"Okay, do you want me to call Sydney and the rest of the council?"

"I think we can wait until communication is back open. We don't need to alarm anyone. And I want to make sure that I'm right."

Anita's expression darkens. "Hiding it from them doesn't serve anyone."

"We're not hiding it from them, Anita." I close my eyes, exhaustion washing over me. "But we have enough to worry about without unsubstantiated rumors."

When I open my eyes again, Anita is staring at me, her gaze stormy. "This isn't some little thing. Mulberry helped found Joyful Justice. None of us would be here without him."

"I know that." I say it more sharply than I mean to and she flinches. "I'm sorry, I'm tired. I just don't want to get everyone upset."

"They'll be more upset if you don't tell them, Dan. I know you like to keep things quiet, keep everything under your control. But this is different. You need to be open about what's happening here, and about what's happening with Mulberry."

"You're right," I say, running a hand through my hair and looking toward the window behind her for a moment before meeting her eyes again. "I'm sorry." Her features soften. "I'll call Sydney after I confirm what's going on, and then we can tell everyone else."

"Good."

Anita stands and I move with her, walking toward the door. She opens it and then turns back to me, half in the hall. "See you down in the command center." I nod and she walks away, the door swishing almost silently shut behind her, the lock clicking automatically into place.

Taking my coffee, I return to my computer and switch back over to the surveillance of Mulberry's house. Or at least what was Mulberry's house until this morning.

Sandy is still sitting at the dining room table. Except her glass is now empty, and she's no longer crying. Just sitting there, staring off into space.

I open a new window and check Mulberry's credit cards—nothing so far today. Next I log into his online banking. He withdrew $1500 in cash. I sit back in my chair, staring at the screen. *He knows I'm watching.*

I dial Sandy's number, it rings on my end, and a moment later Sandy starts, sitting up quickly and turning toward the kitchen. She swipes at her eyes, just staring at the door for a moment before standing up slowly...carefully. *She's had more wine than she is used to.*

Sandy passes into the kitchen and stops in front of the phone on the counter, her head bowed as she stares at it. *Pick up.*

Taking a deep breath, she grabs the handset and pushes the on button. "Hello?" Her voice is ragged, and she keeps one hand resting on the counter, shoulders hunched.

"Sandy, it's Dan."

"Oh," she says. "Mulberry isn't here." Her voice sounds dead. *Emotionless.*

"Do you know when he'll be home?" I ask, hoping she'll tell me what happened. Hoping I won't have to press.

"I don't know if he's coming back, Dan. He remembered some things." Her voice raises, an edge of anger sharpening her tone. Her shoulders straighten out, and she clears her throat before continuing. "He remembered some things that made him have to leave."

"I'm sorry to hear that," I say quietly.

"He's not answering my calls." The edge of anger shifts into pain again...there are tears in her voice. She lets go of the counter and covers her eyes as her shoulders hunch forward again. "Why didn't you just tell him whatever it is he's now remembering? Ease him back rather than having it come in a rush?" Her voice squeezes off into a sob.

I take a deep breath, my heart loud in my ears. "I'm sorry, Sandy. Maybe that would have been better." *Shit.*

"Fuck you." Her rage is fast and quick. "You said you were his friend, but you're not. None of you are." She brings the phone down and pushes the button, disconnecting our call. Sandy places the phone back on the counter and puts her hands on either side of it, bracing herself, head hanging down. I put my phone on the desk next to my keyboard and chew on my lip. *Is she dangerous to us?*

Sandy picks up the phone again and dials a number. When no one picks up, she turns it off, staring down at the handset. Her grip tightens on the phone, and suddenly she hurls it across the room. The plastic smashes into the fridge, pieces flying off before bouncing on the floor. Sandy is breathing heavily, her body shaking.

She turns and races back through her dining room, pausing at the front door for only a moment to slip on her shoes and grab her bag.

Then she's out the door...out of my sight. I rub at the stubble on my chin and close my eyes, leaning back in my chair.

Sandy doesn't know anything...but that doesn't mean she can't hurt us.

CHAPTER ELEVEN

Sydney

MERL DROPS me and my dogs off at Robert's house, and I make my way through the garden, sucking in a deep breath of floral and salt-scented air as I wind along the path to the front door.

A guard named Jorge rustles in the brush, tilting his head to me. I nod back. Frank lets out a happy bark, and Blue silences him with a low growl. *Will Frank ever learn?* A smile crosses my lips as I silently hope he doesn't.

The front hall smells of something delicious, and I make my way back to the kitchen. Jose is humming in front of the stove, a pan sizzling on the front burner.

"Smells good," I say.

Robert's chef turns, giving me a bright smile. In his fifties, with gray-streaked black hair, Jose is originally from Cuba. He braved the passage to America on a homemade raft at the age of seventeen and recently got his citizenship—Robert and I attended the ceremony. "Just onions in butter," Jose says. I take a deep breath, closing my eyes, and let gratitude well inside me. "Mr. Maxim wasn't sure what time you'd be back. I thought you might like an omelet?"

I open my eyes and smile. "That would be so great. Thanks, Jose."

His gaze falls to the dogs, focusing on Blue. "I saved him a chicken liver," he says with a smile. Blue wags his tail as though he understands. Blue loves Jose, who is always saving him special treats and spoiling him. Blue deserves all the attention, but he has a new thickness around his belly Merl recently warned me needed to be watched. *An older dog's weight is very important for his health.*

I refuse to think of Blue as *older*.

Footsteps in the hall draw my attention. Robert looms out of the darkness into the bright lights of the kitchen. "Hey," he says, "how did it go?"

"Fine," I shrug.

A frown tugs at his lips, but he lets it go. *Robert does not like being out of the loop.*

"I need to speak with you about something." There is a note in his voice that raises the hairs on the back of my neck. *Whatever this is, it isn't good.*

"Okay," I say.

Robert turns to Jose. "She can have her omelet in twenty."

"Yes, sir," Jose says as he opens the fridge.

I follow Robert to his office. He gestures to the loveseat and armchairs by the window. "What's going on?" I ask. "The suspense is killing me."

"Sit." I do, my dogs fanning out, surrounding me in a comforting circle. Blue leans against my right leg, resting his head on my lap, Frank settles near my left foot, and Nila lies behind my chair. Robert takes a seat across from me. He settles back into the deep seat, his eyes holding mine. "Your mother—" My heart jumps into my throat, and I'm choking on it. *Is she dead?* "Is getting out of the rehab tomorrow."

I swallow, relief washing through me. "Oh."

"Do you want to see her?"

"No."

He frowns, his eyes darkening with judgment.

"What?" I say, my voice rising.

"You may regret not knowing her one day."

"I *do* know her. She's a crazy bitch."

His lips quirk up for just a moment as he laces his fingers across his stomach. "That doesn't change the fact that she's your mother—your only living family. One day she'll be gone." He pauses, his expression turning serious. "And you'll be alone."

I shake my head, trying to cast off the truth he's speaking. "I'm already alone."

"You're not." His voice comes out harsh, as though I've touched a nerve. *His parents are gone.*

"I'm sorry, but this is none of your business." I stand quickly, knocking Blue back. He harrumphs his displeasure.

Robert rises slowly, unfolding from the chair: a predator revealing its true strength before striking for the kill. "We are friends now, Sydney, right?" The question comes out quiet—sincere—and all my anger evaporates, exposing the deep sadness thinking about my mother causes.

Robert takes my elbow, gentle yet firm. "I consider you a friend."

"Don't get mushy," I warn.

He smiles, subtle and knowing. "So take my advice. Go see your mother. You don't have to agree with her, or even forgive her. But offer her the chance to..." his voice fades out as his attention is pulled somewhere else—his eyes lose focus and a shadow passes over them at the thoughts brewing behind his gaze.

"A chance to what?" I ask, my voice low, almost a whisper.

He returns his focus to me. "I was going to say to know you, but maybe that's asking too much. She fought for you, though. She braved a lot to try to find you. My wrath, her own fear, Isis."

"She's crazy, like I said. I'm sure she thought God had her back."

"That kind of faith can be admirable."

"It's dangerous."

Robert nods, his eyes soft and thoughtful. "Yes, Sydney. Your mother is dangerous. And her surviving this wound is evidence to a lot of people that she is chosen by God to spread her message. A message of equality for women. Of revolution. A message you agree with. Your mother could be useful to you in the future."

I frown. "There is always an angle with you," I accuse.

Robert shrugs, releasing my elbow. "There are many angles to any issue. Forgiving your—"

I cut him off. "I'll never forgive her." Sharp anger cuts through the sadness.

Robert takes a step back. "She's changed. And so have you. Open yourself to the many possibilities the world offers, and you will find the one that best suits you." He steps away, headed for his desk.

"You sound like a Hallmark card."

Robert laughs. "Do you want me to drive you tomorrow?"

"What?"

"To the rehabilitation center."

"I didn't say I would go." I follow him toward his desk.

He rounds it and sits in his chair before looking up at me. His eyes are blank, unreadable. "But you will go see her. It's important for more than just you. Sydney, it is your responsibility to connect with her, to help guide this movement that you started."

My mouth opens and closes. *I'd just gotten used to the idea that I had to help lead Joyful Justice.* "I'm not helping lead a religious movement I don't believe in." *He's crazy.*

Robert's lips tighten. "I'm not suggesting you start giving speeches or making sermons. Just that you speak to your mother."

"I'd rather give a sermon than do that." Anger burns my throat, and I turn quickly, facing the door, my feet swiftly moving toward it, Blue at a heel and the other dogs leaping up to join us.

"I'll drive you tomorrow then," Robert says, his voice soft and assured.

I turn back to him, tears welling in my gaze. I shake my head, but he's not looking at me. Robert's gaze is on his computer, his eyes following text. *He's won this argument somehow.*

EK

I KNOCK on the door of my mother's room, my hands tightly clenched. *I don't want to be here.* Blue taps his wet nose to my coiled fist, offering comfort and strength. My breath eases out.

Robert stands behind me, his phone in his hand, reading something, as if this is all so casual. No big deal—I'm just going to see my crazy mother who almost died.

"Come in," she says.

I swallow the fear trying to climb its way up my throat and turn the handle, pushing into her room, Blue tight to my side, Robert remaining in the hall. My mother stands by the bed with her back to me as she packs things into a small duffel.

Mom's thin shoulders move slowly, the sharp angles of her bones visible through the blouse she wears, making her look frail, almost on the verge of breaking...or maybe just clawing her way back from broken.

I don't say anything, but rather just stand there watching her. My heart beats wildly in my chest as memories swirl across my vision: my mother's gentle touch when I was little; how red her face turned when she drank during my teenage years; the anger, despair, and *disgust* in her eyes after James's death.

The gun gripped in her hands. Her dress, crusted in blood and dirt, the way her eyes shone with light on the battlefield in Syria.

The way she dropped to her knees, dust puffing up around her...the cadence of her voice as she told me I was a miracle, proof of God's righteousness, brought back to life to spread a message.

"Is the car here, Claire?" My mother turns to me with brows raised in question as the door clicks shut behind me. Her mouth drops open as her eyes land on me.

"Joy," she breathes, her voice barely a whisper...practically a prayer.

"It's Sydney," I remind her.

She nods. "Of course." Mom steps forward, her movements inelegant, faltering.

She looks older, as if time has taken a blade and twisted it in her gut, speeding up the inevitable. The lines on her face are deeper, cheeks sunken, and silver dominates her hair. Her body is bent over, being pulled toward the grave, but her eyes are still the same mercury gray as mine—they have that same glow to them—her strange and unshakable faith shining through.

"I'm so glad you came," she says, reaching out for me.

97

I don't want her to touch me.

Side stepping, I avoid her outstretched hand. She pauses, her mouth pulling down into a frown as her hands twine together, holding each other because they can't hold me.

I don't know what to say. I don't know why I came here. My eyes flicker to the closed door. "Where are you headed?" I ask, my voice coming out stilted and strange. Blue's nose taps my thigh in support.

Mom clears her throat, forcing a smile onto her lips. "I've rented a place in town and plan to spend some time resting...I have outpatient rehab. Then I'll be getting back out on the road."

"On the road?"

"Yes, of course." Her voice rises. "I will continue to spread Her message." She raises her hands to her stomach–to one of the places where she was shot. "This was just a test. But I survived. Clearly, I am meant to press on."

"Are you sure? Maybe it's a sign to shut up."

Mom just shakes her head, her smile growing broader. "No, this has brought even more attention to our cause. I am her."

I am her is the saying of those who follow the "her" prophet.

"Yeah, well, Mom,"—disdain drips off each word—"I am your daughter."

That makes her smile. Which wasn't the goal.

She takes a step forward, her eyes widening. She's going to try to touch me again. "Yes, exactly. We are mother and child. Our bond is unbreakable."

"You have so much faith, don't you? Faith God has chosen you. Faith you're on the right path. Faith I will forgive you."

She shakes her head. "I have faith but not in the way you make it sound. It is not some simple, easy thing for me."

"It was easy for you to throw James out. Like he was nothing. Like he didn't matter." Tears suddenly choke my voice, and I hate them.

She flinches as if I've slapped her. Her eyes well and redden with emotion. She shakes her head again. "That was not easy." Her voice is quiet and sharp. As if she's trying to explain something to me, but the words don't even exist.

"Yeah, well, you didn't make it look hard." My whole body is tingling. This is the fight we've needed. These are the words I've needed to say to her.

"I was wrong." Her voice is so quiet now that I barely hear her.

"You should say that more proudly," I tell her. Because it's true.

"I am weak. Like so many others."

"Yeah, you are." Disgust burns in my gut and I turn, headed for the door, Blue pressing against my leg, but Mom jumps forward and grabs my arm. I yank it free, and Blue lets out a soft growl of warning. Mom stumbles, almost falling, but I reach and catch her.

My fingers wrap around her thin biceps—there is hardly anything between my hand and her bone. *She is weak.*

Tears burn my eyes, and I can't seem to stop them from leaking out. She looks up at me, and tears are streaming down her face, too. "I'm so sorry," she says.

"You should be. You should be sorry for the rest of your life. You don't deserve to know me."

She's steady on her feet, so I let go of her. But I don't make another run for the door. I want to hear her admit it. Admit that I'm better than her. *That I was right and she was wrong.*

"I understand why you're angry. You have every right to be. But I still want a relationship with you."

"And why does what *you* want matter more than what I want?" My voice is quiet, lowering to meet hers.

She cringes away from me but does not retreat.

"It's what you want, too." She says it as if she knows me. As if we have some kind of relationship where she can tell me *my feelings.*

My hands are shaking, and I curl them into fists to get them to stop. Blue's wet nose brushes against one balled hand, giving me strength. "You don't know me," I remind her.

"We believe the same things now, Sydney. We are fighting for the same cause." Her gaze finds mine, and I don't look away.

"You are a liar. And a fool. And your faith makes you blind and stupid."

"Your refusal to believe in anything makes you dangerous and sad."

She stands a little taller, knowing she's hit something in me. A soft spot. Something she can push against that will give.

I spent years making myself hard, in both body and mind. And yet, Mom can always find the weakness in my armor.

I shouldn't have come. This was all a mistake.

Again, I turn for the door, determined this time to get away from her. "Wait," she says, but I don't. I pull on the handle, and the door cracks open.

"Why did you come here?" my mother asks, her voice edging on desperate.

I turn and look over my shoulder. She's standing there in her too-big blouse, with her fragile body and her crazy eyes. "I came here because someone convinced me I should try and work on a relationship with you. Because you're my mother. But that's not you. Not anymore. You're just a ghost from my past. My mother died along with my father. And then I died along with my brother. There is no family left here. Just two strangers in a room who don't even like each other."

I rip open the door and storm out, Blue tight to my side. Robert is sitting in one of the waiting chairs out front, and he stands as I head for the elevator. He doesn't speak as I jab the button repeatedly. He just stands behind me, his presence calm and steady.

"This was a mistake," I say, fighting to keep the tears out of my voice.

"No, it wasn't." He says it like he knows me. Like he has some rights over me. *No one controls me.* I clench my jaw so I won't scream at him. So I won't tell him to mind his own damn business.

The elevator doors open, and we step in. Blue sits by my side, and I look over at Robert. He's staring at me with that blue-green gaze of his —so cold and strong.

"She's a crazy bitch. And all I did was get upset."

"Sometimes we need to get upset to realize what's important to us."

"Oh, shut up."

"You can hit me if you want." His voice is a low rumble. *A challenge?*

"What?" I snap at him. *I do want to hit something.* Anything, anyone... except my own mother. I don't want to beat up on some weak old lady.

"Go ahead, hit me. It might make you feel better." He's not smiling, not giving me any clue if this is a joke or what.

The doors open onto the lobby, and I turn to him before walking out. "Nothing is going to make me feel better, Robert. Nothing but forgetting that she even exists. I'd be better off if she died."

I walk out, and Robert follows Blue and me, his strides long and steady. "Maybe you would be, but would the world?"

"Oh shut up," I say again, realizing I'm repeating myself. But I'm more angry than sad now, and that's something. *That's something good.* I can use anger. Sadness is quicksand—I sink in and stay sunk, useless and immobile.

Gathering the anger around myself like a shield, I step out into the bright Miami day. *I'm going to find someone to strike.* There are injustices far greater than my pathetic war with my mother. Watch out, bad guys. I'm coming for you.

CHAPTER TWELVE

Lenox

"YOU'LL BE LEAVING TOMORROW," Petra pouts. She holds a glass of red wine by its stem, twirling it slowly. Her nails are painted the same dark burgundy as the Châteauneuf du Pape. *My favorite.*

I give her a warm smile and reach out for her free hand. "I can come back soon."

"Good," she nods. "But what about Joyful Justice? You never answered me."

I take a deep breath and let it out slowly, as if this has been a hard decision for me. "I can't decide. Please, tell me more about what they are asking for, what they are claiming you've done."

"Not me," Petra says quickly. "I'm not on their radar." *How wrong she is...*

"So, this is the McCain brothers you are trying to protect. And what would you have me do exactly?"

"We are forming a coalition...to stop them. We already have people in place." Petra leans back, a satisfied smile coming onto her lips. I raise my brows, silently encouraging her to go on. But she shakes her head. "I can't tell you anymore until you agree to join me."

"But I can't do that until you tell me more details." I open my palms. *This is obvious.* "I'm a businessman, Petra, not a fighter. Joyful Justice has shown me no ill will."

"But it is only a matter of time," she protests, her voice going high.

"Have you taken action against them?" I ask. She drops her gaze but does not answer. *And that is answer enough.*

"Come," I say. "Let us talk of other things. Enjoy our last evening together."

Petra brings her eyes back to mine and gives me a warm smile. "Yes, lets."

Later, once she is asleep, I draw my arm from where it rests at her waist and slip from under the silk sheets. Naked, I ease from the room in silence, headed toward my guest room. Goosebumps rise on my bare skin as the cool night air wraps around me.

Once in my own space, I dress in exercise clothing and lace up my trainers. *I must check that dungeon in the woods.*

The mansion is quiet except for the wind blustering at the windows, and I arrive at Petra's office without seeing another soul. Moonlight spills in from the windows, lighting the room with its blue cast.

The mother of pearl box is where I last saw it. The beautiful object is smooth and cold against my fingers. I remove the key from its bed of velvet and slide it into my pocket, replacing the box and starting for the back door.

The sound of light footsteps freezes me in the study. Turning quickly I rush to the glass doors, which open to the garden and then beyond to the expansive yard bordered by the pitch-black forest.

"Lenox?" Petra's voice stops me on the threshold.

I look back into the room at her. Green eyes glitter in the darkness as she holds her robe closed against the cold breeze blowing in.

Do I lie?

"What are you doing?" Her voice is as cold as the night and sharp as a blade. *She will not believe me.*

"Going for a walk. Would you like to join me?"

She frowns deeply. "Liar." Moving toward a side table where a phone sits, she picks up the handset. I do not wait to hear who she calls.

Turning to the night, I dash over the loose, white stones of the garden, bursting through the topiaries, hitting the yard at a full run.

The night envelops me, but the moon betrays me as it glows bright enough to see each blade of grass. The black line of trees promises sanctuary, and I run toward it.

The grass, wet with dew, soaks my sneakers and barking in the distance urges me forward. The rumble of an ATV engine joins the other sounds of pursuit as I hit the forest and begin to dash through the trees.

I leap a fallen log. I can just make out the entryway to the dungeon. The pale stone archway, with its moss-covered wooden door, glows softly under the moonlight.

The shouting grows louder. *Do they know where I'm headed?*

I veer off my path. The chances of the girl being there are slim— we're a very long way from Texas. And, in any case, there is no time to save her now. I'll have to come back. But as I sprint through the trees, branches whipping my face and lancing cuts into my skin, the key to the dungeon bouncing in my pocket with each stride, I know I must go back to find out for sure. If she's their prisoner, they will move her or change the lock—I'll lose my chance if I don't do it now.

I'm thus pulled toward the dungeon, first my eyes and then my shoulders, followed by my waist and hips. My hand reaches out and grabs a tree trunk, spinning me around to face the prison. Then I'm sprinting toward it—toward that softly glowing beacon among the trees.

I skid to a halt in front of the dungeon and yank the key from my pocket, fitting it into the lock with unsteady hands. The deadbolt thunks back and I rip the door open, my eyes taking in only charcoal black—the darkness impenetrable.

I step in, closing the door behind me, and grope along the wall for a light switch. One quick flip and a caged bulb in the ceiling glows into a dull yellow. I'm in an anteroom; there is a shorter door with a bolt across it and a narrow barred window in front of me.

I hear scuffling on the other side.

"I'm here to help you," I say.

More scuffling but no response. I pull the bolt back and ease open the door. We don't have much time, but I must be careful—whoever is in there will be traumatized, and getting them to trust me is vital.

The pale light from the single bulb casts my shadow into the cell, long and wide and dark.

A figure presses against the far wall, black hair a tangled mess, eyes bright and wide with terror. "Stay back!" She holds out a bloody palm to warn me off. Her English is accented with a Texas twang. *It really is George's sister, Elsa!*

"I won't hurt you," I promise, putting my palms in front of me.

She shakes her head, nostrils flaring. "Stay back!" her voice is high with fear and desperation. She has no weapons.

I could do whatever I wanted with her.

Taking a deep breath, I force my hands to relax, to lay limp at my sides. "I am a friend of your brother, George."

Recognition flickers in her gaze. Her dirty tank top is stained with soot and smeared with rust-colored bloodstains. Elsa holds up a pair of tattered jean shorts with a white-knuckled fist. *She's lost weight.*

"George sent you?" Her voice breaks a little, but she takes in a deep breath.

"Yes."

She looks around the filthy room—there are seven bare mattresses. "They took the rest." Her voice catches, and a tear breaks free from her red-rimmed eye, leaving a glistening trail as it slides down her soot-stained cheek. "What happened to them?"

"I don't know." She looks back up at me, her pale brown eyes almost yellow in the dim light. Under all the dirt and blood, she's quite beautiful. *So young.* I hold my hand out to her. "Come, we must hurry."

She steps closer and winces. *Her feet are bare and bloodied.* The forest will shred them. "Get on my back," I say. "I'll carry you."

Her expression softens—the offer has won her over. She moves quickly now, and I hunch forward so that she can climb onto me. Her small hands grasp my shoulders. They are icy cold but grip with the strength of desperation. Her thighs hold my waist and her calves bounce against my thighs as I move back through the door.

Turning off the light switch, I step into the forest, closing the door behind us but not bothering to lock it.

Her grip tightens as we enter the night, her whole body shaking when a cool wind blows across us, carrying the sounds of dogs and our pursuers. I don't bother trying to comfort her. *We may be about to die.*

I take off running, moving deeper into the forest. Branches claw at me and the extra weight of the girl slows my steps, but I forge on.

I hunch forward and run faster, my legs burning, my heart hammering. The girl whimpers and holds tighter. *We have to make it. We just have to.*

EK

THE TREES TOWER ABOVE US, the darkness pitch black except for the lights of those hunting us bobbing like fireflies in the distance. My lungs burn, and my legs ache as I run, dodging branches as they come into focus. I fail to avoid half of them and they rip at my clothing, slicing my skin, snatching at me—almost as if they are trying to slow us down.

The girl on my back is thin, and I can feel her bones against me. Her fingers dig into my shoulders, and her thighs continue to grip my waist. She is exhausted and beaten but has not given up.

There is a farm on the far side of the woods, and I am hoping to find horses or some form of transportation. *A pickup truck with the keys in the ignition.*

Dogs bay behind us, their voices cutting through the forest soundscape—alien and dangerous. *They have our scent.* Her blood must be in the air, the welts and scabs and stink of her a thick and pungent trail.

My body is coated in sweat. *I'm running for my life and for hers. I cannot give up.* A root catches my foot, and I stumble forward, my hands reaching into the darkness for purchase. The girl lets out a whimper and her grip on me tightens. My palm smacks into a tree, and I use it to steady myself, then push myself off it, my pace quickened by the rev of an engine behind us.

The pale green of a field under moonlight twinkles through the trees.

My already hammering heart beats even faster at the sight...the anticipation of escape.

The revving engine is growing closer. There are quads in the woods. Faster than me, but not as agile in the thick trees. But once we reach that open field...

At the tree line, I pause, looking out into the waving blades of wheat. The farmhouse, squat with a thatched roof and stone walls, is dark. The barn, twice its size, hunkers behind it.

There must at least be a plow horse in there.

The girl slides off my back, landing on her injured feet with a grunt of pain. Her hand grips my bicep, as if she is afraid to lose me. I turn to look at her and though her face is shadowed, I can see that her lower lip is pulled between her teeth.

"Will they catch us?" she asks in a whisper.

"No," I promise her. "We'll head to that barn. Stay low. We are most exposed here in the wheat, but if we stay low enough they shouldn't be able to see us." My whole body is tingling now that we are still.

An engine rumbles closer, and she trembles. "Come on." I take her hand in mine and tug gently, crouching down so that my head is beneath the fluttering tips of the grasses. She follows me, her size making it easier for her to hide.

We move quickly, our exhaustion not as deep as our fear. Her fingers twined with mine are delicate and thin. *She is just a child.* Anger bubbles in my chest. How could Petra do this? Even if she believes that Joyful Justice is wrong, how could she justify taking this innocent girl captive?

The barn looms up before us, the doors closed, but the soft sounds of animals make their way to us. We have to dash across an open lawn to reach it. We pause before making the break for it. Elsa squeezes my hand and I nod once, then sprint, pulling her behind me across the open space. *Please let the darkness shield us from the eyes of our pursuers.*

We reach the barn door and I push it aside, opening it only as far as we need to slip through. The scent of hay and animal musk fills my senses as we step into the dark warmth. I quickly close the door behind us.

Blinking, I wait for my eyes to adjust. The girl's hand stays locked in mine. Animal hooves shift in hay. A soft whinny of concern rises from a nearby stall.

The animals know that strangers have entered their home. But these are domesticated creatures. *Their fear is not that of the hunted.*

The girl leaves me, her footsteps silent as she moves down the aisle, whispering quietly. "Shh, it's okay. It's just us. We won't hurt you."

I can barely make out her form, a black shadow in the darkness. A horse's head leans over a stall, the white star on its forehead visible as it reaches for her palm. It sniffs her, breath loud in the quiet of the barn, then bends forward, allowing her to pet its long snout.

The horse is large, a draft breed gelding meant for labor in the field so it should be able to carry both of us. I feel along the walls, searching for a bridle, but find only a halter and rope.

It will have to do. I approach slowly and the horse whinnies, his eyes widening in fear.

The girl whispers to it calmly, reaching out and soothing it with her palm. I hand her the halter, and she slips it easily over the giant horse's head. Unlatching the stall, she leads him forward.

The horse's tail is cropped short, and his back reaches to my shoulders.

I look around for a mounting block but there is none. There is no saddle. The girl stands on her tiptoes and grabs a fistful of mane. I lean down and boost her up. The horse whinnies and shakes his head but does not protest further.

The other side of the barn leads toward a dirt road that can take us into the village. There is more forest on the far side of the road and we could enter there and hide in its darkness but the dogs would find us...

I cross back to the door we came in through and peek out the narrow opening.

There are lights dancing at the edge of the forest.

We are out of time.

I hurry back to the horse and, taking it by the halter, lead it to the far door. Pushing it aside, I move us out into the night.

Cool air hits the drying sweat on my body, and a shiver runs through me, raising goosebumps. The girl whispers to the horse and it nickers, bobbing its head.

I look up at her, and it occurs to me that I should let her go. She and that giant horse could get away faster without me on its back, increasing the load. *But she could never navigate her way out of the country.*

She needs me.

I take a deep breath and look around, seeing a fenced pen for pigs. Leading the horse over, I climb onto the fence and then onto the horse's back, settling behind the girl. My arms around her waist, both gripping the mane tightly, we move forward. I can hear the engines of the quads as they zip across the field, and she urges the horse into a trot as we reach the dirt road.

They still can't see us, as we are shielded by the barn, but that won't last long. "To the forest," I whisper. She pulls at the makeshift reins, and the horse enters the trees, finding an animal path and breaking into an easy lope.

Can they see us? Or does the darkness hide us still?

They have dogs, lights, and the speed of engines. But we have stealth, darkness, and the will to survive.

CHAPTER THIRTEEN

Sydney

BLUE'S GROWL WAKES ME. I sit up in bed. The glass door is open, and the moon hangs big and bright—it's probably around 2:00 a.m. The curtains sway in the warm breeze, dancing between the indoors and out.

Blue stands and walks to the door. I slip from under the blankets, following him in bare feet. The house is protected by security men, cameras, and alarms. No one can break in. *There is no danger here.*

But Blue is pointing out into the night, and when I follow his gaze, I see a dark, broad figure moving along the stone patio.

My heartbeat resounds in my ears as he gets closer, but no lightning strikes or thunder sounds disrupt my concentration. A smile parts my lips. *Thank you, Dr. Munkin.*

The sheer white curtains billow out in the breeze, making the broad man pause, his head turning toward me. "Sydney."

His voice wraps around me, warm and yet cold—hot with anger, frozen in time.

"Mulberry?" It comes out a question, even though I know the answer.

He walks forward quickly, his movements sure and fast. The pale light hits him for just a moment as he steps in front of the open glass door so that I can see his jaw, coated in stubble, his nose, his lips, and for just a flash, the gold-green eyes of the man I love.

My throat closes and I stand motionless, desperate to embrace him, terrified of the cost.

"You coward," he snarls, moving toward me in steady strides, his gait only slightly tilted by the prosthetic on his left leg. He grabs my shoulders and pulls me close so that his eyes—flashing with anger and passion—bore into me. "How could you just leave me?" I can't reply, just stare at him. He shakes me. "Answer me, dammit."

My voice unlocks on a wave of regret and pain. "I was broken, and I wanted you to be happy. Thought you could have, that you could…go back. I don't know." I force myself to hold his gaze. To not look away. To be brave. "I saw you kiss her, and you two looked like you were in love, and I thought maybe you could be free of me." The last words come out a whisper.

His lip raises in a snarl. "You're—" He cuts himself off, tightening his jaw.

"I'm sorry." His eyes widen in surprise—I'm not known as a big apologizer. "I'm better now. I've gotten treatment. I wouldn't make the same mistake again. But then…I couldn't ask you to remember me, Mulberry. You were better off without me."

He barks a laugh, it's bitter and pissed. "You know what happened to me yesterday?"

"Dan said you were doing well…"

"*I remembered you.*" Mulberry leans in closer, his breath brushing my nose. "I woke up next to my ex-wife, and I remembered why she and I broke up. And I remembered I was in love with you. I woke up, and my heart ripped out of my chest, and then I had to rip hers out, too. Because she let me back in. Sandy thought we were going to be together forever, again. No one told her. No one told me." He stops talking, his eyes sobering, the anger melting away and deep sorrow filling his gaze, rimming his eyes in red and softening his grip on me.

"I'm no good for you," I whisper, pain constricting my voice.

Mulberry lets go of me and takes a step back, turning to look out at the ocean. It's calm now, the storm hovering at the horizon all day having finally blown out to sea, leaving the water still and black. The moon's reflection is a broad white stripe down its center.

"I want back in," Mulberry says, his back to me—he's just a silhouette again, a shadow of a man.

I'm not sure what he means. "To Joyful Justice?" I ask. He gives a curt nod. His hair is longer, curling at the nape of his thick neck. That tiny difference tugs at me even more than his missing leg. *I was there for that horror.* But I missed his hair growing. I left him to heal alone. "I'm sorry," I say again. The words leave me without permission, and I bite my lip to try to stem the flow of admissions. But I can't. "I love you," comes out, strong and loud. Like I mean it. Like I'm no longer afraid of it.

His shoulders tense. "Are you fucking him?"

I'm confused at first, but then realize he must mean Robert. It's not an unreasonable supposition. I am living in his house, and we've become close in a strange, wonderful way. "No. We're friends."

"He's in love with you."

I shake my head, even though Mulberry can't see it. "I think he was in love with the idea of controlling me, but he's changed." Mulberry barks another one of those bitter laughs. "What?" I raise my brows. "You don't think people can change?"

He turns quickly, so fast for a guy his size. The moon is bright behind him, keeping his features in shadow, but I can *feel* his eyes on me. Mulberry stands there, his shoulders rising and falling, the rasp of each breath loud in the quiet. Then slowly, as if moving through deep water, he walks toward me.

I stand my ground, lifting my chin slightly to keep my gaze on his face. It comes into focus as he reaches me. His eyes are hooded, dark. And when his left hand comes out and rests on my hip, I lean into him, melting into where I belong. His free hand comes up and cups my face, his fingers lacing into the hair at the base of my skull as his thumb runs along my jaw.

Slowly, so damn slowly, he lowers his lips to mine, and time stands still. There is nothing in the universe but us. There is nothing that matters but him. We are everything.

We fall into each other, into the past, the present, and the always. My back sinks into the mattress, his good knee pressing into it next to me, and his bad leg between mine. He hovers over me, his hands in my hair, holding my head like he never wants to let it go. Like I'm a dream. A hallucination.

And I grasp at his waist, my fingers running up his back, memorizing every detail of the muscle there, every curve and dip of his anatomy. I can't breathe. I can't think. I'm making sounds; small noises and breathless pleas. He leaves my lips and I'm bereft, but he finds my chin, my neck, worshiping me.

Tears burn in my eyes, and I can't find words. I guess I don't need them, but there are so many left unsaid between us.

His lips meet mine again, and his tongue invades, dominating me. My leg comes up and wraps around his waist, the rough material of his jeans penetrating the thin layer of my pajamas. "I love you." The words fly from my lips on gossamer wings—so delicate and fragile.

"Shut up," he growls, taking my mouth again, not giving me a chance to respond. His fingers dive under my shirt, and he breaks the kiss to tear it over my head. I meet his anger with my own bold movements, pulling at his clothing, demanding equal access. He lets me take his shirt, exposing the hard flesh of him, the scarred, sacred expanse of his chest, rising and falling with desperate, starving breaths.

I grab his face and pull him back to me, and his hands run up and down my sides, his calluses rough against the softness, the contrast sending a shiver of need and desperation zinging through me.

I want him so badly.

A hot tear escapes and is gone, lost in our movements. His hungry hands find my pants and cloth rips as he pulls at them. He growls at the sound, liking it, and ripping more. "You're mine," he claims, and I don't deny it. *Can't deny it.*

Bucking my hips and rolling, I force Mulberry onto his back, my thighs on either side of his waist, chest pressed against his. "Then fucking take me," I challenge.

His eyes light, the green in them almost a neon glow. There is still anger there, a hard stone of it set among the crystals of yellow and dashes of blue. But desire and love flame around it, trying to burn that stone to ash.

Can we burn hot enough to destroy it and clear our path?

EK

Lenox

THE WARM MUSK of the horse mixes with the fetid scent of the girl.

The cold, dark forest presses in on me but I take comfort in the animal's long, sure, and fast stride. *It knows where it is going.*

Behind us lights glimmer, shaking in the darkness, spots of danger swaying in the night. The rumble of engines and the echoing bays of the hounds grow soft with distance, but the sounds continue as we wind our way through the darkness. *They are not giving up.* The ATVs can't navigate this narrow path, but the dogs and men can.

My fingers hold the mane tightly, and my hips move with the swaying motion of the horse's gait. The girl in front of me is a small defense against the chill night wind. A shiver passes over me, and I grit my teeth against the cold.

Dawn is still hours away, and we should make it to the village long before that.

My mind traces over the maps I examined of the area. It seems we are on a path that will take us out to the main road and from there on to the village, probably a shortcut the farmer uses regularly, and so the horse knows it.

The girl speaks to the gelding softly, her voice a mellow and welcome sound compared to the clacking of the trees branches swaying in the wind and the howling dogs chasing us.

A shimmer of moonlight ahead, and then the path opens into a meadow with long, silver grasses waving back and forth, almost as in greeting. The horse stops, bowing his head to eat, munching his way toward a stream that winds through the open space.

We don't have time for this.

The girl urges him forward, but the horse pays her no mind, making his way lazily toward the water's edge and lapping at the crystal clear rushing stream.

Elsa digs her heels into the horse's side, her voice rising, and he whinnies, raising his head to bolt forward a step into the water so that I almost lose my balance. He trots through the water, head high, snorting with displeasure.

The lights of our pursuers grow larger, and my heart beats faster, panic tightening my muscles.

Reaching the far shore, the horse bows his head, again going for the grass. I dig my heels into his side, but he just snorts. Elsa kicks, but he ignores us. Adrenaline surges as the gap we managed to make closes.

I slip off the horse's back and, yanking at his halter, pull him toward the forest where the narrow path continues. He rears up with an outraged snort, and I stumble back into the wet grass as his hooves paw the air, just missing my face.

"Leave him. I'll get him to go," Elsa says, still on his bare back. The dogs are close, and my heart is thundering. Elsa's legs flail against his sides. The horse shakes its head, refusing to continue.

I move to the horse's side and grab Elsa around her waist, dragging her off the beast's back. She lets out a squeak of alarm but does not fight me. Her bare feet hit the grass, and my hand finds hers.

I take off running, and she follows, the horse remaining in the field, chewing its grass happily.

We dive back into the shelter of the forest, continuing on the path. Elsa slows as the rough ground meets her bare, wounded feet. I stop, and gesture for her to climb onto my back. Her thin arms come around my shoulders and warm thighs wrap my waist. My elbows under her knees, I begin to run again.

The rest I got while riding the horse renewed me, but my muscles feel tight. Frantic barking is followed by a sharp whinny of fear, and suddenly hooves are thundering behind us.

Leaving the path, I move into the thick trees to avoid its approach.

The gelding races past, the reins flapping against its neck, hooves throwing up clumps of dirt and sticks. The dogs bark, the timbre of their voices raising in excitement.

They are so close.

Fighting through the underbrush, branches pulling at my clothing and tearing at the girl's bare legs, I return to the path. Glancing back, the dark outlines of the men chasing us are clear behind the glow of their lights.

A flash of light reaches us, and a man cries out in victory. My heart hammering, I sprint after the gelding. The girl clings to me, her heart beating so hard I can feel it against my back.

We're not going to make it.

The horse has disappeared into the night, and I wish I could do the same—but I don't have the speed. *I am just a man.*

The pounding of horse's hooves behind us confuses me for a moment —my panicked mind incapable of comprehending how the gelding circled around. Then I realize Petra's horses must be chasing us as well.

"Lenox!" Petra's voice reaches me over the pounding of my blood in my ears and the sound of her horse's hooves on the path. It reaches me over the strained barking of the dogs as they choke against their leashes to reach us. "Lenox, stop!"

But I can't. She'll take the girl back. She'll kill me. My only chance at survival is to keep going, to put one foot in front of the other until there is nothing left of me. Because soon, if I'm not fast enough, there will be nothing left except the memories I leave behind.

A bullet whistles through the air, thunking into a tree, sending splinters of shrapnel across the path. A fresh burst of adrenaline surges through me, making my stomach flip and urges my legs to move faster. "Do not shoot them!" Petra screams at her men, her voice weak in comparison to the deep woofing of the dogs.

They are right behind us now. *I can't even look back.* The horse will run us over. We will be trampled.

But the horse's hooves slow to a trot when it reaches us. Petra doesn't shoot us. She doesn't try to stop us. She just follows us.

"Lenox." Her voice is harsh, but not with anger so much as with fear. It's the fear that slows my steps. "Lenox, please."

My lungs are on fire, my feet unsteady and I trip forward, stumbling to a stop. I turn to face her, the girl clinging to my back, her breath warm against my neck.

Petra is astride Tarzan, the giant black horse's coat as dark as the forest around us. Behind her the dogs still bark, and the men follow so close now that I can see their breath steaming in the cool air.

Petra turns in her saddle, looking back, and yells for them to stop. "Stay where you are," she commands before returning her attention to me.

"Lenox," she says again, her face is in shadow and her voice is soft. "Please, Lenox. Return with me to the house. Let's talk about this." I take a step backward.

And Tarzan follows.

There's no way I can escape her.

"You know I can't," I say. "I can't let you have her."

Petra, backlit by the men behind us, stiffens. "She's mine."

"She's nobody but her own. Since when do *you* own people, Petra?"

"Lenox," her voice is tight. "I do not want to have to kill you."

"You don't have to do anything Petra. It's all a choice." My breath is slowly returning to normal, and a calm is coming over me. *Maybe Petra is still the woman I know. Maybe she has not become a monster.* "I can't let you take her." I take another step back and she follows again.

The low hum of a diesel engine rumbles behind me. *The road is closer than I'd thought.* We almost made it. Maybe the girl still can.

I let go of her legs, and she slides off my back. I keep a hand on her waist, to keep her from coming out from behind my bulk. My body can shield her for a little bit longer.

"Petra, I won't let you have her. But you can have me if you let her go."

Petra shakes her head. "Don't be ridiculous, Lenox."

"You used to be so brave," I say. Petra stiffens in the saddle. I glance to the side, where headlights twinkle through the forest from the road. The sound of that distant diesel engine grows closer. I turn a little further and whisper to the girl, "Run."

She takes off like a deer in flight. Petra screams for her to stop, but she does not falter.

Petra urges Tarzan forward, but the path is too narrow for him to get past without trampling me. He's a pleasure horse, not a war horse, no matter what his breeding says, and I hold my arms out to keep him at bay. Tarzan stomps impatiently as Petra kicks his sides.

"What are you doing?" Petra hisses.

"I'm making sure she survives. It's my responsibility, as someone bigger and stronger and more powerful."

Petra grunts in exasperation. I take another step back, and this time she holds Tarzan's reins. Another step, and again Petra does not follow. The brake of truck tires wheezes from the road. I turn and sprint toward the sound.

Breaking out of the thick forest, I see the girl climbing into an idling vegetable truck. Sprinting, I reach her before the door can close. She looks back when my hand touches her waist, her eyes filled with fear and desperation that evaporates when she sees me. She scoots into the truck, and I follow her.

The driver, a man in his fifties with a hat pulled low, stares at me with wide eyes. "Go!" I yell. He just sits there. But then he hears the dogs and some kind of awareness comes into his eyes. The awareness of any man who's ever been chased, ever been oppressed. His jaw tightens, and he puts the truck into gear. The truck eases forward. *We made it.*

I look back and see lights in the forest still, but they are not chasing us. *Petra let me go.*

Maybe she can still be saved.

Sydney

WHEN I WAKE the next morning, Mulberry is gone. There is no note, just a few hairs on the pillow next to me and memories I hold tight as I stare around my empty bedroom.

It wasn't a dream or a hallucination.

My phone rings, and I grab it off the side table, glancing at the screen as I bring it to my ear. "Dan, what's up?"

"Mulberry is gone. He left his apartment, and I can't find him. He's off the grid."

"He remembered." I say it quietly, my gaze holding the ocean—it is a sparkling blue this morning, welcoming wind surfers and sailors to enjoy its majesty. "And he's pissed."

"You saw him."

I nod then force words past a lump in my throat. "Yeah."

"Shit. I worried we should have told him. So, he's with you?"

"No, he…was last night. But he's gone this morning. I don't know where."

Silence stretches between us. "What did he say?"

"That because of us, he had to rip out Sandy's heart. That remembering ripped out his own."

Dan sighs. "Fuck."

"At least this bad decision didn't get anyone killed."

Dan let's out a jaded laugh. "That's the bar now? Ruining a man's psyche is no big thing?" There is an accusation in his tone. *I hurt him.* But I warned him. Dan never believed me—but I'm no good. Or at least I wasn't.

I can't burn fiercely enough to erase my past.

"He said he wants back into Joyful Justice. So I'm sure we'll hear from him soon. He probably just needs time to process."

"Okay," Dan sighs. "I guess. Just let me know if you hear from him."

"I will."

We hang up, and I climb out of bed, stretching toward the ceiling, enjoying the warmth of the sun streaming through the glass doors on my bare skin.

A knock at my door gets Blue up from where he's been sleeping on his bed. Grabbing my robe, I pull it on before answering. Robert waits in the hall, looking down at his phone. "You had a visitor last night."

I lean against the door frame and can't help the smile that tugs at my lips. "Yes." I draw the word out. He looks up at me, his brows raised. "What? You want to gossip about it?"

"How is he?"

I shrug. "Pissed."

"I bet. Come on." He jerks his head. "Let's have breakfast. I want to hear all about it. And we need to discuss Hugh's wedding."

I laugh and Robert furrows his brow. "What?"

"You've just—you've changed so much."

"That's a bit of the kettle calling the pot black, my dear." He smiles and turns away, headed down the hall. "Want pancakes?" he asks over his shoulder.

"Sure," I agree, as I close my door to get dressed.

Robert is out on the west patio, his coffee by his side, the paper next to it, his phone in his hand. He glances up at me. "Going blading after this?" he asks, referencing my bike shorts and tank top.

"How else can I afford to eat so many of Jose's pancakes?"

"That's why I stick to Muesli."

I laugh again. "We really have changed."

Robert grins, the expression making him look somehow older and younger in the same breath: younger because the joy radiating from his gaze is innocent, older because the lines around his eyes crease. He's spent a lifetime squinting into the sun, suspicious of what the light hides.

"So," Robert looks down at his phone again. "You told Hugh he could have the wedding here."

Hugh and Santiago came for drinks last night and I'd offered the house again. "You were sitting right next to me."

Robert looks up at me and nods then reaches for his coffee. "You had already offered before they even arrived. Also, I learned in my many marriages never to disagree in public."

"Oh really?" I laugh as he sips from the elegant white mug. Jose comes out onto the patio, his dark hair ruffled by the playful breeze.

"Morning, Ms. Rye," he says, placing a steaming plate of pancakes in front of me and a pitcher of hot syrup next to it.

"Morning, Jose, thank you. This looks and smells amazing."

Jose grins and nods before heading back inside. I pour the syrup liberally over the butter-laden, fluffy deliciousness before returning my attention to Robert. "So, you're saying you don't want to have the wedding here."

Robert puts his mug back on its saucer. "I'm saying that it's not your place to offer my home up for a wedding. You are not, in truth, my wife." There is something in his tone I choose to ignore, but Mulberry's harsh laughter seems to ring in my ears.

"You're right. I'm sorry. I'll call Hugh and tell him we have to find another venue."

Robert shakes his head. "No, don't do that. I'm happy to host. I just would have liked you to discuss it with me before offering."

"Fair enough. I'm sorry."

He smiles. "Look at you apologizing." He shakes his head. "I never thought I'd see the day." My mouth is filled with pancake so I can't answer, instead just grin around the sweet, buttery goodness. "I know a good wedding planner."

I swallow down the pancake, trying not to choke as I bark out a laugh. "I bet you do!"

Robert picks up his phone, the salty sea air fluttering his newspaper and toying with the collar of his pale blue linen shirt. He glances up at me, his eyes taking on the colors and excitement of the sea beside him. "I do love a good party." Heat comes into his gaze, and I shake my head.

"We need to get you a date."

CHAPTER FOURTEEN

Dan

GEORGE IS out of sick bay and resting in his room. I knock on the door because I'm polite, not because he deserves it.

When he opens it, George looks wrecked: dark shadows under his eyes, hair sticking out every which way, and a beard covering his jaw that wasn't there a few days ago. *He's given up hope.*

"Can I come in?"

He clears his throat. "Yeah, please." He steps back.

George's hands are still bandaged—the white gauze the cleanest-looking thing about him. His room smells musty, the blinds are closed, and there are no lights on. Sympathy churns in my stomach. *He's not a bad man. Just a coward.*

"Can I get you anything?" George asks, gesturing toward his kitchenette.

"No, I came to tell you that we've found and rescued your sister. Lenox called twenty minutes ago. He found her in a makeshift prison on an estate in Romania owned by a sex trafficker named Petra. They managed to escape through the surrounding woods and wave down a driver willing to take them to the closest city with an international airport."

George's mouth drops open, his eyes instantly glazed with tears. He raises one of his wrapped hands up to them, looking almost like an animal swiping with a paw. "Thank you," he says, his voice tight. He keeps his head bent, hiding his tears from me.

I nod, my own throat tightening. He risked all of us for her. *To spare himself the pain of losing her.* My hands itch to comfort him, but I fight my instincts, refusing to offer any consolation.

I'm still not sure what to do with George in the long term. Given what he knows, he's far too dangerous to release, but we are not set up to hold him captive. George hasn't asked to leave—appears to be willing to take any punishment we mete out.

I don't want revenge, though. I just want everyone to be safe. *Shit.* Turning, I head for the door. "Can I tell my parents?" George asks, his voice choked.

Standing at the door I look back at him. "Your sister already called them. She'll be back with them soon. Lenox is going to escort her back to Texas himself."

"Will she be safe?" he asks, straightening.

Worry pulls my lips into a frown. "I hope so."

He takes a step forward and then stops. "Can I talk to her?"

My heart aches at the pain in his voice. "Maybe tomorrow."

He nods, accepting my decision without argument...without even a sigh of resistance. I let myself out and close the door, hearing the lock click automatically into place.

Hank, a tall African American guy, sits in a folding chair in the hall, guarding George. "Everything okay?" he asks.

I nod. "Yeah, has he given you any trouble?"

Hank shakes his head. "Super quiet in there."

"Has he been eating?"

"Not really," Hank says with a frown. "He looks depressed to me."

"He should be." Hank nods, silently agreeing. "You need anything?"

"Nope."

Looking back at George's room one more time, I take a deep breath. *I don't have the time or bandwidth to worry about him.*

Back in my rooms, I boot up my computers before grabbing a pizza out of the freezer and throwing it in my toaster oven. Communication with the outside world is open again but with a lot of controls. Every email is being read, every conversation listened to. It's like we've become a freaking apocalyptic novel. Next we'll be burning books and controlling thoughts.

But how else can we trust each other?

We've learned nothing so far, though. It's so frustrating. Anita suggested this morning that maybe there wasn't another mole. That perhaps the people blackmailing George lied.

In a way, that would be worse. Because if there is another traitor or two in our midst then we can find them and end this. But if there isn't, then the doubt will remain forever.

I head back to my computer and check the logs. No new emails or calls since I went to talk to George. Mitchel is in the control room and has everything in hand.

Checking in on Sandy's feeds, I find her getting ready for work. She seems to be doing okay. Hasn't heard from Mulberry but also isn't staring at empty wine bottles in the evenings. She even went out with some girlfriends last night. Nothing like bitching about your love life with friends to make things better.

Switching screens, I look in at Mulberry's bank and credit card accounts. No action. *He'll turn up eventually.* He's pissed but at the end of the day will call, even if it's just to yell.

My hand hovers over my mouse for a moment. Then I give in to my urges. I haven't indulged since this all started. But I *need* to check in. *Just to make sure she's safe.*

Sydney is living with Robert Maxim—a snake in tailored suits. I log in and the video feed opens. She's sitting on her bed, hair falling over her face as she leans down to put on a pair of shoes. Blue sits by her side, and his two puppies are lying behind him.

Sydney sits up and reaches out to pet Blue.

The bed is made, and the room tidy. A dress is draped over an armchair. *That must be what she's wearing to Hugh's wedding.*

A smile pulls at my lips. Sydney Rye is helping plan a wedding. Maybe she is finding some peace. A knock at my door makes me jump, and I quickly turn off the feed, guilt making my fingers clumsy.

Taking a deep breath, I stand and head to the door. It's Mitchel. "Hey, man," he smiles. "I've been sent to drag you outside."

I lean against the doorway. "Yeah?"

"Yeah, your mom"—he laughs—"I mean Anita, pointed out you've been missing your paddleboarding." He punches me on the shoulder. "How you gonna think clearly without exercise?"

I shake my head, smiling. "Fine, let me get dressed."

"I'll wait in your living room. I don't want you trying to weasel out of it."

I laugh again, leaving the door open and stepping back into my space. "Fine."

"Anita is scary when she's serious," Mitchel says, following me in.

"Tell me about it." I head to my room to get changed.

It's good to have people who care about you. Watch out for you. That's all I'm doing with Sydney. Keeping an eye on her.

EK

Sydney

A storm blew in this morning, the sky churning with clouds and lightning flashing, illuminating the sky in deep purple, pale yellow, and the sickly green of a fading bruise. Gray swirls still hover off the coast, turning the ocean into glinting silver, ruffled and dangerous, the wind pressing down upon it—almost as if the sky has taken temporary dominion over the sea.

Hugh paces nervously, sweat lining his brow. The heat and humidity surround us like an electric blanket with the dial turned all the way up. "Where is he?" Hugh asks, his voice high and worried.

"I'll find him," I say, standing up from the loveseat, my skirt swishing around me. Hugh nods, his eyes worried.

Stepping out of the guest room, I make my way down the hall and peek out to the patio where Hugh and Santiago's wedding guests are gathered. Santiago's mother and grandmother are here—he must plan on showing up. *He wouldn't stand Hugh up at the altar.* Would he?

No. No way.

He's probably in traffic. Or something happened to him...

Footsteps behind me draw my attention. Robert is coming down the hall. He's wearing a light gray tailored suit and his green-blue gaze flashes with concern. He pulls at his left cuff, straightening it, and frowns at me.

"Santiago?" I ask.

"There's been an accident." My heart hammers. "He's on his way to the hospital. Get Hugh. We'll take him there now."

I nod but don't move. "Was it really an accident?" I ask.

Robert doesn't answer for a moment, the lilac on his lapel making his gaze almost violet. "I don't know."

"Could this be *our* fault?" I ask, my voice low, a whisper.

"I don't know," he says again, his eyes hard. *Robert does not like not knowing.* "Go get Hugh."

I suck in a deep breath and nod again, turning back to the bedroom where Hugh waits. "Did you find him?" he asks as I enter. Hugh's hair has fallen over his brow, and his eyes are frantic.

"There was an accident." Hugh's face crumples into a pained grimace, and tears well in his eyes. I hold out my hand and Hugh grips it. "Let's go. We need to get to the hospital." I tug, leading Hugh forward. He follows blindly, holding onto me like I'm a life preserver and he's just pitched overboard.

My phone rings as we climb into one of Maxim's SUVs. Brock is driving, Robert sitting in the passenger seat. I pull my phone out of the little clutch—it's a blocked number. *Fuck me.*

"Hello."

"Ms. Rye," it's a woman with a thick accent.

"Who is this?" My voice comes out harsh and low, almost angry except with a note of fear that I loathe.

She laughs, low and quiet. "You are as brash as they say."

"Who says?"

Robert turns around in his seat and is watching me, his gaze sharp, the flower on his lapel fluttering in the air from the vents.

"Your friend...Santiago. I have him."

My breathing slows, and I force my eyes to stay straight, to concentrate on the flower. To not look at Hugh. *I can't be responsible for another person he loves getting killed. No fucking way. Nope. I refuse.*

"What do you want?"

I hear her shifting, the sound of leather wheezing as if she's resting back into a chair. "Your organization. What do you call yourselves?"

"I'm a Rotary Club member. Used to be in the Girl Scouts, but they kicked me out. Couldn't sell enough cookies."

She laughs, louder this time. "Oh, you are fun."

"Am I?"

Robert begins to text on his phone, his jaw tight. *He's guessed what's happening.*

"Joyful Justice." She drops her voice—there's almost a sneer in it. *She's not a fan of vigilante justice.*

"Bless you."

"You are the one who needs a blessing."

"You're the one who sneezed."

Robert is smiling, his fingers flying. I've got to keep her on the line. Somehow Robert is going to trace this. Somehow he is going to figure out where Santiago is being held. And we are going to get him back. *Somehow.*

Faith is a powerful drug.

"Do not play games with me." The first hint of anger edges her voice.

"Then how about you cut to the fucking chase?"

"I have Santiago. And he will die unless you back off."

"Back off who? What? I have no idea who you are or what you want. Is this your first time blackmailing?" Hugh turns to me quickly, but I refuse to look at him. "Get to the point and stop wasting time. I am busy."

My free hand is fisted so tight that my nails are cutting into my palm. "My associates received one of your packages."

"Your associates must be scum bags."

"Your friend will be dead if you don't listen closely."

"Threatening me and the ones I love never works out for anyone. You know my name. Do you know my reputation?" Anger wells in my chest, and suddenly my mouth is running with it. "You will die. Your associates will die. Don't fuck with me, bitch."

"You don't know my name." Her voice is quiet, still, flat...dangerous. "You don't know my reputation. And that's because I am wise, I am dangerous, and I am the boss. So, you will stop any and all activities against the McCain brothers. You will pack up your little operations and go back to the Brooklyn hipster neighborhood you crawled out of, and you will disappear."

These McCain boys are going down.

"You need all that before you return Santiago?"

Hugh lets out a little whimper.

"You do all that, and I'll consider letting him go. I'll consider letting you live."

"Petra, Petra...you underestimate me." She doesn't react to my using her name. *Have I guessed wrong?* "Usually it's just men who do that. But I guess that's because women are usually on my side. The McCain brothers are buying women from Isis." *The same bastards who took George's sister.*

"They are not." She snaps at me, that edge of anger cutting through like a samurai sword slicing butter.

"Believe their lies or believe my truth. Either way, you'll die, and Santiago will live. This is *my* city. You can't hide him from me."

"I don't need to hide him. I can just kill him."

"But then you'll have no leverage. Let's meet. I can show you evidence of what your business partners are doing. Then you can decide if you want to fight me...or join me."

"You are a fool."

"Really, Petra?" I decide to double down. How many female super villains with thick Czech accents can there be freaking be? "You choose the location. I'll show you what your friends are up to. Then you can return my friend and the wedding I've squeezed myself into a tight ass dress for can go on."

She laughs. "He's in no shape to wed today."

"If he dies, you will suffer." My voice comes out strange, strangled yet terrifying in its own way. Petra doesn't answer. *She can hear the truth in my words.*

I stare at the flower on Robert's lapel—so delicate yet strong, holding its own against the force of the air trying to loosen it—as I wait for her reply.

There is more shuffling. "Okay, I'll meet you." There is a smugness in her tone. "There is an abandoned parking structure at the shuttered mall."

My eyes jump up to Robert and I mouth *pen*. He produces one from his inside pocket and I write the address on the palm of my hand. "Meet me there in an hour," Petra says.

We hang up, and I glance at Hugh. His eyes are wet, his hands shaking, and I swallow the lump in my throat, banishing my emotions. *There is no place for them here, now.*

Turning to Robert, I show him my palm. "It's Petra," I say. He nods, his eyes scanning the address. A smile plays across his lips, and he turns to his phone, texting quickly. "We have sixty minutes."

"Take us to the office, Brock."

The security officer nods and exits the highway, headed toward downtown Miami and Robert's offices there.

"What's happening?" Hugh asks, his voice wavering.

"Santiago is being held; we are going to get him back." I don't tell him not to worry because that's impossible, but I do reach out and take his hand. I hold his gaze. "I will not let him die. I promise."

Hugh takes a stuttering breath and nods, my promise sinking in. He trusts me.

I will prove I am worthy of it.

CHAPTER FIFTEEN

Sydney

The abandoned parking garage's gray, decaying concrete floor is littered with broken glass, empty beer cans, and the occasional glinting, spent needle. A burnt spoon lies next to a stained mattress separating our two groups.

Petra is surrounded by ten hulking men, accentuating her diminutive size. High-heeled boots give her a few inches, but she's still shorter than me in my soft-soled sneakers. Petra wears all leather: black, shining slickness hugging every tight curve. My T-shirt and loose linen pants let me move like water; her leather protects her like a second skin.

You only need multiple skins if you fear getting cut.

"Nice spot," I say, gesturing to the crumbling walls and broken light fixtures. The sun pierces through the holes in the walls, lighting our meeting in dramatic spears of gold. There are three floors above us, the ceiling open in many places.

Blue is pressed tight to my left side, Nila to my right. Robert stands to my left, Merl to my right, with his three dogs fanning out from him. Dust sprinkles from above, and Petra's gaze is drawn to it for just a moment before returning to me. *She hasn't guessed we have snipers up there.*

She doesn't know who she's up against.

No weapons are drawn, but I can see the bulk of pistols under the ill-fitting suit jackets of the men ringing Petra.

"Let's talk," I say, waving a hand between Petra and myself. "Privately."

She shakes her head slowly, smiling. "No, I am not here to talk. And you— you are here to die."

I can't help the grin that pulls at my lips as her men begin to fan out. "You forgot something, Petra," I say, as the first man drops, his neck exploding with blood. She spins toward the dying figure as her other minions try to pull weapons, only to be dropped in their tracks. The thudding of bodies is louder than the soft pops of the silenced sniper rifles.

Suddenly, Petra is all alone. A pistol gripped in each fist, lips drawn back over her teeth, eyes narrowed. *She is ready to fight but not to die.*

"It didn't need to go down like this," I say quietly, the silence of so much death around us seeming to make my voice louder. "Are you ready to talk?" Her eyes, bright green, lined with charcoal black, hold my naked gaze. "Drop your weapons."

She straightens, her chin high, eyes never leaving mine. "You"—she nods slowly—"You were right. I underestimated you." She drops the pistols; they land with a clatter onto the filthy floor.

"I'm trying not to return the favor. From what I understand, you're a good woman. Smart. Ruthless. Yet fair. Moral."

She gives me a half smile. "You compliment me, and yet the scent of blood is thick in the air."

"You should have talked with me." I take a step forward, my dogs moving with me. Her gaze drops to them for just a moment and then comes back to me. "I think we can come to an agreement without any more bloodshed."

Petra shrugs, looking almost casual despite the slumped, lifeless corpses surrounding her. "The McCain brothers will never stop coming at you. They will never relent. We are not doing anything wrong. All the women we work with want to change their lives. They want to be free."

I nod. "Yes, they want to be free. But what they are is slaves. Prisoners."

She shakes her head vehemently, loosening a curl from the tight bun at the back of her head. "No. I do not trade in slaves."

"You might not, but the McCain brothers do." I step around the abandoned mattress, with its depressing stains and forgotten tools of addiction. I'm only a few feet away from her now. "Come with me. I can prove it."

She lets out a jaded laugh. "As if I have a choice."

"There is always a choice." I say it quietly, so she can barely hear. And I hold her gaze. *You can die.* She shrugs again, looking cool and unaffected in all that black leather. "I'll need to search you before we go." Petra raises her arms without protest, her gaze challenging me. *Touch me, I dare you.*

As I run my hands over her body, I can't help but remember that I'm supposed to be at Hugh and Santiago's wedding right now. This woman totally fucked with the new normal life I'm building.

A tickle of rage blushes up the back of my neck as I feel a knife in her boot. Extracting the long, thin blade, I toss it onto the mattress. "That was a gift," she says.

"You can come back for it, if you live." Grabbing her bicep, I jerk Petra forward. She matches her stride to mine. Merl and Robert fall into step with us as Robert speaks quietly into his radio, controlling his men.

Blue's nose taps my hip, reminding me he is there. Nila stays close to Petra, her blue eyes trained on my prisoner. *She won't get away. And I will get Santiago back.*

EK

Petra's arm feels thin in my hold. She follows me easily, her expression defiant.

We walk down the nondescript hallway of the office building, and I push open the unmarked door. Inside there is a black metal folding chair facing a TV screen and a security camera blinking in the corner.

Leading Petra over to the seat, I push her into it. She lands with a thump and a hiss of a threat. *Try me. Just try me.*

"You are going to show me a movie?" Petra asks, her voice thick with sarcasm.

"Yeah, *The Princess Bride*, ever seen it?"

She makes a sound of disgust and crosses her arms, staring at me with narrowed eyes. The screen glows to life, showing a paused video. The footage, from an HD camera hidden within Lenox's clothing, is crisp. Through shoulders and heads we see a young woman kneeling on a low stage.

Her bound hands lay limp on her thighs. She wears loose-fitting clothing in dark colors. Her thick black hair is tied back at the base of her neck. Tears stream down her young face from under closed lids.

I hit play, and an auctioneer's voice speaks in rapid Arabic. Subtitles translate on the bottom of the screen. I've seen the video several times. Lenox made it three months ago while researching the McCain brothers —Petra's sometimes partners and recent crusaders against Joyful Justice. Nothing like getting called on your shit to bring the bad guys together.

I don't watch the video. Instead I stare at Petra. She shifts in the metal folding chair, sitting up straighter, her eyes focusing on the screen. Her gaze flicks to me and then back to the image of the girl now being led off screen as her new owner makes his way through the crowd toward the pay station at the side of the stage. "What does this have to do with me?" she asks, challenge lacing her accented voice.

"One of your buddies is about to make a star appearance," I say.

Her lips purse and she shakes her head. "They would never. The McCain brothers are good men."

"Joyful Justice doesn't go after good guys. We *are* the good guys." I smile at her. *I'm a good guy who's going to punch you in your evil-doing-fucking-face.*

Petra settles back into the chair, recrossing her arms, her gaze drawn back to the screen. It's mesmerizing, the way the auctioneer stands so still behind his podium as two more girls are brought onto the stage. They are pale with fear, wearing that same dark clothing, hair drawn back. Everyone in the room shifts to get a better look. *It's fascinating the way they can just pretend the girls are salable objects. That they can fool themselves into believing they are better than them. So much better, in fact, that they deserve to own them.*

My blood heats at the self-imposed superiority. *I want to kill them all.* Taking a deep breath, I consciously relax my clenched fists and return my gaze to Petra. Spots of color have appeared on her cheeks, and she is slumped in the chair, her arms over her gut, as if she is trying to protect herself. As if there is any protection from the world we live in.

The auctioneer points to the winner, and the camera turns to him. I glance back at the screen briefly. *This is the moment.* A white man in a sea of brown stands up, his light hair, blue eyes, and wide shoulders making him a stereotype of an Irishman. *All he needs is a four-leaf clover pinned to his chest.*

Petra shifts, sitting forward, her eyes riveted to the screen, her face transforming. A moment ago she looked sick, now deep anger is sharpening her features, glittering in her eyes, and blushing up her neck. She uncrosses her arms and grips the edge of her seat, as if she is ready to launch herself at the screen and kill Ian McCain herself.

"Enough?" I ask.

"Not yet," she answers, her voice low…not trembling, but not steady either.

On screen, Ian McCain stalks toward the stage as the war prisoners are lead off. The camera captures him paying for his new merchandise. "When was this shot?" Petra asks, her voice quiet and cold.

"About three months ago."

Petra sucks in a deep breath and turns from the screen, where another woman, this one older and limping is being forced onto the stage, her hands bound behind her back, teeth bared at the crowd.

"And you did nothing to stop it?" she asks me, her voice filled with accusation.

I let out a bark of a laugh. "Says the woman on Ian McCain's side. The woman who is holding a totally innocent man hostage to let that shit—" I point the screen—"continue. You just tried to kill me to protect that guy. *I'm* the one trying to take him down."

"You were there," she says, her voice rising, pointing to the TV. "Why didn't you stop them?"

"We did," I say quietly.

She starts, her eyes going wide, and recognition blooms in her gaze. "He said he got into a bar fight."

"Our operative freed those girls, maimed Ian, and destroyed the auction house." *Lenox is what we refer to as a bad ass.*

"Good," Petra says.

"So, you're on our side now?"

"I understand your position. Lenox should have been honest with me. Men always lie." I can practically taste the bitterness in her voice—it's like dark chocolate if the chocolatier forgot to add the sugar.

"I'm sure he would have if he wasn't so busy trying to save your prisoner."

"I was told she was an operative for Joyful Justice." Petra's voice turns defensive, and her legs tense as if she is about to stand.

"Her name is Elsa. And she's a sixteen-year-old high school student from Texas."

Petra does not look repentant. Her eyes on the paused screen, she looks pissed. "I want to kill him." She is staring at Ian McCain's broad back.

"Fantastic. Let's do it."

"Do his brothers know?" she asks, her eyes still on the screen.

"We believe so."

"But you have no proof?" Her eyes find mine, a spark of hope igniting. *Maybe she isn't the only one who got fooled.*

"What do you think?"

"Ian is the only one who speaks Arabic."

"Wouldn't you notice if all the women your brother brought home from the Middle East were young, terrified, and crying most the time?"

"Many willing girls cry, too." She says it calmly. *It's just a fact.*

"Nice business you're in."

Petra almost stands this time, but a sharp growl from Blue gets her butt back in the seat. "I provide an escape for many women who are trapped at home. They can prostitute themselves and get paid, save up and do what they want in the future. Or have their parents give them away to the first man who offers enough cattle. There is more than one way to be a slave." I grind my teeth, knowing she's right but hating it anyway. "But this," she points to the screen. "This is unacceptable. And they must pay."

I nod, feeling our missions align. "So you'll work with us?"

Petra turns her green gaze to me, her eyes are sharp, angry. "Abso–fucking–lutely."

I can't help the smile that stretches across my face. *We are going to kick some ass.*

"Now tell me where you're holding my friend."

"At the Bay Shore Marina. On a yacht—*The Tempest.*"

"Let's go," I gesture for her to lead the way.

Two of Robert's men escort her down the hall, and I hang back to talk with Merl. "I've spoken with Lenox," he says. "He is on his way. Should be here by morning. Looks like she is going to be helpful."

"Yes," I agree. "Once Lenox gets here, we can come up with a clear plan. You spoke with Dan?"

Merl nods. "Yes, he is relieved that we have her in our control but is still concerned about the breaches in his security."

"Understandable."

"He still hasn't found any other moles?" Merl shakes his head. "I guess that's just another question for Petra."

"Yes, if she knows. It looks like she is just one spoke in this wheel."

"Right, we need to talk to the hub. The person at the center of all this."

"Ian McCain and his brothers," Merl says, absentmindedly tracing a hand over Chula's head. The dog leans into him with a sigh.

"I'd like to go to Ireland with Petra for that conversation."

Merl's focus returns to me, his eyes sharp. *I'm not known for my conver-sation skills.* "We need information from them."

I smile with only one side of my mouth and raise my brows. "What? You don't think I'm a good conversationalist?"

Merl watches me for a long moment—so long I begin to grow uncomfortable. "You've changed," he states.

"Yeah."

"Maybe this will be good for you."

"What?"

"Getting back in the field."

"I think so."

"Sydney!" Robert calls from the end of the hall. "We need to go."

"Coming," I squeeze Merl's arm in farewell and jog toward Robert, Blue tight to my side.

Time to go save Santiago.

CHAPTER SIXTEEN

Declan

THE CAMERA, with its zoom lens, is pressed to my eye, focused on the front door of the nondescript office building. From my perch in the parking structure across the street I can see everyone who comes and goes.

The door spins, sun glinting off the glass, blinding me for a moment. I blink against the glare, and there she is...Sydney Rye, Blue heeling at her hip. A woman in all black walks next to her. I have a better angle of the stranger's face than when they entered the building and quickly capture several shots. The light is soft from the setting sun, casting a pink glow over the city.

Sydney, Blue, and the stranger move quickly, climbing into the black SUV that idles at the curb. Brock Johnson is behind the wheel. He eases them into the evening traffic, and I capture a few more shots—a profile of Brock's stern face, the license plate number of the vehicle, and one final parting shot of the bumper as it turns around the corner.

I sit back on my haunches and just breathe for a moment, waiting for Robert to appear. It's hot as Hades and humid as fuck up here. *But I can take it.*

The deep rumble of the Ferrari's engine pulls my attention back to the street. Black and sleek, the sun glinting off its windshield, the super car emerges from the parking area. I click the shutter of my camera as it turns, and the driver is revealed: Robert Maxim. He's wearing aviator shades and a smug, satisfied smile, like driving that car feels good. *I bet it does.*

He too disappears around the corner, the vibrations of his engine melting into the city soundscape. I stand up, stretching my back, reaching for the sky and then my toes.

Sweat moistens my hands, and I have to wipe them on my jeans before taking my equipment apart. Returning the camera to its case and folding up the tripod, I head back to my rental car, a white Toyota Camry with gray cloth seats and the scent of pine woven into the fabric. It's cheap and nondescript, but isn't going to get me laid or put a smug smile on my face.

Placing the camera on the passenger seat, I start the thing up, causing lukewarm air to blow out of the vents. I roll down the window, letting the thick humid air stinking of urine and concrete into the car. It mingles with the pine, and I put the car into reverse. *Can't sit here one more second.*

Navigating across town to my apartment, I shower off the stench of my surveillance shift, and then pour myself a glass of ice-cold rosé before settling in behind my laptop. The air-conditioning blows onto my wet hair, sending a chill over me. *It feels good.*

Downloading the day's worth of photographs onto my computer, I start at the beginning. The first wedding guests arrived at the security gate to Star Island at 5:17pm. I pick up the invitation that lies on the glass dining room table next to my computer. Cream linen, simple black print: Hugh Defry and Santiago Sanchez request your attendance at their wedding…ceremony at 6:00 p.m. followed by dinner and dancing.

Sydney is hosting weddings now.

But it didn't work out that way. Because at 5:57 p.m., Brock drives out looking even more constipated than usual, and Robert Maxim is in the front seat with him, his body turned to the back. I zoom into the image and can see Blue clearly in the middle seat, the white of his fur bright in the darkness.

A series of images captured on the run shows how the evening unfolded. The group went first to Robert's office downtown, taking a circuitous route that suggests they changed their minds about ten minutes into the journey. Then, having traded Hugh for a couple of unidentified figures and changed out of their wedding clothes, they set off again an hour later for an abandoned mall.

The shots inside the mall are partly obscured—I had to shoot through a door that was slightly ajar. I didn't dare open it further. Not with Blue there—he'd have heard or smelled me.

I zoom in on the image of Sydney's back, flanked by Merl and Robert. She's facing a woman in black, who is surrounded by ten armed men—I'm guessing it's local muscle hired for the job.

I scroll quickly through the images of the men falling and Sydney taking the woman by the arm. The men who joined them after that first stop must have been snipers who took out the hired guns. *It was all so perfectly orchestrated.* I couldn't help but admire the ease at which Sydney took the woman hostage.

The next image is back at that nondescript office building. I make a note to check the leases—does Joyful Justice have an office there now? Or does Robert Maxim keep one there for interrogations?

I click through the final images of Sydney coming out with the woman. She does not look injured in any way. No limp, no bruising. I sit back and sip my rosé, scanning the photos.

I almost spill my wine as I bolt forward. *What the hell?* A tall, lanky figure is on the edge of one of the images—a man walking away from them, with bright red hair.

Is that?

I click to the next image, but he's out of the shot. So I go back two and there he is, in full view of the camera: Billy Ray Titus's right-hand man, Nathan Jenkins.

What the hell is he doing in Miami following Sydney Rye?

Sydney

SANTIAGO BLINKS against the bright light spilling into the small room. He holds up a hand to cover his eyes and turns away from the door. Santiago's sleeve is ripped, stained with blood, and his usually perfect hair is rumpled and curled. There is a ligature mark on his wrist and the red line makes my heart beat faster.

Petra promised he wasn't hurt.

"Santiago," I say and he drops his hand, scrambling to stand.

"Sydney!" He blinks, recognizing me. "I knew you'd come." He steps forward, not limping or wincing in pain, and embraces me.

"Are you okay?" I ask.

"I am now that you're here." He steps back. "How is Hugh?"

A warmth spreads in my chest. Bound and held against his will in a tiny, pitch-black room, and Santiago is worried about Hugh. "He'll be fine as soon as we let him know you're with us."

"He's safe?"

"Totally."

Santiago nods. "Thank God."

"They didn't hurt you?"

He shakes his head, holding up his torn sleeve—there is a deep scratch on his forearm but nothing serious. "The worst damage was to my suit."

"We can get that fixed." Such a small and stupid thing to say. Santiago forgives me with a smile. "I'm sorry," I say.

"Make it up to me?"

My brows lift. "Anything."

"I want to get married today," he says, looking past me into the hallway of the boat. "What time is it?"

"After midnight," I tell him.

He nods, his jaw tightening with determination. "Then we have twenty-four hours before another circle around the sun. I'm not wasting one more moment not married to the man I love."

The words bring tears to my eyes, and I have to turn away. Blue's nose touches my hip, and I rub his head, finding comfort in his presence. *There is beauty and love in the world, not just evil and revenge.*

"Let's do it," I say.

Santiago nods and follows me as I start down the hall. Robert waits on the upper deck with three men, all of them in matte black, their weapons holstered, but their deadly natures evident just in the way they stand. *They are killers.*

Santiago touches my arm, and I glance back at him. He's gone a little pale. "Don't worry," I say quietly. "They are on our side."

He nods, relaxing. *Trusting me.*

It's my fault he ended up imprisoned on his wedding day, and he still trusts me.

"Santiago," Robert says. "Good to see you well."

"Thank you."

Robert pulls out his phone and presses a button before passing it to Santiago. "I know Hugh will want to hear your voice."

Santiago takes the phone, his eyes suddenly red-rimmed, and he turns his back to us, putting the phone to his ear. Robert gestures with his chin for his men to step onto the deck and we follow, giving Santiago privacy.

"He wants to get married today," I tell Robert, the brine-scented breeze pulling a strand of hair free from my ponytail.

Robert nods, lit by the electric lights coming through the salon's windows, his gaze following one of the loose strands of my hair as it tangles against my lips. I tug it free, pushing it behind my ear, only to have it lift and float away again.

His mouth quirks into a smile. "My life/ How much more of it remains?/ The night is brief."

I raise my brow, recognizing the poem. "Masaoka Shiki?"

"Very good." His voice is a deep rumble.

I let out a laugh, but it is cut short when Robert catches the strand of hair and places it gently behind my ear, his palm cupping my jaw. "What are you doing?" I strive to keep my voice even, but it is high with fear and anticipation.

He just shakes his head ever so slightly, all relaxed pleasure. "Nothing."

The door of the salon opens behind me and I turn, Robert's hand dropping away. Santiago joins us on the deck. Tears glisten in his eyes. "Thank you," he says, holding out the phone.

Robert brushes past me. "Let's go," he says. "I hear we have a wedding to attend."

Santiago breaks into a grin and nods, emotion brightening his eyes. He links his arm through mine, and we follow Robert off the boat toward the waiting vehicles.

We start for Star Island, Blue's weight heavy against my side. Santiago, his energy sapped, quickly falls asleep, snoring softly next to me.

I wake with a start when Robert's hand touches my arm. *I fell asleep?*

Blue is watching me. "We're here," Robert says. Out the window, the familiar gardens of Robert's front yard glow under the warm light of strung lanterns. They swish back and forth in the sea's breeze, throwing shadows. *It's beautiful.*

Santiago climbs out his door, and I open mine, joining him on the path. Blue leaps out and leads the way toward the house's front entrance. The door swings open, and Hugh bounds out. His hair is wild and his eyes wide.

He lunges down the steps, and Santiago races toward him. Robert takes my elbow, slowing me to a stop. The two men embrace, a shared sob rising up between them.

Tears prick my eyes and I turn away, giving them privacy. Robert tugs on my arm, leading me away from the main entrance and around to the front patio, where the sea wind blusters hard enough to pull a tear from my eye. We enter Robert's office through the sliding glass doors, and he closes them behind us, silencing the wind.

The room is dark, the familiar furniture and bookcases just shapes in the dimness. Robert moves around and turns on the desk lamp.

The tears start slow and hot. I swipe at the first, but two take its place. Robert's jaw tightens as he watches me, his fists on the desk, shoulders hunched forward. I take a stuttering breath, desperate to banish this swelling tide of grief, but it rises like a storm surge—unstoppable, powerful, and impermanent.

Robert moves around the desk so fast my breath gets caught for a moment—a brief pause in the midst of the cyclone.

"Don't cry," he says, close to me, his voice a deep rumble. Robert's strong chest, straining against his black T-shirt, is right at my eye level.

I cover my face and turn to him, falling against all that strength. His arms come around me, gently at first, but as my tears transform to sobs he holds me tighter, squeezing me, crushing me against his chest.

"Shhhh, it's okay," he tells me.

I shake my head. I'm not crying because anything is wrong. *It's just all so much.*

His hand rubs up and down my back. My hands leave my face and scrunch into his shirt, pulling the soft material, crushing it in my fists so I can feel his muscles underneath.

Robert's lips brush my forehead—once, twice…warm and soft. The bristle of a day's stubble is sandpaper against my skin.

I raise my gaze to look up at him. His eyes hold mine. *God, he's so human.* There is hunger in his expression, along with deep sadness and sharp intelligence. His hands still on my back, fingers curling and gripping my shirt as mine hold his—knuckles digging into muscle and skin.

"I'm sorry—" I say but he cuts me off, his lips pressing to mine, fast and hard, stealing my breath and my thoughts.

I try to pull away but he's holding me too tight…or I'm holding him too tight. Breathless—mindless—I pull back, caught in a tangle of arms and hands and lips and tongue and pure electric fire.

"No," I plead, quietly, so quietly…but he hears, and he stops. I duck my head and press it to his chest. It's heaving, his heart hammering. My lips are raw, tears still seeping hot and steady from my eyes. "I'm sorry," I say, my thoughts coalescing, forming out of the fog of upset swirling in my mind.

His fingers loosen, and his lips brush my hair again. "You don't need to apologize."

"I'm in love with Mulberry." The words come out weak—low— almost unsure. But my heart is hammering his name. *I do love him.*

"If you say so." Robert's voice thrums through his chest, right into my ear.

A spark of anger ignites, and I want to pull back to look into Robert's face again, but I can't risk it. *If he kisses me again, I don't know what will happen.*

Robert's hands drift up and down my back in a comforting stroke. "You left him."

His words energize me, and I pull back this time. Robert lets me slip from his hold easily, his eyes searching for mine. "For his own good. I loved Mulberry enough to let him go."

Robert doesn't move or speak for a long moment—just stands there breathing, his eyes bright and lips glistening. A tug on his mouth almost breaks into a smile, but he turns away, tracing one long finger along the edge of his desk as he moves around it.

Robert reaches his seat and looks up at me again. His eyes are shuttered, dark. "I'd never leave you." He says it quiet and sure. *It's true.*

"Even if you thought it was best for me?" I take a step forward, anger and righteous indignation propelling me into his desk, my palms hitting the hard wood with a slap.

That tug turns into a smile, and Robert nods slowly, ever so slowly, his eyes holding mine, and it's then that I realize... *he just told me he is in love with me.*

And that he'll never let me go.

The force of the realization drives me back until my legs knock into one of the armchairs.

There is more than one way to be a slave.

I turn to the door, my hands fisting. *I have to get out of here.*

Lenox

PETRA SMILES AT ME, her expression easy—a predator in disguise. She looks like any sophisticated, wealthy woman sitting at an outdoor café enjoying coffee: hair pulled back into an elegant twist, silk blouse moving subtly in the breeze, diamond necklace sparkling in the sun. The security men in the SUV watching her could just as easily be her own hires as opposed to those paid by Robert Maxim.

Petra watches me as I wind my way through the sparsely populated tables. She sits up a little taller and reaches for her water glass. A sign of unease. "You look well," she says, when I reach her.

Taking the seat across from her, I catch the waitress's eye. Young, slim, and tan, she raises her brows and begins to move toward us. I point to the iced latte in front of Petra, and the waitress smiles and nods, veering off toward the bar. I sit back into the chair, stretching my legs out in front of me. They are still stiff from all the flying. "I'm sure I look well compared to the last time you saw me," I say to Petra, my voice low, neutral. Not unfriendly but lacking warmth. "Last time we met I was running for my life."

Petra purses her lips. "You looked good then too. You always look good, Lenox."

Unbelievable. A laugh bubbles up in me, but I control it. The fear of that night drawing it from me as a cold compress draws heat. "Why am I here?" I ask her.

Her eyes flick behind me, and the waitress approaches with my coffee. "What else can I get you two?" she asks, looking between us.

"I'll have the yogurt and granola," Petra says, holding out the menu —her sleeve slips back, revealing a faint bruising around her wrist. *Sydney must have bound her at some point.*

The waitress takes the proffered menus and turns to me. "Just the coffee."

Petra frowns as the waitress leaves. "You're not hungry?" she asks, lips pouty.

"I don't plan to stay long. I have nothing to say, but Sydney asked me to hear you out."

"I suppose you expect me to apologize," she sits back a little as she says it, her jaw setting into a stubborn line.

"That's up to you. Say what you want. I'm listening." I glance down at my watch. "But I'm leaving soon."

"Oh Lenox, don't be mad. I let you go." Crossing my ankles, I fold my arms and wait for more. "The McCain brothers lied to me." Her voice is firm, as if that's an acceptable excuse for kidnapping a young woman and holding her hostage, then chasing an old and trusted friend through the woods with the intent to kill or capture him.

"What did they tell you about Elsa? How was that young girl ever a threat to you?" I keep my voice even despite the anger simmering in my chest. *Elsa is a child.*

Petra breaks eye contact, her shoulders slumping forward under the weight of her mistake. "I regret what happened."

"Your regrets are not my concern."

Petra's eyes find mine again. "Does our history mean nothing?"

"Our history makes this betrayal that much worse." I suck in a breath, attempting to regain control of myself, but I've shown my anger. *Exposed my hurt.*

Petra reaches for her bag, a red leather clutch with a gold chain. She opens it and hesitates for a moment before glancing up at me again. "Can I make it up to her?" she asks.

"You'd have to ask Elsa that. But I'd guess not."

She leans forward, her hands still on the purse in her lap. "Can I ever make it up to you?"

"Which part? The exposure of how low and callous and greedy you are?" I shift toward her, my legs coming under me and my arms landing on the table, so our faces are close. "Or the attempt to kill me, chasing me through the woods like a hunted animal? How can you ever make that up to me?"

Petra wets her lips. Her emerald green eyes are still beautiful, still bright...how is it I can see her so differently yet she looks so much the same? "I want your help." This time I let out the laugh. Then just shake my head, sitting back, my arms crossed over my chest. Petra pulls her phone out of her purse and places it on the table. She looks down at the blank screen. "I need you."

"You lost me."

Her eyes jump to my face, and the pain in them is reflected in my own heart. She takes a breath, settling herself before she continues. "I'm going to help take down the McCain brothers."

"Yes, I know." Sydney and Merl informed me of the plan.

"That will leave a vacuum."

I puff out a breath. "One I'm sure you'll be willing to fill."

"Will you partner with me?"

"Partner with you?" I shake my head, a laugh dying in my throat— crushed by a sudden wave of despair. *We are so far apart.*

"Lenox. Be reasonable."

"I am." I say it quiet, gentle. "Who wants to partner with someone who has tried to kill them?"

"I did not." Her voice rises, and she glances around, but no one is looking at us. The only other occupied table is at the far side of the patio, and the couple seated there is very much involved with each other. Petra returns her attention to me. "I could have killed you, Lenox, and I did not. I never wanted to hurt you. Never." Her voice is fierce, hard. *She means it.* "I'm sorry."

I lean forward again, and our faces are close. "It's far too late for that."

Petra sighs. "You're right. Lenox," she reaches out, touching my forearm, but I retreat. Petra purses her lips for a moment, taking a breath, and then continues. "Someone will take over their business interests. Wouldn't you rather it be you than someone less scrupulous?"

"Like you?"

"You can help keep me in line." A spark comes into her eyes—a challenge, the hint of a game.

"I don't deal in women."

"You haven't. That doesn't mean you can't."

My mother's face—alive, laughing, her hair wet from the sea—bursts across my vision. *Is there anyone who could have kept her safe?* "Lenox, think of how much good you can do..." I drop my gaze, looking down at my hands, resting on the white linen cloth. They are still covered in tiny wounds from my escape. "Please—" Petra cuts off as the waitress arrives to deliver her meal.

"Can I get you anything else?" the young woman asks. I force myself to meet the waitress's gaze, both to acknowledge her presence and drag myself from my own thoughts.

"No, thank you."

She walks away, and Petra sips her coffee. "At least think about it."

"I will. If you tell me who is working for you on the island?"

She picks up her spoon and dips it into the creamy yogurt, bringing it to her lips before she responds. "I will tell you, in good faith that you will join me. As I am joining you."

"Tell me because it is the right thing to do, and I will consider working with you."

She nods. "His name is Mitchel Swan."

The name is instantly familiar: Dan's right-hand man. I've met him a few times. Tall, almost nondescript, but his eyes are lit by a rare intelligence.

"What do you have on him?"

Petra casts her gaze down to the bowl of artfully designed breakfast. "I don't know."

"Is he the only one?"

"I think so."

"You *think* so?" Disgust leaks into my voice.

"How can I be sure of anything now?" Petra asks. "They lied to me—never in a million years did I think they would be dealing in"—she lowers her voice to almost a whisper—"war slaves. It's disgusting."

"Yes, it is." *And so are you.*

Her eyes jump to mine, as if she's read my thoughts. Petra's jaw tightens. "I did what I thought was right."

"And you were wrong."

Her cheeks brighten in a rare blush. "I know that." She holds my gaze. "And I will do whatever it takes to make amends."

I nod once, believing her intention but not sure if what she seeks is possible. "I have to go," I say, rising. She does not try to stop me.

But as I turn to leave, she says my name. "Lenox." Her voice is high, almost childlike. I turn back to her. "Please," she says. "Think about joining with me. I won't do this alone."

I don't respond. I can't. She's backed me into a corner. There is no right way out. I either have to scale the walls or blow a hole through them. Taking over the McCains' business is of no interest to me, but if we leave the vacuum then another bad actor is likely to take their place.

So I don't answer. I just turn and walk away, reaching into my pocket for my phone. I've got to call Dan and give him some bad news.

CHAPTER SEVENTEEN

Dan

THE PHONE IS light in my hand, but I'm gripping it like the thing is an anvil. My mind is tripping over itself. *I knew it was possible.* But I didn't want to believe.

I must have missed signs.

Anger flushes through me, washing away the confusion. *The bastard is one hell of a liar.*

Mitchel. What the fuck?

I stand up, adrenaline shooting through me. Leaving my office, I race down the spiral steps and rush through the command center to the elevator. Waiting for it, I tap my toe, gritting my teeth, repressing the urge to punch at the metal doors.

They finally open, and I step into the empty space, flashes of my ride with Tom pinging through my mind. *I assumed my enemy was a stranger. Should have known it was someone closer.*

Once on Anita's floor I break into a jog, headed to her room. My fist pounds on the door, louder than I mean it to be, my furious frustration needing an outlet.

Blood is rushing in my ears, and when there is no answer, I knock again, even harder this time. *I need to hit something badly.* The door swings open, and Anita, her usually silky hair mussed into a teased mess, stands on the other side, wearing a robe and a look of concern.

"It was Mitchel," I say, my jaw clenched to keep from screaming it.

Anita's eyes widen, and she glances over her shoulder toward the bedroom. It's then I realize what I've interrupted. *Shit.* It's the middle of the freaking day. Anger flares anew. Irrational this time, misplaced and tinged with the scent of jealousy. "We need to go," I tell her.

Anita turns back to me and nods. "Yes. Give me a few to get myself together."

"I'll wait right out here." *I don't need to be in there with that smell.*

In the few minutes it takes her to get dressed, I call Tanya and tell her to locate Mitchel. It's his day off, and he usually goes out paddle-boarding in the morning then hangs in his rooms. This would all go much easier if we could confront him in private.

I must find out what he did to my systems.

As Anita steps into the hall, her hair brushed and pulled back into a ponytail, wearing jeans and a bright blue tunic, Tanya calls me back. "He's in his room."

"Meet us there," I say. "Mitchel is the mole."

Tanya's intake of breath is the only hint of her surprise. "On my way." Her voice is hard. *Ready.*

We convene outside his door, and I knock, my anger leashed. I've found my control now. With Tanya and Anita by my side, I am grounded. Supported.

But can I trust it?

Mitchel answers, and when he takes in my expression he steps back into the apartment, looking suddenly exhausted. "Why?" I say as I follow him, Anita and Tanya flanking me. "How could you?"

His tired eyes harden. "I had no choice."

"There is always a choice," Anita says, her voice steely.

"What did you do?" I ask.

"I haven't done anything yet." Mitchel is in the center of his living room now. He stops backing up, his spine straightening. "But if anything happens to me, the whole thing goes down." His eyes light with

154

triumph. I recognize the spark in his gaze. The sense of power—it's a hacker's drug, the power we take. We control the machines, and the machines control the world.

But Mitchel can't beat me.

Anita steps forward. "Tell Dan what you did now, so he can fix it."

His gaze falls on her. "No. I'm sorry, Anita." his voice drops low. "But I can't. If I don't follow through, they will kill my mother."

My own mother flashes across my mind's eye. Her voice over the Alexa stream fills my ears—the soft sound of her weeping. Would I betray all this to save her? No. I've betrayed *her* to create this.

To create justice.

And this asshole isn't going to take it all away.

Tanya moves forward with fluid strides and grabs him by the collar before Mitchel can backpedal. "If anything happens to me," he says quickly, "Joyful Justice will be destroyed. All our data—the names and locations of our operatives—everything will be sent to Interpol, the CIA —" His voice cuts off as Tanya punches him in the stomach, and he bends over, gasping for air.

Tanya gives a short laugh. "You cannot destroy Joyful Justice," she says, her accent thick but her words clear. "We are not our computer system. We are not individuals. We are a collective vision. We are justice."

"How could you do this?" I ask. "Why didn't you come to me?" The hurt in my voice is terrible. Anita looks over at me, and deep sympathy wells in her gaze. *Shit.* I sound pathetic.

Not taking her eyes off Mitchel, Tanya says, "He is a coward, Dan; that is how he can risk us all. This is a great act of cowardice." She lets him go but only long enough to step back and deliver another nasty blow to his stomach. "Give me your phone," she says. "I'm not fishing around in your pockets."

Mitchel stumbles back, both hands to his gut. His eyes are bulging. Mitchel is not used to physical confrontation.

"If you take my phone then the virus will go off. Only I can stop it."

Tanya steps forward and grabs his shirt, straightening him again. "Give me your phone." Her voice is steely.

Mitchel looks over her shoulder to me. "You know, Dan. You know I've got you trapped."

"Give her your phone," I say. We don't have much time.

Mitchel reaches into the pocket of his shorts and takes out the slim device, handing it to Tanya. She passes it to me. It's warm and light. *And dangerous.* "What do you want me to do with him?" Tanya asks.

"Take him down to George's rooms. They can stay together." I've secured that room. There is no way for them to communicate with the outside. No escape.

She grabs Mitchel's arm and starts to move him toward the door. "Dan!" Mitchel says, his eyes wide. "It will go off if I don't stop it. I have to manually extend the time every six hours."

"Why haven't you set it off yet?" I ask.

"They told me to wait for their communication, and they have not contacted me."

"Who?" I ask, needing to confirm what we already know.

"I don't know their real names." He says it like it's obvious.

"But they know yours." I shake my head. What an idiot. How did he let this happen? His face goes red at the implied insult. "We found them," I say, my voice weary.

"Do you have my mother?" he asks.

Should I lie and say we do? Blackmail him into giving me the code to his bomb? "Yes, she is in our custody, so you can turn it off now." It sounds like a lie even to my own ears. *Shit, I should have thought this through before storming up here.*

Mitchel's lips tighten into a straight line. "You're lying. I want to speak to her. Then I'll end it."

Tanya jerks him. "I'll kill her myself," she says, close to his ear. "She will die a painful death if you do not give Dan the information he needs."

Mitchel shakes his head. "Threaten me all you want. I'm not risking her."

"You'll risk all of us, all the operatives in the field?" Anita asks.

"She gave me life," Mitchel says, his voice almost a whine.

Anita lifts her chin to Tanya, indicating to get him out of here. Tanya pulls him forward and out the door. I watch them go down the hall, stunned into inaction for several seconds. "You okay?" Anita asks.

No.

"I have to go."

I leave, headed for my private rooms. I have a bomb to defuse. *Fuck me.*

EK

Declan

THE RESTAURANT IS ALMOST FULL, and the view of the square—one of Savannah's most beautiful—sparkles through the tall casement windows. The hostess seats me at a two-top with a clear view of the fountain at the park's center.

Scented of butter and garlic, Amelia's is bustling with brunch customers on this sunny Sunday. The worn wooden tables and Ball jar water glasses contrast with the elegant height of the ceiling and fine linen napkins. It's the kind of dichotomy America loves at this moment: the old and new, the rustic and urban, the casual and formal all mixing together.

Below me on the square, a few guys are gathering around the statue of a Confederate leader known for his bravery on Civil War battlefields and dedication to his country: the Confederate States of America.

Organized by a blogger who calls himself Darth Vengeance, the Men's Rights rally is set to begin in about thirty minutes. My contact within the movement, Troy Richardson, will be there. Troy agreed to meet when it's over so I can talk to him about why the fuck Nathan Jenkins is following Sydney Rye.

Consuela Sanchez's theory that the MR movement might be more organized than we think is niggling at the back of my mind. They seem like such a rag-tag team of losers. But with two mass killings and an assassination attempt under their belts, maybe what we've been seeing as lone actors is actually much more. Could they really have their shit together enough to organize—and raise money for—terrorist operations?

My waiter, a tall, slim African American man with a big smile, interrupts my train of thought. "How are you today?" he asks brightly. I glance back down at the all-white crowd of men swirling below us and suppress a sigh.

"I'm good, and you?"

"Very good, thanks for asking." His accent is local, lyrical, and friendly. "Can I tell you our specials?"

"I'll have the shrimp and grits; it's my favorite." I smile, letting him know I'm a returning customer.

"Wonderful. I love that too. Anything to drink?"

"Just coffee."

He takes my menu and moves away, navigating the tightly packed tables as elegantly as a dancer sashaying through a crowded nightclub.

I pull out my phone, checking again to see if there is an ID on the woman Sydney took hostage. Almost thirty hours have passed since I sent the images to a friend at Interpol. He owed me one—but if he can tell me her name then I will be in his debt.

As my email loads, I glance at the crowd below. They have signs I can't read from this angle, but the women who walk by react with wrinkled noses and dirty looks, which just make the protesters smile. *Dickheads.*

My phone pings with fresh messages, and I scroll through. *Yes!* My contact came through. I open the email and scroll past his gloating.

Petra Bokan:

38 years old, Czech-born but resides in Romania. Suspected of human trafficking—she has brothels all over the world.

My eyes narrow as I stare at the brief paragraph. *Could she be connected to the McCain brothers?* They are in the same business.

Nathan Jenkins attends a meeting with Ian McCain in Istanbul, then I see him in Miami...maybe he wasn't following Sydney. Maybe he was following Petra.

The waiter appears with my coffee, and I thank him before sending a reply to my friend. *Thanks so much, can you check if she has any connections to the McCain brothers—Ian, Michael, and Murphy, Irish Nationals involved in sex trafficking.*

I reread the email and hit send. There has to be a connection. This is too big a coincidence. Putting my phone next to my plate, I sip my coffee, returning my attention to the gathering crowd below. There are about twenty or thirty protesters now. A stage has been erected next to a statue of the Confederate officer, and someone is making final adjustments to the microphone and loudspeakers.

My gaze scans the rest of the park. A perfect square in the center of this block of graceful mansions, it is planted with mature live oak trees —their gnarled branches dripping with silvery green Spanish moss. Hundreds of years old, the trees shading today's rally stood here when the last slave ship to deliver human chattel to American shores docked in Savannah in 1859—a half century after the importation of slaves had been outlawed.

Sitting under the cool whisper of air-conditioning, listening to the clink of silverware and the soft rumble of conversation, a shiver passes over me as I think of the history haunting this city...this nation. My gold watch bumps against my wrist bone as I replace my coffee cup on its saucer.

An inheritance from my grandfather, the Rolex is nothing compared to the vast wealth left to me. Generations of freedom and privilege afford me the luxury to choose my own course. *It is my duty to help foster freedom for all.*

My eyes drift to the men below again—stirring now, as a speaker steps onto the stage. I lean forward. *Is that a woman?* Yes. About average height, wearing a power suit in burgundy, with long blonde hair that reaches to the middle of her back, she steps up to the microphone as the men cheer.

I can't make out her words, but the men press closer to the stage as she begins to speak. Some of them are nodding along. Others clap and whistle.

Local people and tourists are avoiding the men now, taking any of the other shaded paths available to bypass the gathering. The rally is concentrated in the center of the square, the small crowd filling the space between the fountain and the statue.

I'm distracted as the waiter brings my food. The buttery scent of the grits and the brine of the shrimp bring a smile to my face. "Thank you."

"Enjoy," the waiter encourages. His eyes pass over the window as he turns to leave, and he pauses for a moment, looking down at the rally below.

I follow his gaze. A dark, draped figure is moving toward the men. It's a woman in a burka. She is alone, walking slowly but purposefully toward the center of the park. My heart beats faster, and I tense to stand. *Something is wrong.*

As the covered figure reaches the edge of the crowd, the men she meets step back, surprise evident in their postures.

The waiter leaves me, moving on to another table. Riveted, I watch the woman as she pushes through the crowd. Finally reaching the front of the stage, she raises a hand as if to ask a question. The speaker looks down at her, eyebrows raised in question, her mouth turned up into a condescending smile.

A man in the back yells something, and the rest of the crowd cheers him. A sudden flash of light is followed by a loud bang, causing the casement windows to shudder in their wooden frames. Everything is happening so fast that I'm standing, my chair knocked over behind me, before I even fully realize what I'm seeing.

Men are lying on the ground, smoke is swirling, and the speaker is missing. As the air clears I see her—or rather, a part of her. Bile rises in my throat. Where the burka-clad woman stood in front of the stage is now just a wet, charred horror. *A suicide bomber. The woman was a suicide bomber.*

Other diners are crowding around me, staring down at the carnage. My heart hammers, and my palms are slick with sweat. Sirens begin to wail in the distance.

Is this the beginning of a war between the Men's Rights activists and the Her Prophet followers?

CHAPTER EIGHTEEN

Sydney

HUGH AND SANTIAGO stand under a canopy of flowers—the fragile blooms windblown and wilted compared to the fresh brightness they presented yesterday. But the two men are radiant, making up for any delay and all the complications.

The crowd of guests is smaller, only the most intimate gathering now, rather than the larger event planned.

Santiago isn't wearing his custom suit—the sleeve was beyond repair at such short notice—but he looks dashing in a blue seersucker, a white flower tucked into his lapel.

Hugh beams at his fiancé—soon to be husband—as the officiant, an African American woman named Maude Flanders, quotes Maya Angelou.

"Love recognizes no barriers. It jumps hurdles, leaps fences, penetrates walls to arrive at its destination full of hope." Maude, a justice of the peace that Santiago knows from the soup kitchen where he volunteers, beams at the two men. "Those of us who know and love you can't help but admire the bond you two have formed. And even though this wonderful day had to be postponed"—she smiles—"nothing can stop the two of you." The crowd nods in agreement. "Meeting at a support group for people who have lost loved ones to violence, you found not only healing, but also each other. In part, that shared history of pain is what helps you both live so fully today."

The woman sitting in front of me, Santiago's aunt, a stout, strong-looking woman who flew in from Colombia two days ago, murmurs her agreement.

"Are you ready for your vows?" Maude asks.

Hugh takes a deep breath. "You help me see beauty every day," Hugh begins, his voice strong and sure. "In every moment that I have." His lips purse as his eyes well, and my own eyes burn. "Almost losing you yesterday..." He stops, and Santiago squeezes his hands, tears slipping down his face.

"Just a fender bender," Santiago says—the cover story we came up with to explain his absence. "Nothing serious."

Hugh hiccups a laugh and nods. Taking a deep breath, he returns to the vows he prepared for the day before, the day before violence almost ended their relationship. "I've always thought of marriage as a partnership, as having a confidant and friend along on the ride through life with me. Someone who always had my back, and who I'd defend with my life."

Santiago smiles, and the two men just look at each other for a moment. The love between them is almost palpable. It's floating in the air, same as the briny scent of the sea and the sweet floral of the bouquets.

"You are strong, funny, warm, and brave. And I'm honored to take this journey with you. I promise to stand with you, my love, forever."

Santiago bends his head, looking down at their joined hands as he pulls himself together. Maude waits until Santiago looks up again, shaking his head a little and giving a teary smile. "Hugh Defry." He breaks into a grin that sends ripples of laughter through the crowd. "You are my best friend. My favorite person. And your food makes me fall down at your feet." The gathering laughs again. "Your bravery, resilience, and artistry remind me every day that this is a beautiful world." Santiago bites his lip, holding back emotion. "No matter what is happening outside us, what the world is doing, we will always have each other. And that is such a comfort to me."

Tears are falling down Hugh's face, and he lets go of one of Santiago's hands for a moment to swipe at them. "I love you, Hugh Defry. And I'm honored to become your husband."

The officiant smiles, turning her attention to us. "You," she says, "are here to support and witness this union." Someone cheers and clapping breaks out. Santiago and Hugh inch closer to each other. Maude produces the rings and hands one to each man. "Repeat after me, Hugh." He nods. "Santiago Sanchez, I take you to be my lawfully wedded husband, to have and to hold, for better or for worse, until death do us part."

Hugh repeats the words, slipping the ring onto Santiago's finger.

"Now you, Santiago," the officiant says.

He nods, looking the most serious I've ever seen him, and makes the same vow to Hugh. He slips the ring onto Hugh's finger, and I clap along with the rest of the guests.

"I now pronounce you married!" Maude declares. The cheers rise up so loudly that a group of sea birds take off, squawking loudly, from where they'd rested on the bulkhead.

Hugh and Santiago embrace, kissing madly.

My heart aches with joy and a soft sadness. There is a part of me, tiny really, but still there, that can't help but think... *that should be my brother's happiness*. It was stolen from him. And that thought ignites an old rage—a rage at how many other people's happiness is being stolen as I stand here watching my friends marry.

There is still so much injustice in the world that it is a weight on my shoulders, a heaviness around my soul. What Santiago said, about how no matter what was happening in the world, they could always turn to each other to know that there is goodness...I can see that. But I also know that celebrating the good won't make the bad go away.

No matter how much I wish it would.

Robert comes up to me afterwards, as I stand watching the sun slip below the Miami skyline while the guests sip cocktails in the living room. "Nice ceremony," he says. I nod, feeling both melancholia and joy while barely tasting the rosé I'm drinking. "I don't suppose you've looked at the news?" I turn to him, my brows raised. His skin glows in the soft light, his eyes flashing green-blue...the same as the ocean. "There was a Men's Right's Rally in Savannah today."

I roll my eyes. "Those idiots."

"A suicide bomber killed six and injured another twenty."

"A suicide bomber?" My mouth goes dry.

"Apparently, it was a woman wearing a burka." He holds my gaze, knowing I'll jump to the same conclusion he has. *It was a Her Prophet follower.* "Maybe you should call your mother."

I step back involuntarily, knocking into the railing. "She didn't have anything to do with that. It's not her style."

Robert's lips tighten, and he looks back into the house where most of the guests are mingling as a musician plays the piano and waiters move through the crowd passing hors d'oeuvres. "Maybe," Robert says, "but,"—his gaze lands on me again—"I think it's worth the call."

"No way."

Robert's lip tightens, but he does not argue. Instead he turns to look seaward at the horizon, resting his arms on the rail. I join him, and we silently watch the sky darken and the stars begin to come out. A chill steals through the night, and he moves slightly closer, buffering me against the evening breeze. Blue leans against my other side, warming my leg.

It is then, with lucid certainty, that I know my time here is up. *I can no longer hide in this shelter.*

I must begin to fight again.

CHAPTER NINETEEN

Sydney

THE BARTENDER NARROWS his eyes when Blue, Petra, and I walk into the pub. It's in one of the shabbier neighborhoods of Drogheda, a midsized Irish city where the McCain brothers were born, raised, and still reside. The bartender doesn't close the paper he looked up from. "Can't bring a dog in 'ere." His accent is thick and brawny just like his bulging biceps and hairy forearms.

"Let me take care of this," Petra says quietly, sauntering toward the barman, her hips, clad again in tight black leather, swinging in a way that only Eastern European and Latin women can pull off—I've tried but end up looking like I'm on the verge of a seizure. *Not sexy.*

We are the first customers, but it's still early on a Wednesday. *The punters are not out of work yet.* Petra leans against the bar, practically melting over it, and the barman puts down his paper, coming to rest his elbows across from her, bending down to meet Petra's posture.

Blue and I take a booth, my banned companion slipping under the table, turning so he can see most of the room. I slide around so my back is to the wall, and my view of the door is clear.

The place reeks of cigarettes, sweat, and spilled drink. Soccer plays on a television crammed onto a shelf behind the bar—it isn't even a flat screen. *What year is this?*

The wooden tables and booths are dark and worn. Wide floorboards scuffed and aged with filth match the scent of the place.

Low yellow lighting keeps any of the dirt from being too obvious—it's a thick, beaten-in crust rather than a fresh coat of dust. Taking in a deep breath, I close my eyes and think back to my life in London years ago. The scars on my face stood out sharp and new, but my body didn't ache with old wounds…though my heart still burned with the newness of James' death.

Petra puts a pint of beer on the table, pulling me from my thoughts. It's piss yellow with a few spare bubbles at its head, warning me the thing is barely carbonated, in the traditional style of shitty Irish or English beer. *This place is traditional.*

I sip it—noting, as expected, that it's room temperature—with a smile. I like this pub; no pretense, no updating, none of that fancy customer service with a smile or beer with the kind of fizz the rest of the world seems to prefer. Who needs perfumed cleaning products, or artisanal ales, when you can have Mr. Beefcake and a game of footie that fuzzes in and out of service?

In the back, through a darkened archway, I spot a pool table covered in red felt. "Fancy a game?" I ask Petra as she slides into the seat next to me—her back is also to the wall, her view of the door as unobstructed as mine.

She takes a sip from her own pint, following my gaze to the pool table. "Only if we can make it interesting."

I smile. "You want to bet?"

"Gamble?" She flashes me a smile, her green eyes bright. "You like risks, no?"

"What are we gambling for?" I ask, my old Madonna-style British accent coming back with a vengeance.

"If I win, we kill them." I huff out a laugh, but she continues "And you let me do the talking."

"And what will you say? 'I'm going to kill you now'?" I smile at her.

"That I know what they've been doing, and now they are going to pay."

"I was joking. But you seriously want to warn them before we kill them? Besides, we have to get information out of them first."

She nods slowly, taking a sip of her beer. "I like to warn them. That way I can see the fear in their eyes."

"You think you frighten them?"

"They are not fools. Just liars."

I nod my head, raising my own pint. *It makes sense to be afraid of Petra.* "And what do I get if I win?"

"What do you want?"

"Good question." I look down into the beer, its amber depths offering me nothing. "How about if I win, I get to do the talking?"

"We kill them no matter what?"

I nod. "After we get the information we want."

She grins. "I'll take that bet."

Blue comes out from under the table as we stand, making our way to the darkened back room. Petra flips a switch, and a low light over the pool table flickers to life, bathing the red felt in a warm yellow. Its glow reaches the few tables around it but doesn't penetrate the dark corners of the room.

The bathroom door hangs open on drooping hinges, the smell wafting over us. Petra's nose wrinkles as she pulls coins from her purse —a small red satin thing with a gold chain for a strap.

Grabbing a pool stick, I find the chalk and rub it over the tip. Petra pushes in the coins, and the balls are released in a clatter. Blue sits beside me as Petra gathers the balls into the triangle. Her face is expressionless, her eyes concentrating on the task at hand.

"Do you play often?" I ask her.

A smile creeps onto her lips, as though a memory is crossing her vision. "Not as much as I used to." All the balls in their place, she looks up at me. "I started hustling at a pool hall when I was thirteen. It was something my father and I did together." *How nice.*

We agree on a game of 8-ball. She plucks a pool stick off the wall then turns and, with a wave of her hand, offers me the break. I shrug and step up to the table. Petra takes chalk off the rail and steps back to give me room.

I grab the cue ball and line it up. Bending over the table, I aim and then fire.

The balls come apart in a satisfying crack, racing across the table, but none of them sink into any of the pockets.

"You play often?" she asks me, humor in her voice.

"No, haven't in years. Never was much of an aficionado."

I think back to the few games I played when I frequented bars in Brooklyn. I was always half drunk and terrible.

This wasn't a bet I particularly wanted to win.

Petra bends over the table, her leather pants lending her an air of sophistication and danger. She looks perfect like that, her gaze fixed on the ball, her hands holding the stick gently. *Like a real professional.*

The white cue ball strikes a striped ball and sinks it. She moves around the table, wetting her lips and lowering herself near the cue ball again. She doesn't bother calling out her shots, but she sinks them all. A second striped ball, a third, a fourth. I drink my beer and wait.

The pub door opens, and my heart leaps for just a second until I spot two women coming in; teased hair, short shorts, and halter tops. They aren't here for us. They are here to get free drinks and maybe play some pool. Just girls out for a night.

They frown at the empty bar, but when the bartender puts down his paper and greets them, they perk up.

He'll keep them busy until the rest of the crowd arrives.

Having finally missed a shot, Petra speaks to me from across the table. "Your turn."

"Is there any point?" I ask with a smile.

"You don't strike me as someone who gives up, no matter how bad your odds."

I let out a short laugh. "And I always wanted to be one of those people who knew how to pick their battles."

She laughs, leaning against the wall, her pool stick in front of her, eyes tracking the women at the bar.

Turning my attention to the table, I find the solids well outnumbering the stripes. I pick a ball that looks like an easy shot—the deep-green 6-ball sitting right next to the side pocket. One more sip of my pint, and I put it down on the ledge. Blue's nose touches my hip in a gesture of support. I lean over the pool table, knowing my jeans don't look nearly as alluring as Petra's leather pants. Maybe I should get a pair.

I sink my ball and smile at the small victory. Petra nods at me, encouraging. I move around the table and take aim at the 3-ball, missing this time. The cue ball bounces off my intended quarry and rolls slowly toward a pocket, stopping just shy of the edge.

"Your turn," I say.

Petra sinks the rest of the stripes and has only the black 8-ball left when the door opens again. Her head rises toward the sound and, standing to her full height, a predatory smile crosses Petra's face.

Four men, two of whom I recognize from the photos we looked at before we left Miami, stand in the entry—the last rays of the sun outline them in a brief golden glow before the door swings shut.

Two of the three McCain brothers: Murphy and Michael. The older one, Michael, is shorter and darker than his younger brother, Murphy, but more striking. With his thick black curls and eyes so blue they seem to pierce through the gloom of the pub, Michael surveys the space like he owns it. *Maybe he does.*

Murphy's blond curls, wide shoulders, and impressive height are softened by an easy, dimpled smile and wide aqua blue eyes that sparkle with good humor as he nods to the bartender.

Both are wearing pressed denim with faux fading and crisp button-down shirts.

The two other men are broad and tall, their heads square and their brown hair cut short. Their muscles bulge against thin black T-shirts and their heavy brows hunker over narrowed eyes.

"Just one more shot, and I win," Petra says, pulling my gaze to her.

"True," I answer.

She leans over the table, her gaze remaining on the men as they head to the bar and order pints. She strikes the cue ball, and the eight disappears in a corner pocket. Petra stands and leans the pool stick against the wall and picks up her empty pint. "Can I get you another?" She asks.

I look at my half-full mug and refuse. Swaying her hips in that way she has, Petra heads over to the bar.

When the McCain brothers see her they smile. Murphy opens his arms, and she steps into them. *He dwarfs her.* His hands span her lower back, and Petra's thin arms barely reach around his neck.

The henchmen are introduced, and she nods at them but doesn't offer her hand. The men stand back from their bosses, no drinks in their meaty fists.

A fresh pint in her grip, Petra leads the brothers back to the pool-room where Blue and I wait in the shadows, surrounded by the stink of urine.

"Sydney, this is Michael," Petra gestures to the dark-haired, medium-height brother with the striking blue eyes. "And Murphy." The younger brother with his blond curls, paler blue gaze, and big smile reaches out a thick-fingered hand, and I take it. His skin is calloused, his grip strong. But not that *I'm a man and I'll crush you* strong. More *I'm such a powerful man that I don't need to crush your hand to prove it* strong.

Michael takes my hand next and gives me a tight smile, not as jovial as his brother, more suspicious and harder. Where Murphy is big with rounded muscles, Michael is wiry with corded strength and hard angles.

Petra sips her drink and gestures for us all to take a seat at a four-top in the corner of the room. The henchmen close the pocket doors, sealing us in the pool room, then stand with their backs to us, facing the closed doors, hands clasped behind them in what could be mistaken as a military stance.

"So," Michael starts, addressing Petra. "While it's always lovely to see your beautiful face, I wonder what we're doing here."

He's not nervous. This is his turf.

Petra leans back in the old wooden chair, her smile friendly. "Sydney here has been telling me about some things you boys have been up to."

Murphy lets out a half laugh. "And how exactly would she know?"

"She says," Petra continues, ignoring Murphy's question, "you've been buying women from Isis. Using my channels to move them, then selling them for a profit." She gives a little shrug. "Of course, after earning a little off them yourself."

Michael's brow furrows, and his bright blue eyes go stormy. "Those are lies." His gaze is locked onto Petra's.

She shakes her head no. "I've seen evidence."

Michael's attention shifts to me. "Who the fuck are you?" he asks, his tight muscles stiffening even further, a vein in his neck beginning to pulse.

Murphy's knuckles are white around his pint, but he keeps his relaxed pose, leaning back in the wooden chair, long legs stretched out in front of him.

"I'm Sydney motherfucking Rye," I say.

"What the fuck does that mean?" Michael asks, his voice dropping an octave as his accent thickens.

"That means," Petra leans forward, her elbows on the table, fingers wrapping around her pint. "You shouldn't fuck with her. And that I believe her."

Murphy folds his hands onto his stomach, keeping up the appearance of a man who's not nervous—who's not coiled for a fight. "Petra, we've worked together for years. Why would we start doing something so stupid as that?"

"Because you're greedy. And you're men. And you think with your dicks instead of your heads."

Michael tenses, while Murphy laughs, putting his hands behind his head, making his broad chest one big-ass target. There is no fear in either man's gaze, but in Michael's I see the recognition that Petra did not come here to talk. That this will end in blood.

Murphy seems to still be under the impression that this can all be worked out. That we can resolve this in some way that is not violent. If only that were true. If only violence was a choice instead of a destiny.

I take a sip of my flat, warm beer and wait for Petra to give me a cue. These men are going to die, and I'll do my part in killing them. But first we need to get some information.

EK

Dan

EMILY KIMELMAN

IT WILL RELEASE *the names and locations of all our operatives to Interpol, Homeland Security, and the CIA.*

Mitchel is a bastard. A coward.

But brilliant.

The bug is wound through our system like DNA through a cell. In order to stop it, I will have to destroy the entire system. This is not a cancer that some amount of poison can burn out. This is a fatal flaw.

I sit back in my chair and stare out the glass walls in front of me to the wide screen displaying surveillance video, maps, and other information vital to Joyful Justice's mission.

What are we without data?

My hands are shaking, tapping against my desk, so I bunch them into fists. Closing my eyes, I take a deep breath, and let it out slowly. Opening my eyes, I check the time. Thirty minutes until either Mitchel puts in his code, or our people are exposed.

I can't let that happen.

My phone vibrates, drawing my attention. *My mom.* "Hey," I answer, trying to sound normal.

"Oh honey, I'm sorry to bother you." I can hear her fiddling with something in the background, cans clink against each other. She is in her pantry. The scent of it comes over me suddenly—the dry powder of flour mixed with the bite of spices. *I should bring her some cardamom...*

"I love talking to you, Mom, thanks for calling."

A pause in her movements. "Well, that's nice to hear." There is a smile in her voice, and I fight sudden welling emotion. *Would I kill for her? Yes. But not my own people.*

Mitchel had to betray someone—he chose me.

"I'm going to come visit soon," I say, not thinking it through, just needing it to be true.

"That's wonderful!" Her joy pierces me, leaving a burning pain. "I can't wait."

"Me either." My voice sounds strangled.

"You okay, honey?" she asks.

"Yeah, just tired." I run a hand through my hair and sit up, forcing myself to sound normal.

"I'd love to come visit you some time." Her voice is quiet, like it's not really true, but she wants it to be. Mom is not a traveler—she's a cat lady who likes to watch her shows when they are live, none of that DVR or streaming for her.

"You would?" A smile pulls at my lips.

"I want to see how you live." Her voice is stronger. "I try to picture you, and it's like you're in this void all by yourself. Just a black space. I can't see anything around you."

My chest clenches. "It's not like that. It's beautiful here. Tropical. Bright. Lush."

"Well, I need to see it for myself. Maybe I could come visit you instead of you coming here?" Her tone pitches up in question.

"Sure…" *Should I tell her the truth about my life and move her to the island? That would keep her safe.*

A crash on her side of the line makes my heart jump. She lets out a yelp. "Mom! Are you okay?"

She laughs, light and airy. "Oh, I'm fine. Rascal just got into the pantry with me and knocked down a bunch of cans." She tsks at him and laughs again.

"I'll let you go Mom, but we'll plan a trip soon."

"Promise?"

"Yes." *And I will.*

"I love you, Dan. Be good."

"I love you too, Mom." I don't promise to be good. I can't. Not right now. There is too much at stake.

Grabbing Mitchel's phone and my laptop, I shove them in a bag and head to the elevator. The guard outside Mitchel and George's makeshift prison nods to me as I walk up. She opens the door, and I step into the bright space.

The two men are sitting on the couch, and both stand when I enter. George's hands are still bandaged but in less gauze than before, so he no longer looks like a sad bear.

His sister's rescue lifted his spirits, and from the tentative smile he offers, I assume he does not resent his imprisonment.

Mitchel, on the other hand, glares at me. *As if I'm being unreasonable.*

"George, give us a minute," I say.

The younger man nods and heads into the bedroom.

I pull out my laptop and put it on the coffee table then place Mitchel's phone next to it. Fifteen minutes until all our people's information is released.

"Put in your code," I say. We are standing across from each other, the low table between us.

Mitchel glares at me. "I can't risk my mother."

"I found your bug, and I'll destroy everything before I let you expose us. Either way, you don't win. Either way, your mother dies."

His face pales but he shakes his head.

"You'll risk all of us for one person?" My voice is a low growl.

He gives one strong nod. "Yes."

I shake my head. "You are a coward."

Mitchel's face goes red. "You're the coward," he says, his voice venomous. "With no real connections to anybody. You sit up in your office above it all. You don't know what it is to love."

Anger rushes through me, and I've grabbed his shirt and hauled him close, banging his shin into the coffee table before even thinking about it. Mitchel's bright blue eyes go wide for a second but narrow quickly. He doesn't try to defend himself. "I know what love is," I say.

"You're afraid of it because you got hurt. But I'm not. I won't kill my mother to save you."

"It's not just me!" I shake him, and he pulls at my fist holding his shirt. When I release him, he stumbles back, falling on the couch. "Reset the damn clock."

He just shakes his head.

"Fuck you." Sweeping the laptop and phone back into my bag I storm out. *I have no choice.* I will destroy all our servers, all our information. Joyful Justice will just be the people. The network must be destroyed to save them.

Half way down the hall, my legs pumping, my face hot, eyes burning, I stop.

The world around me disappears, and I'm sucked into space. *A solution clicks into place before my eyes. Fake it. I have to fake it.*

When I burst back into the room, Mitchel is standing by the window, staring out at the ocean, but he turns quickly as I cross to him.

"We will find your mother. And we will save her. You know we can do it. We did it for George." Mitchel opens his mouth to speak, but I keep going. "But until then, we fake our demise. Like a predator fakes an injury to lure its prey closer. We can do this, Mitchel. You and me, we can do this together. Reset the clock."

Confidence oozes through my blood. *This is a brilliant idea.*

Mitchel's brows are raised, and I can see him thinking. I know him so well. "We release fake information?"

"Yes, and we shut down all our websites. We go dark. As if you won, and I panicked." A slow, predatory smile is pulling at me—it is reflected on Mitchel's face. I put the laptop on the coffee table again, next to his phone. "Reset the clock. Give us a little time."

Mitchel hesitates for only a moment then joins me, picking up his phone and entering code.

Joyful Justice is not just people or a network. We are an idea. *An ideal.* And nothing can stop us.

CHAPTER TWENTY

Sydney

I SIP my beer and eye the beefcakes guarding the closed doors to the pool room. They are almost the same height and width, though one has a curl to his hair—it laps at the collar of his T-shirt—whereas the other has a buzz cut. There is a scar on the back of his head in the shape of a C. The short hair shows it off. Does he like people to know that he can get knocked on the head and keep going? Why else keep his hair so short?

My attention is pulled back to the conversation at the table when Petra says my name. "Sydney has proof."

Michael shakes his head. "You've got this all wrong. Petra, you know us. We don't deal in slaves."

I sit forward, and Blue shifts under the table, tapping his nose against my knee. "You brought Elsa to Petra. Told her Joyful Justice was threatening you—"

Michael cuts me off. "Are you a member of Joyful Justice?" His lip sneers in disgust. "That stupid packet you sent us. What a joke."

Murphy laughs and sits forward, his big forearms coming to rest on the table. "We didn't do those things you accused us of."

"Yes, you did."

"Sorry, sweetheart but you've got the wrong guys. We don't deal in slaves. All our girls are there by choice. Some of them even love it."

Bile rises in my throat at the tone in his voice. "They love it?" I raise my brows. "Are you sure?" He just nods, a twinkle in his gaze. My fists tighten in my lap. "You are a dumbass."

He laughs and takes a sip of his drink. "We might be dumbasses, lass, but we do not deal in war slaves."

"She showed me footage of Ian at a slave auction," Petra says, her voice tight. "I saw it with my own eyes."

"That kind of thing can be manipulated." Michael waves his hand in dismissal.

"What about Elsa?" I ask.

"Who?" Michael questions, cocking his head.

"The girl you had me hold," Petra says, her voice so low I can barely hear it.

Michael shakes his head. "All is fair in love and war. Joyful Justice threatened our business—you prudes don't like what we do," he says to me.

"I don't have a problem with sex workers," I say. "I have a problem with sex slaves. A big problem."

"How many times do I have to say this? We don't deal in sex slaves!" Murphy's voice raises enough that Curls looks over his shoulder, checking on his bosses. Is it possible Murphy doesn't know what his brothers are up to? I glance at Petra, and she is chewing on her lip, brow furrowed.

"You didn't tell him," I say to Michael.

His blue eyes glitter with anger. "What are you blabbering on about?"

"Murphy doesn't know," I say. The truth is written all over Michael, exposed in the hard lines of his face and the tense grip of his hand. The reason Murphy thought this wouldn't end in violence is he thought he was innocent. *How sad.* "You and Ian did this without him knowing," I say with a note of awe in my voice. *What assholes.*

"That's ridiculous," Michael says, but he doesn't sound convincing.

Murphy turns to his brother and then to me. "Bullshit. Don't try to drive a wedge between us. We're family. That won't work."

I can't help the laugh that pops out of me. "Boy, you are in for a big surprise. You didn't know."

"You're full of shit," Murphy says, showing the first signs of anger...of doubt.

"This is just sad," I say to Petra.

She doesn't respond, too busy staring daggers at Michael.

"Do you know they kidnapped Mitchel Swan's mother, Matilda?" I ask Murphy. "Just like they kidnapped Elsa."

Murphy shakes his head. "Fuck you." He stands quickly, knocking against the table and making the beer in our pints dance. "I'm done here."

"Sit down," Petra says, her voice low but commanding. "We are not done until I say we are."

Murphy turns on Petra, hulking over her. "You come here, to our city, and bring an enemy with you to accuse us of..." He sputters for a moment. "Of dealing with fucking Isis, and you expect me to sit down and take it?"

"You can talk to us or you can die," I say, raising my gun.

Murphy laughs, turning as if to leave. The silent thwap of a bullet exploding through the silencer beats at my ears milliseconds after I pull the trigger. Murphy's eyes go wide, and he looks at the wall right behind him where the bullet penetrated a painting of dogs playing cards, tearing the canvas and sending slivers of plaster floating into the air.

"You crazy bitch," he says.

"Sit down, or I'll kill you."

He turns to Petra. "You're letting her get away with this."

"Sit down," Petra says, keeping her eyes on Michael. The older brother is frowning but does not look afraid. Blue growls low, and I flick my eyes to Curly and Buzz at the door. They are facing us, their bodies stiff, but well trained enough to know not to make a move when a marksman has their boss in her sights.

"We should go," Petra says. "You two will come with us."

"Do you have a death wish, woman?" Murphy asks.

She stands, eyeing him. "Do you?" She grabs his bicep, her hand not able to get even halfway around it. Petra has no weapon, but she starts to push Murphy toward the goons at the door with the confidence of a person carrying an Uzi.

Blue lets out a sharp bark, but Michael is already moving. Exploding from his chair, he wrenches the table up, tossing it at Murphy and Petra, and diving for me. His hands wrap around the gun as Blue knocks into him, and we all go down in a pile.

Michael's breath is hot on my face, my weapon pressed between us. A brief waft of sandalwood and spice overtakes me as my nose is pressed into his neck. I open my mouth and bite, keeping my hand tightly around the gun, my finger slipping between the trigger and the handle so it can't be fired.

Michael grunts as my teeth sink into him.

He is on top of me, Blue on top of him. I can't see a thing, but I hear crashing and thuds of impact around us.

Michael tries to pull away from my teeth, and I release him. Blue yanks on his arm and the man is off me, his fist pummeling at Blue. The taste of his sweat is thick on my tongue. I didn't break the skin, but a red mark in the shape of my teeth is outlined on his neck.

Petra is in a corner, Murphy and Curly circling her as she swings the gold strap of her purse. Where is Buzz?

A blow from behind knocks me forward, off my knees and onto my chest, landing on my stomach with a grunt. Buzz is on my back, the gun under my stomach.

I can't breathe.

Hands wrap around my neck, and, leveraging himself up, Buzz smashes my face into the filthy floor. I'm stunned for a moment, but with a last gasp of air I try to twist over. Buzz is too strong, and with his weight on me, I'm paralyzed.

Blue barks a warning, and suddenly Buzz is knocked off me. I roll over, my gun automatically coming up. Michael, stumbling to stand, sees me and the gun aimed at his chest and freezes, one hand on the pool table, the other dangling by his side, blood dripping off it from a wound in his forearm. I don't fire. Can't kill him yet. First I need answers.

Buzz is under Blue, my dog's jaws wrapped around his neck. The goon is laying very still as Blue keeps up a low and threatening growl. He won't rip out the man's throat unless Buzz does something stupid... like try to move.

Picking myself up I glance over my shoulder to see Petra lash out with her purse strap at Curly, who shies away with a yelp, holding his left eye, blood welling between his fingertips. Murphy lunges at her, and she disappears behind his bulk. *Shit.*

I can't kill him yet either. Keeping my gun on Michael, I circle to the pool stick I left leaning against the wall. Taking it in my free hand, I notice the cue ball by the corner pocket. Putting down the stick for a moment, I pick up the white orb and hurl it at Murphy's head. It strikes him, and I feel a small wave of triumph. *Good fucking shot.* He lets out a grunt and reaches one hand to touch the back of his head.

Picking up the cue stick, I push my gun into my waistband. Michael's eyes go wide when I put the weapon away, and he lunges for me, running right into my stick. It catches him across the throat, and he stumbles back, choking. "I'm actually more dangerous with this thing," I say, twisting it back and cracking him in the side of the head. He crumples like a demolished skyscraper.

Curly sees his boss go down and looks at me with his one good eye. Dropping his hands away from his injury, he falls into a fighting stance. *Oh.* He is trained. I can tell from the set of his shoulder, the placement of his loosely curled fists, and the way he's ignoring the blood dripping down his face.

A smile tugs at my mouth, accepting the challenge, falling into my own stance, bringing my stick under my arm, ready.

Curly moves closer to me—slowly, cautiously. Petra and Murphy are in the corner of my vision; I see the gold strap of her purse flash but can't take my eyes off Curly long enough to check what she is doing.

Curly eyes Petra's pool stick where she left it on the table. I step forward quickly and lash out, he reacts lightning fast, throwing up a block so that my weapon smacks into his forearm. That will hurt tomorrow but isn't going to slow him down today.

He spins away, grabbing up the other stick and whipping it toward me. I knock it down with my own then step forward, using the downward momentum of my weapon to bring the far end up and around to smash into his head. He stumbles back but doesn't go down.

I keep moving forward, not wanting to let up and allow him to move onto the offensive. Kicking out with my front leg, I keep him off balance then bring my stick around again to smash into his side.

The pool stick splinters at the impact. *Fuck.*

I jump back as his weapon whips forward, aiming for my face. I feel the breeze of it on my nose as I retreat around the pool table. Catching my breath, the wide expanse of red felt between us, I take stock of my stick. It's cracked right in the middle. Bringing my knee up, I break it the rest of the way and, with a shorter stick in each hand, smile across at Curly.

Blood drips off his chin from the slash on his left eye, and a red welt is rising on his forehead where I got him. He smiles back at me, a nightmarish figure in black. But I am not afraid.

I take a split second to glance at Petra and Murphy. She's got her chain around his throat—I can see it tight on the back of his neck, making the skin bulge. His arms are up, so I'm pretty sure his fingers are between it and his windpipe.

Curly is circling around the table, and I return my full attention to him. He steps over Michael's collapsed figure and past Buzz, still subdued under Blue, and keeps coming, his stick light in his hands. I fall back into my fighting pose. Left leg forward, right back, arms up, sticks gripped. He settles in across from me, and we begin to circle in the tight space.

When my back is to Michael, Curly lunges forward, and I duck, lashing out at his knees as his stick swings over my head. I hit him in his right knee, and it buckles. As he falls, our faces are at the same height. Twisting, I bring my other stick around and into his nose. Blood explodes and he flies back, his bad knee bending awkwardly, and his other leg splaying out.

I slide forward on one knee and bring an elbow down onto the side of his head. His eyes roll, but he does not lose consciousness. Fumbling, he brings his weapon up, but the guy is dazed, and I easily knock it back. His fingers go slack and the stick drops, rolling away. I bring one of my sticks around, cracking him on the temple. This time his eyes roll into the back of his head and his lids shut. But he's still breathing. For now, anyway.

Panting, I stand up. Michael is still out. Buzz is still under Blue. And now Murphy is on his knees, Petra holding her golden chain tight around his neck. She is looking down into his face, her eyes glittering, blood seeping from a wound on her cheek that is quickly swelling. Damn, she took a punch from that behemoth and is still standing.

"Wait," I say. She glances up at me. "Don't knock him out. We need him to carry Michael."

Petra and I might be able to kill the brothers, but no way are we strong enough to carry them anywhere.

Petra looks down at Murphy for another moment and then releases the tension on the chain. He falls to the side onto his hands and knees, choking for breath.

Petra kicks him in the stomach hard enough that he falls to the side. He rolls away from her, and I pull my gun, aiming it at his head when he stops at my feet.

His eyes are bulging and there are deep, livid impressions in his neck from the thin gold chain. "Come on, sweetheart," I say from behind my gun. "Pick up your brother and let's go."

"What about him?" Petra asks, gesturing to Buzz as Murphy stumbles to his feet.

"You'll fucking pay for this," Murphy wheezes at me.

"You're so not the first guy to say that to me," I tell him before turning to where Blue is still holding Buzz by the throat.

"I guess we should knock him out," I suggest to Petra. She nods. Raising a hand to her face she probes the wound on her cheek and winces. Anger clouding her features, she crosses to the pool table and, reaching over Michael, pulls a ball from the well. "Blue, come," I say as Petra approaches them.

Blue steps back and hops over the prone Buzz to my side. "Get on your knees," Petra says. Buzz rolls onto his side, facing her, and begins to rise to his knees, but lunges out before he gets there, tackling Petra around the waist. As she falls backward, she brings down the 8-ball, cracking it right onto the scar on the back of Buzz's head.

They smash into a table, which collapses under their combined weight, and land with a crash on the floor.

Buzz lies still, and Petra wriggles out from under him and stands, breathing hard. She looks down at her leather pants and silk blouse—the delicate fabric is stained with blood and wrinkled. Her lips go into a tight line as she surveys the damage. Then she picks up her purse from where it landed in the wreckage, reattaches the gold chain with a click, and slips the strap over her shoulder before turning to Murphy. "Pick up your brother. We're leaving."

CHAPTER TWENTY-ONE

Lenox

THE SLIDING door of the van flies open with a loud whoosh, and the damp night air billows in. Four shadowed figures darken the opening. Twisted in the driver's seat, the wheel pressing into my side, I aim my gun at them.

"It's us," Sydney says, the dome light catching the waistband of her indigo jeans and gray T-shirt—a thin spray of blood arching across it. "Put him in." Her voice is a command, rough and low.

An unconscious man is pushed onto the bench seat behind me, helped by a large man with light-colored curls I recognize as Murphy McCain, the youngest brother. I reach back with my free hand to try to help. "Keep your filthy hands off my brother," he growls. My eyes rise to meet his gaze. His eyes, the same blue as a shallow sea over white sand, narrow as they meet mine.

I take my hand back, clenching my jaw to keep from answering. "Shut the fuck up, Murphy," Sydney says, echoing the voice in my head. The smile that pulls at my lips can't be helped. Her East Coast accent is tinged with a British lilt—she used to live in London, and the cadence of their speech is catching, even here in Ireland.

Murphy sneers, climbing into the van and sitting on the bench seat next to his unconscious brother. "You'll all pay for this," he promises.

"I'm pretty sure you said that already." Sydney climbs into the row of seats behind them, the scars on her face, one under her left eye and the other running over that same brow into her hairline, stand out stark under the light until she sits back into the darkness. Her eyes meet mine, and she aims her gun at Murphy before giving me a nod. *She's got them covered.* Blue leaps onto the seat next to her, his ears flattened so as not to brush the ceiling.

Petra gets into the passenger seat and I face forward, trusting Sydney and Blue to have my back. "Where to?" I ask.

"I'll direct you," Petra says.

She leads us through the narrow, crowded streets to the edge of the city. The air is misty, and our headlights are white beams in the night. "Here," she says, pointing down a narrow lane. The road leads out of the city and into the countryside. The houses fade away, and farmland rolls out in dark waves on either side of us.

"Next driveway," Petra says.

A moan from the back draws my attention, and checking the rearview mirror, I see the other brother, Michael, is waking up.

Petra wants me to take their place—steal their business. Make it my own. My lips tighten at the thought. I don't want to be like them.

"What the fuck?" Michael gingerly touches his temple. "Murphy, what the hell is going on?" His confusion is tilting into anger quickly.

"They are taking us hostage, brother. Looks like Petra is leading them to our safe house."

The driveway appears on my left, and Petra points. Taking the turn, we pull onto a gravel drive, the stones crunching under the van's tires.

Tall crops tower on either side of us. The drive leads to a darkened house. The headlights illuminate a stone facade and glinting metal roof. I pull around the circular drive until the side door of the van is facing the entrance to the home.

Petra climbs out and heads to the house as I twist in my seat again, bringing my gun up from where I rested it in my lap. "Who the fuck are you?" Michael asks. His dark blue gaze is shadowed by a large bruise on his temple. With the dome light on, I can see the resemblance between the two brothers. They share strong jaws and straight noses—but where Murphy's eyes are the light blue of shallow waters, Michael's are the navy of deep ocean. Where Murphy is large and bulging, Michael is compact and corded.

Petra returns to the van, sliding back the side door. Beyond her, the house door is now open, yellow light spilling out from the hall. "Come on," she says.

Murphy and Michael climb out, standing sullenly in the drive as Sydney and Blue follow. I turn off the engine and come around as they start up the steps to the house.

It has the musty scent of a place rarely visited. Dust has settled on the empty coat hooks by the entrance, and as we head down the hall to a sitting room, it is obvious no one lives here. The large room is furnished with a sagging couch and several wooden dining room chairs but not a hint of personal effects. Petra has placed rope on two of the chairs, and she gestures for the brothers to sit.

They make eye contact. Will they try to fight their way out of this?

Already having been bested by Sydney, Blue, and Petra, without me even there, the men don't risk another defeat. As they settle into the chairs and Petra begins to bind them, they do not look frightened or nervous. Michael's brow is furrowed in annoyance, and Murphy's jaw is clenched in anger.

Petra, done tying their arms and legs to the chairs, comes around to face them, cocking one leather-clad hip and resting a hand on it. "Well, boys," she says with a smile. "I always did want to tie you up."

Michael glowers at her.

"You've been bad boys," she says, beginning to pace in front of them.

A shiver runs over me. We will never get them to betray their brother, not without torture. But we don't need betrayal. All we need is the location of Mitchel's mother.

Then we can kill them—quickly. With mercy. Ian will come to us once his brothers are gone.

"We have not," Murphy says, sounding almost like a petulant child.

"I wonder," Petra says, stopping her pacing and turning to Murphy. "Do you really not know?" She looks at Michael. "You do."

The older brother does not answer, just stares at Petra, hate burning in his gaze.

"Yes, I thought so. But you Murphy." She shakes her head. "You might actually not know."

That would make killing him a harsh punishment. If he really has no idea what his brothers are up to...

"Let's not worry about that for now, though," Petra says, beginning to pace again. "We need some information from you."

"I'm not telling you shit, you fucking bitch," Murphy says.

"You don't appear to know anything dear," Petra says. She turns to Sydney, raising her brow. "Can you take Murphy into the bedroom? He looks like he could use a nap."

"Sure," Sydney says, looking at me. *Grab the meds from the car will you?* her gaze asks.

I nod before heading for the door. "You her errand boy?" Murphy calls after me. I can't help the smile that creases my face. He is such a Neanderthal. As if getting something for a friend makes me her servant. Sadly, he may never know the pleasure of worshiping a woman from head to toe.

I don't bother responding, just head to the car and grab our bags. Bringing them in the front door, I go to the kitchen, putting the smallest duffel on the empty counter.

Inside, I find the black case, and entering the code into the lock, I open the dart holder. There are two tranquilizer guns inside and ten rounds. We have more in the duffel. Robert Maxim's own design, the weapons have long barrels and large stocks. With exceptional aim, they deliver a dose of tranquilizer large enough to take down a man of three hundred pounds in 1.7 seconds.

I load both guns with the largest vial—one that will make the victim sleep for approximately six hours—and return to the living room. Nodding to Sydney, she turns to Murphy. "Come on," she says. "Time to go."

Blue follows her as she moves behind him and works on the knots

Petra made. Murphy tenses as his hands are released, but I'm standing right in front of him, my weapon trained on his chest. He stands slowly, keeping his gaze on mine. "You're going to die," he says.

"We will all die," I remind him.

"Down that hall to the left," Petra tells us, pointing to a darkened doorway at the far side of the room. Sydney and Blue go first, the restraints dangling from her hand. She flicks on a light, illuminating a bare hallway. Murphy follows her, and I bring up the rear.

Sydney finds the bedroom and steps into it, turning on another light. A single bulb in the ceiling glows to life, bringing into focus a naked mattress and stained pillow.

"Have a seat," Sydney says.

Murphy shakes his head. "Rather die standing," he says.

"I'm not going to kill you now," Sydney assures him, pushing him toward the mattress. He takes a step forward but does not lower himself. "It's your call," Sydney says, firing the tranquilizer into his back. He lets out a sound, not a yelp of pain or surprise, more a grunt of annoyance, before folding up like an accordion, his head landing on the mattress, his legs splayed on the floor.

I pull out my phone and set a timer. *We have six hours until he wakes.*

Sydney crouches at his ankles and begins to tie them together, her movements sure and graceful. Her ponytail has come loose and sprays of blonde hair—brightened from her time in the sun—dance around her face as she works.

Should I help her? A smile plays on her lips. *Then it would be harder to admire her.* And I do so enjoy the artistry that is Sydney Rye. A woman who is so soft-hearted it has made her hard, strong, and dangerous.

She pulls Murphy's ankles up so she can bind them to his wrists. Sydney wraps the rough rope around him, her focus complete. When done, she stands, pulling the band from around her ponytail and scrunching her fingers into her scalp for a moment before wrestling it all back under control.

I laugh when she looks at me. "What?" she asks.

I step forward, and she does not flinch away. *She trusts me.* Her scent wafts over me as I pull the band loose again: the musk of effort, the sweetness of soap, and the spice of a beautiful woman. Inhaling, I run my fingers through her hair, and she stays still, letting me care for her.

The locks detangled, I pull them into a tail, gripping it strongly as I wrap it tight. "There," I say, stepping back. "That's better."

She raises a hand and feels the flat planes of her head. "Thanks," she shrugs. "I've never been good at that kind of stuff."

"Yes." My voice is low and warm. "I know. It's one of the things I enjoy about you."

The slap of palm against flesh draws our attention to the living room, and we move in unison toward the doorway. Petra stands over Michael, her breathing heavy as she raises her arm again, the next slap louder than the last. "You lying son of a bitch," she says, her voice tight with anger and edged with despair.

The sound of a phone pinging comes from Michael's pocket. Petra leans forward and digs around in his jeans, pulling out a slim handset.

She turns to me, her eyes lighting with victory. Holding out the phone, I take it. A text on the screen reads: *Shipment to port at midnight.*

I pass it to Sydney as Petra looks back to Michael. "Is it slaves?" she asks him. Michael, blood staining his lip, does not respond. "Are you using my channels? My houses?" He still doesn't answer.

She holds out her hand for the tranquilizer gun. Sydney hesitates. *We don't know where Mitchel's mother is yet.* Petra lifts her chin, a silent request for Sydney's patience and faith. Sydney turns her gray eyes to me. *Can we trust Petra?*

I give a nod, sending up a prayer that I'm right.

Sydney hands over the weapon, and Petra shoots Michael in the chest. He slumps forward against his binds. "I know where the shipment is arriving." She starts toward the door.

"But what about Mitchel's mother ?" Sydney asks.

"They are all hostages," Petra reminds her. Sydney grabs Petra's arm, dragging her to a startled stop. "Trust me," she says. "They are moving slaves tonight. We stop them, and we will get more answers."

"You said they could be hiding Mitchel's mother anywhere in the city," Sydney reminds Petra of her warning before we left on this mission.

She nods. "But we are getting closer. I promise."

Sydney narrows her eyes. "You better be right. If this is a trap, I'll kill you myself."

"I'm not like them," Petra says, indicating the brothers. "I am a woman of my word."

"We'll see," Sydney says, letting her go.

I follow them out into the night, believing both of them, but unsure of what dawn will bring.

EK

Sydney

THE SEA IS black as ink, the clouds a gray mist, pale and swirling. The wooden dock extends into the fog, disappearing into its depths.

The rumble of the engine reaches us, traveling across the water as clear as a bell calling the faithful to pray. The black bow of a ship emerges from the wall of white, a fog light mounted on the bow barely penetrating the thick mist.

Sitting in the van, hidden by the dark shadows of the parking lot, we watch men jump down to the dock, rope lines stretching behind them. They move quickly and elegantly—choreographed dancers on a dark stage—tying the boat to the dock. The engine cuts, and the night falls quiet again.

Petra climbs out of the front seat. Lenox, Blue, and I follow. The four of us stand in the cool night air, watching. "These men work for you?" Lenox asks Petra, his voice as low a rumble as the ship's engine.

She nods once sharply. "Some of the women will work in my places to pay their passage." By *her places* she means brothels. "Others are passengers paid for by the McCain brothers."

"What are we waiting for?" I ask. These men work for Petra, shouldn't we just walk up to them and find out what the hell is going on?

"The McCains' transport should show up soon. I want them here before I reveal myself." She checks her purse, looking inside the compartment for something then closes it. "I think if they see me, they won't stop."

Time ticks by, and soon a van, bigger than the one we rented, enough seats for probably about fifteen, pulls down to the dock.

Two hulking figures climb out and make their way down the dock, greeting one of the men from the ship. A soft laugh carries to us, then the men from the van head up the gangway onto the boat. *To retrieve their goods.*

Petra starts forward, her breath blooming white around her. Lenox, Blue, and I follow, the gravel of the parking lot crunching beneath us.

As we approach the dock, a guard there, a young man with a thick neck wearing a pea coat, shouts for us to stop.

"Dimitri, it is me, Petra," she says, stepping onto the dock. It sways under her weight, sending ripples out across the water. The guard's shoulders relax, and he grins, his teeth white in the lowlight.

"Petra, what a wonderful surprise." She stops in front of him and takes the clipboard he's holding. "How many do we have tonight?"

"A total of thirty-two. Twenty for our own locations, and then twelve for the McCain brothers."

"Their people are on board getting the girls?" Petra gestures with her chin toward the boat. It's about sixty feet long with a wide beam and rounded at both ends—good for open ocean passages. Dmitri nods in answer to Petra's question.

"And where are the passengers coming from?" Petra asks.

Dimitri's brow furrows in confusion, as if she should know this. "They are coming from Gibraltar."

"Okay, I will wait for them to come out." Petra looks back at us. Her eyes are hard with unspoken anger. The clinking of boots on the deck precedes a tall man appearing at the top of the gangway. Catching sight of Petra, he startles slightly but quickly regains himself. "Who are you?" he barks down the gangway.

"I am Petra Boken," she says, her voice traveling clearly over the still water.

"What are you doing here?" His accent is Irish and thick, his shoulders broad, and a bulge under his coat indicates that he's armed.

"A woman can check on her own business, can't she? Who are you ?" Petra places a hand on a cocked hip.

"Seamus O'Donnel," he answers. "I work for the McCain brothers." A line of shrouded figures, indistinguishable from each other in the night, file behind the man, driven by a second man in the rear.

Seamus starts down the gangway, and the women follow. He reaches us, bringing the scent of tobacco with him. His teeth are stained yellow and his eyes are deep brown. "It's nice to meet you." He holds out his hand, and Petra takes it, shaking once.

"Where are you taking them?" she asks.

Seamus gives her a half smile. "Not at liberty to say."

"Tell me," Petra demands, her voice sharp.

He just shakes his head, laughing it off. "Is this some kind of test?"

"Tests don't usually have such dire consequences if you fail," Petra says. Seamus shifts on his feet, his hand moving closer to his jacket.

"Don't," Petra says, slipping a small silver pistol from the folds of her purse. Lenox and I both stiffen, not expecting it to go this way so fast.

Dimitri, standing beside me, is even more surprised. Seamus's back-up is leaning over the side of the boat behind the line of women, trying to figure out what the holdup is.

"We are going with you," Petra tells Seamus.

He narrows his eyes. "Don't threaten me," he says, keeping his voice low and calm.

"It's not a threat, it's a fact," Petra says. "This is my ship and my passengers. I demand to know where they are being taken."

"The McCain brothers pay the bills for this group. Get your information from them."

"My gun says differently." Petra steps forward and reaches into Seamus's coat pulling out a gun. He puts his arms up, a smile on his lips. Almost like he enjoyed her touch. Petra waves with her weapon, stepping aside so Seamus can lead the way to the larger van. Lenox and I move over, both drawing weapons. Seamus starts forward, Petra stepping close behind him while Lenox and I wait for the man in the back.

The women file past, stinking of body odor and fear. They wear dark, oversized clothing, and their hair is tangled.

Big brown eyes, dark skin, full lips. These women look like friends of mine. They look Yazidi; the preferred religious ethnic group to be enslaved by Isis.

Seamus's back-up pauses halfway down the gangway, pulling a gun.

"What the fuck is going on?" He asks in a broad North English accent.

"I'm not entirely sure," I answer honestly. "Petra is here, and she wants to know where these women came from and where they are going."

He frowns. "Petra?"

"Yeah, it's her boat," I say, gesturing with my gun. "Put the gun away, and I promise we won't hurt you as long as you don't do anything stupid."

The guy is young, with blue eyes and crooked teeth. He looks at the retreating back of the last girl as she makes her way down the dock. I point my own weapon, gesturing for him to follow. He is still holding his gun, a good ten feet from me. I don't ask him to give it up, just to come along.

"It's fine," Dimitri yells to him. *They must know each other.*

The guy continues down the gangway, pausing in front of me for a moment. I keep my weapon down, holding it casually. He does not put his away as he moves past me. Lenox follows, raising up his pistol and clocking the guy in the back of the head hard enough that he drops.

Dimitri lets out a grunt of displeasure.

"Tie him up. Keep him away from phones and weapons until Petra calls you," Lenox says. Dimitri nods.

We follow the women off the dock to the waiting van. They are climbing into the back as we reach the road. Seamus is in the passenger seat, the door open, Petra keeping her gun on him.

"You'll drive," she says to him as we approach. Seamus nods, his expression sullen as he goes around and climbs into the driver's seat. Petra keeps her gun trained on him as she gets into the passenger seat.

Lenox, Blue, and I climb into the back with the women. Their scent fills the enclosed space, their fear ratcheting up now that they've seen the guns. Clearly, something has not gone to plan, but they don't yet realize it's a good thing for them.

I turn around to face them and smile, trying to look nice. Trying to look like I'm there to help them.

"Everything is going to be okay," I say, grinning like an idiot. None of them respond. "Anyone speak English?"

Again, no response. Lenox turns in his seat. "Parlez vous français?"

One girl stirs, seeming to understand, but does not speak up. Her eyes latch onto Lenox, though.

"Tell them we are here to help. Explain we're not going to hurt them," I say.

Lenox speaks in French, and the girl sits forward, her hand coming to rest on the seat back in front of her. *She only has three fingers.* The girl next to her places a hand on Three Fingers's arm, trying to hush her. Three Fingers tightens her lips for a moment, her gaze determined. She answers Lenox, her voice high—she sounds like a child.

Lenox interprets for me. "She asked who we are."

"Tell her we are from Joyful Justice," I say, a knot in my stomach. *How old is she?*

Seamus turns in his seat slightly to look back at me. Petra gets his attention with the gun, gesturing for him to watch the road. "You're working with Joyful Justice?" Seamus hisses at Petra.

"You're dealing in war slaves," she spits back, disgust dripping off each word.

Seamus stiffens but does not respond. Lenox speaks with the girl more, her gestures becoming animated. Blue leans his weight against me, and I close my eyes for a moment and breathe deeply, welling with gratitude that I am me. That I chose this life. That I am here to help these women. That I am not a slave. That I have the power to make the men who did this pay.

THE VAN TURNS into a narrow alley behind a block of townhouses. We are in a residential neighborhood, where the windows all need painting and the stoops droop from decades of use.

Seamus stops the van and cuts the lights. "This is it," he says, meaning the two-story home we've parked behind.

Squares of light from the windows fall onto trash cans where rats scavenge. When Petra clicks her door open, they rise up on their hind legs to watch but do not flee. *This is their home.*

"I'll stay here," Lenox says. "We shouldn't leave them alone." He is turned in his seat, looking back at the women. *They won't be going into this house.*

"Thanks," I say.

Petra nods and climbs out, coming around to open Seamus's door for him. Lenox gets out to let Blue and I onto the street. He waits by the open door of the van as we join Petra and Seamus on the other side.

I glance back at Lenox; he gives me a nod and a breath of a smile. His dark skin almost sparkles in the low light, and his eyes are bright. *That is one powerful man.*

The rats finally flee, bald tails held high, nails scratching on the broken concrete, as Blue starts toward the back door. Unpainted wooden steps wheeze under Seamus's weight as he climbs them. His knock is loud, and the bark of response that comes from the other side is angry.

Clomping footsteps and low grumbled curses filter through the door. The curtain shifts, and a woman peers out at us: sagging cheeks, gnarled knuckles, dull russet brown eyes that narrow as she takes us in.

The lock thunks, and she eases the door open slowly. "You brought friends, Seamus?" Her voice is sharp and rough—like whiskey before it's had time to mellow in a barrel for a decade or two.

"Let us in, Mary, I haven't got time for this tonight. Petra here"—he jerks a thumb at the petite woman holding a gun on him—"wants to see where her cargo lives."

Mary raises a brow and quirks a smile, exposing the dark hole of a missing tooth. "Petra, eh?" Mary's eyes travel down to the pistol in Petra's grip. "You here to take over?" Mary leans against the door, her stained shirt pulling tight against her lumpy body. "Finally getting rid of the McCain brothers." Seamus stiffens and clenches his fist. "You kill them yet?" Mary asks. "Or did you want to see their whole operation before deciding what to do next?"

Petra doesn't answer. She looks almost bored. "Let us in," she says, her voice flat.

"By all means," Mary says, opening the door wide. "We've got nothing to hide, do we, Seamus?" She grins at him, exposing the rest of her yellow teeth—there is another dark hole on the bottom row. *The McCain brothers are not paying this woman enough, clearly.*

We enter into a kitchen; the linoleum floor is yellow with age, the counters stained with generations of cooking. The cabinet doors hang loose on their hinges, giving the whole place a feeling of movement, as if we are on ship that's had a couple rough days at sea.

Blue lifts his nose, scenting the air. It smells of cleaning product. Despite the place's worn appearance, it's kept tidy—no crumbs on the counter, no dishes in the sink. A worn table with three chairs is pressed against one wall. At one place setting, a gossip magazine sits open next to a cordial glass of amber liquid. *Mary must have been having a nightcap while she waited for Seamus.*

"Is there anyone else here?" I ask Mary.

She nods, folding her arms over sagging breasts. "Two girls who came in last night. From the Ukraine, I think. And that old one we've been keeping for a while now. She's in the cell."

"The cell?" Petra asks, her voice a low thrum of anger.

Mary's gaze falls on the younger woman and a smile creases her face. "Yeah, the cell. You sure you got the stomach for this business?" Petra doesn't answer, and Mary lets out a laugh that reeks of liquor. "She tried to escape. Nearly killed herself climbing out the second story window. I didn't have a choice." Mary grins enough so that we see both missing teeth. "Can't have the neighbors asking questions."

"Shut up, Mary," Seamus hisses.

This "old one" doesn't sound like the rest of the girls. We may have just found Mitchel's mother.

Thumps above yank my attention to the ceiling: cracked and water-stained, it's vibrating under heavy footfalls.

"Mary!" A man's voice calls down. "What's the hold up?"

"Keep your mouths shut," Petra warns, then glances at me. I give a nod, and Blue and I head out of the kitchen through the only doorway.

We enter a living room. Directly across from us is the front door. It has two deadbolts and a chain. To my left is a sagging couch, covered in part by an afghan. It is indented at one end as if someone had been watching the TV, which is still on but muted. A twenty-four-hour news station plays. Images of refugees in a tent city flash across the screen, then a female reporter wearing a wind jacket with her network's logo on the breast, and enough make up to hide any humanity, talks into a microphone. To my right are stairs leading to the second floor.

Thumps warn of a descending figure. I draw my weapon and step close to the wall so that anyone coming down the stairs won't see me. Blue presses to my side. A big man in a wife beater and sagging sweatpants appears, rubbing at his balding head. There is more hair on his shoulder than his scalp.

He reaches the bottom of the steps and turns toward the kitchen.

His eyes go wide at the sight of me, his gaze dropping to my weapon. His hands come up automatically. "Hi," I smile. "What's your name?"

"Tom," he answers. "Who are you?"

I grin but don't answer. "Come and join us in the kitchen." He nods and passes me close enough that I can smell the stale sweat and old beer that make up his personal cologne. Blue taps my hip as we follow him to the kitchen. "Have a seat," I suggest. He takes Mary's empty chair in front of the gossip magazine.

"I'll go upstairs," I say to Petra, "And check it out."

"You'll need keys," she says, her gaze landing on Mary.

The older woman nods and goes to a drawer in the kitchen. I stiffen as she reaches in, but all she pulls out is a ring of keys. She really appears to have no loyalty to the McCain brothers. *Is she smart or so beaten down she doesn't care who her master is?*

Mary crosses to me and hands over the keys. "Mind if I sit?" she asks Petra. "I'm thirsty."

Petra nods, and Mary pulls out another chair, reaching for the cordial glass as Blue and I head back to the stairs.

We ease up to the second floor, moving slowly, cautiously, Blue in the lead, his ears perked forward, hackles raised slightly—ready for whatever we find up here.

It's warmer on the second floor, the air stale and stuffy. The disinfectant scent of the kitchen is gone, replaced with the fetid musk of unwashed sheets and old pillows. There are four closed doors. The keys in my hand jingle as I stop at the first. It takes two tries to find the right key but then the lock gives with ease. *It gets used a lot.*

I open the door slowly, the sound of frightened shuffling warning that there are people inside. Two women are huddled together in the far corner. There is a light in the ceiling, and two single beds made up with patchwork quilts. "Hi," I say as Blue passes me, making his way slowly toward them. They grip each other and close their eyes. Tears leak from one—she looks younger. "Blue," I say quietly, stopping him. "We are not here to hurt you," I say to the girls.

There is no recognition in their eyes—they don't speak English. They have mousy brown hair, pale skin, and enough family resemblance to make them sisters or at least cousins. The Ukrainian girls, perhaps. Slaves not of war but of circumstance. I back away, leaving the door open. Letting them know they are free to go.

The one not crying watches me, her brow furrowing slightly, an expression of curiosity fighting the fear. Standing in the hall, I gesture back and forth, some pathetic attempt at miming freedom.

Maybe Lenox will be able to speak to them.

Continuing down the hall, I stop at the next door. Finding the right key, I get it open. The lights are off and the air is still. I find the switch and discover an empty bedroom bigger than the last, this one lined with mattresses on the floor. They are made up with a random selection of sheets. It could almost be the setting of a slumber party except for the bars on the windows, which look new. A lesson learned from Mitchel's mother, perhaps.

Leaving that door ajar, I move on to the third door, and find a very similar scene inside. The fourth produces another empty room filled with mattresses. But no more captives. *Mary said "the cell."* Maybe there is a room in the basement.

There are three more keys on the ring.

Blue and I head back down the hall, and I peek into the first room, finding the sisters still together in the corner, whispering to each other. They gasp when I poke my head in, but when I smile, the older one returns it tentatively. "I'm going downstairs now," I say. "You're safe. And I'm going to help you."

They don't respond, but I get the sense that they've gotten I'm on their side. I'm not going to hurt them. What they have not yet grasped is I won't let anyone else hurt them, either. They've fallen under my protection.

Back downstairs, I find the door to the basement under the stairs. A switch at the top of the steps illuminates a low-ceilinged, unfinished, damp space. Blue goes first, and I hear the scurrying of rodents as they flee him. My steps echo in the narrow space, and when I get down to the concrete floor I have to duck to avoid hitting my head on an exposed beam. Pink insulation puffs between the raw boards. I'm in a dark room with a tiny, filthy window that faces the street out front. To my left is a step down into the utility area, a boiler and pipes snaking to the rest of the house. On my right is a rough wall with a door set into it.

The cell?

Blue sniffs at the gap under the door and then sits, his tail swishing along the filthy floor. I fiddle with the keys until I find the right one. The door wheezes open. It's pitch black on the other side. I reach into my back pocket for my phone to use the flashlight when Blue lets out a low growl of warning. I freeze, holding my breath and listening.

There is tense breathing in the darkness. "I'm here to—" but I don't get to finish my sentence. A figure launches from the blackness, barreling into me. I stumble back, barely keeping my balance before tripping down the one step and slamming into the boiler with a clang that jolts my head.

A fist strikes out, and I block it, instincts kicking in. Another fist flies as a feral scream fills the basement. I grab the wrist and twist, turning my attacker so she lands on her knees, hand behind her back, arm bone at my mercy.

She's panting and struggling, her fear and survival instincts making her a powerful opponent. "I'm here to help you!" I yell. But she doesn't seem to hear me, still struggling to twist away. Blue is sitting next to the door of the cell, his head cocked in question. He does not consider her a threat and appears curious as to why she is acting so crazy.

"Are you Mitchel Swan's mother?" I ask.

That gets her to slow down. She stops struggling and looks over her shoulder at me. Pain and bruising twist her features, but I can see the family resemblance. Mitchel and I worked together in China, and they have the same intelligent, aqua eyes. I recognize them despite the swelling around her gaze—the woman's nose was recently broken, and a storm cloud of colors has ballooned across her face.

"I'm Mitchel's friend." Or at least I was before he betrayed me. "And I'm here to free you."

Her entire body sags, and I let go of her arm, letting her fall forward onto her hands and knees. She starts to sob. She's wearing jeans a size too big and what looks like a man's flannel shirt, the hem ripped in places. "It's okay," I tell her, "you're going to be okay."

She doesn't answer, just continues to cry.

EK

"WE FOUND HER," I tell Dan, keeping my voice down as I stand in the alley next to the van. Blue sits by my side, leaning against me, warming me against the damp night. "She's safe and not seriously harmed."

"Mitchel will be relieved."

I glance back at the house, unable to see anything through the drawn curtains. But I know Mitchel Swan's mother is in the bathroom getting cleaned up. And Lenox is upstairs, trying to speak with the sisters.

"I'll send you our GPS coordinates for the pick-up." Expecting to find prisoners, we arranged with a shelter to take the women in. Joyful Justice has contacts with rehabilitation centers all over the world. We fund several, including one in London, but nothing in Ireland. So, we are working with a local Catholic group tonight.

A pale gray is leaking over the sky. Day is approaching.

My stomach twists and lurches, and I have to swallow against the nausea. *I'm exhausted, and this alley smells like ass.*

"Let me give you the number instead," Dan says. "We can't have any action being initiated from this area. Our systems are supposed to be destroyed."

My stomach gives another lurch, and I start to pace. "They are expecting us though, right?"

"Yes. Don't worry, it's all arranged."

I nod even though he can't see me. "Thanks, Dan."

"Of course." He sounds almost insulted; no gratitude is necessary for doing the right thing. He gives me the number, and I put it into my phone.

"How are you feeling?" I ask.

"Fine." He pauses. "Weirdly excited."

I let out a breath of a laugh. "It's always fun when they think they have us on the ropes."

"Yeah," he says. "I guess that's it. How are you doing?"

"Kind of feel like shit right now, actually," I answer honestly. The image of Mitchel's mother's bruised face, the echoes of her wretched sobbing in that dark, damp space, coming back to me on a wave of nausea. *We'll never do enough.*

"Get some sleep. You'll feel better in the morning."

We hang up, and I turn back toward the house as Lenox opens the door and nods to me. *He's communicated with the frightened girls.*

I dial the number for the shelter and hold my breath as it rings.

The day will be bright before we are done.

CHAPTER TWENTY-TWO

Sydney

ROLLING OVER, sharp pain in my shoulder cracks through my haze of sleepiness, and I moan. A wet tongue licks at my nose, and I roll again, avoiding Blue's ministrations. He whines softly. "I'm okay," I assure him, my breath coming in quick, pain-filled pants. *My lungs hurt too. Actually...everything hurts.*

Blue's nails on the wood floor click around until he's facing me again. He sits, swishing his tail back and forth, staring at me. "What?" I say.

He whines again. *He needs to pee.*

I nod. "Got it." I push myself into a sitting position and wait a moment for the dizziness to subside. Getting my feet onto the floor, I stand, reaching out to hold onto the wall as I make my way to the bathroom.

The mirror tells a sad tale of an abused young woman. My left cheekbone is swollen and there is a gash on my shoulder surrounded by a blooming bruise. Both my hips are bruised. *I hit the ground hard a couple of times last night.*

My knuckles are cut and swollen—the knuckles of an abused woman who fought back. There is a splinter in my palm that I didn't even notice last night. Finding a pair of tweezers in my bag, I pull it loose, sucking air through my teeth. *Why does the littlest shit hurt the most?*

I dump some alcohol on the cut, sprinkle a little on the wound on my shoulder, then pop four Tylenol. Dressing in loose clothing not appropriate for the rainy, cold day, I leash Blue—who looks at me like I'm a traitor for the indignity—and leave the hotel room, trying to walk like I wasn't in a hell of a bar fight last night that ended up with two goons in the hospital and two others tied up in a safe house on the outskirts of town.

They deserved it.

On the street, Blue takes care of business, and then we head to the bakery across the way. *Yeah, coffee is gonna fix this.* The young woman behind the counter is wearing a black apron, thick glasses, and a look of horrified fascination—she pours my coffee and hands me my muffin without mentioning the bruising, but I can tell she'll be thinking about me for days to come.

For a moment, I envy her—a life devoid of violence, where the biggest threat to her survival is an accident. *An accident.* What a wonderful way to live, where fate is the most dangerous adversary.

I worked in a coffee shop once...and I quit. I chose this life. And I choose it anew every day. Fighting for justice hurts like a bitch, but it's worth it every damn time. The faces of the women we saved last night float through my mind. I can't even picture them all clearly. They are a blur of innocence, a sea of features, all worthy of a life free from slavery.

Back in my room, I find Blue's kibble and pour him a big bowl, then reconsider. *He deserves a special treat.* I call down to the front desk and ask for an order of steak and eggs.

Before Blue's breakfast arrives, Petra calls. She and Lenox went back out to the safe house after dropping Blue and me off. They needed to talk, and I needed to sleep. I sip my coffee and spit it back into the cup. *Gross.* The cream must be spoiled.

"Sydney," Petra says for the second time.

"Yeah, sorry, hi."

"The shelter expects us in an hour. I'll knock on your door?"

"Sure. How did it go last night?"

"We will tell you on the drive."

A bellboy arrives with Blue's steak and eggs. I pick at the hash browns while he devours the protein. *I should have ordered a cup of coffee.*

My phone rings again. It's Merl. I catch him up on last night. "Glad you found Mitchel's mother. And it's great you're going to visit the girls in the shelter. Always good to see the positive side of what we do, and not just the bloodshed."

Yeah. My stomach swirls from the few potatoes I had. *Maybe that spoiled milk in the coffee isn't agreeing with me.*

"Any sign of Mulberry?" I ask, a lump forming in my throat.

"He hasn't reached out to anyone."

"Okay."

"Hey, he'll turn up. I promise."

My gaze shifts to the window—it's misty out, and I shiver just looking at it. "Yeah," I agree.

A knock at the door draws my attention. "I've got to go."

"Be brave." Merl ends our call with the saying of Joyful Justice.

"Be brave," I answer back before hanging up.

A wave of exhaustion crashes over me, but I push through it, headed for the door. *There is no time for rest now.*

EK

Declan

IT'S *like being in a cloud. A cold, miserable cloud.*

The air is white with mist. It isn't raining. Just wet. A chill has set into my bones, and all my hours of surveillance under the hot Miami sun are looking like a cakewalk compared to the past few days in Ireland.

Even inside it's damp. Even pressed up close to the fire, a cup of coffee in my hand, two pairs of socks in my new boots, and a scarf snug around my throat, I can't get warm.

My phone vibrates on the table. *Consuela Sanchez.* "Hey," I say, guilt stirring. I didn't call her after the attack in Savannah, just dropped cash on the table for my food and left. I couldn't explain why I was there without explaining what I was up to…and that was not an option.

"Declan." Her slight accent turns my name from something Irish into something Latin, and I like it.

"Just one more question?" I ask, humor warming me. "You're a regular Colombo."

She snorts, and I settle deeper into the cushioned bench, pressing the phone to my ear, practically smelling sunshine.

"I'm assuming you heard."

"About?" *The attack on the McCain brothers' ship last night?* How did *she* hear?

"Joyful Justice. It's gone dark."

I jolt into an upright position. "What?" *That makes no sense.*

"Their website is gone. Not a single peep in twenty-four hours."

"Weird." I'm trying to sound almost uninterested. "Thanks for letting me know." I clear my throat. "What does this have to do with your case?"

"We've rolled the suicide bombing into our task force."

"What does that have to do with Joyful Justice? Was the bomber associated with them?"

The creak of Consuela's chair as she sits back with a sigh reaches across the ocean. "She posted on their forum about 8 months ago, but it doesn't look like she got further than that. Stacy Marcus. Ever heard the name?"

It means nothing to me. "Nope. That's the identity of the bomber?" *It hasn't been released to the press yet. Is she testing me? Or does she trust me?*

"Yes, she was staying at a domestic violence shelter. Left her boyfriend around the time she posted on the JJ forum. Looks like she got into the Her Prophet soon after."

"From what I've read she was wearing a burka, so I suspected as much. She didn't leave a note?"

"Can't say." *That's a yes.* The chair wheezes again. "Just wanted to check in and see if you knew anybody in Joyful Justice you could ask about Stacy."

"Not their style," I say as the waitress approaches with my breakfast. I smile as she puts it down in front of me—a greasy plate of eggs, bacon, and sausage. I wait for the waitress to get out of hearing range before I continue. "Joyful Justice is careful in its targeting. They would never risk civilian lives like that." Memories of the attack come back to me: the acrid scent of smoldering plastic mixed with the stink of burnt flesh.

"It sounds almost like you respect them," Consuela says.

"They are a worthy adversary." She gives a harrumph I can't quite interpret. Either she agrees or thinks I'm being a romantic. "Anything new on your theory?" I ask, my gaze wandering to my iPad. The minivan is still where they parked it last night in the hotel parking lot. Sydney Rye came home alone...where did Petra and Lenox go? Silence stretches. *Consuela is not supposed to talk to me about it.* But she wants to.

"I've confirmed a connection."

"Wow. I'm impressed." *Does she know about Petra?* "How?"

"Can't say."

"Of course not."

"How are you enjoying your vacation?" She changes the topic.

"I'm in Ireland; it's cold and wet. But the landscape is beautiful."

"Discovering your roots?" she says, a smile in her voice.

"Something like that," I answer, my eyes drawn to the iPad as the van begins to move.

"I've got to run," I say. "My tour bus is leaving."

"Enjoy the sights."

"Good luck with your case."

We hang up, and I take another sip of coffee before turning to my breakfast, one eye on the van as it starts through morning traffic.

CHAPTER TWENTY-THREE

Lenox

DARK CIRCLES SHADOW Sydney's eyes, but she gives me a warm smile as she climbs into the van. "How did it go?" she asks.

I shrug. No decisions were made. We left them tied up. Petra wanted to kill them, but without knowing for sure what Murphy knew, how involved Michael was...I just can't murder them. Not like that.

Sydney reaches out a hand and squeezes my forearm, giving me a soft smile. I bow my head in gratitude for her silence. She does not push me.

Petra climbs into the back seat, and I catch her eye in the rearview mirror: sparkling green emeralds in a porcelain mask. She is a classic beauty, delicate features and sharp lines. Her hair is spun up into an elegant twist, and she is wearing a dark, cashmere coat that gives her an air of wealth and sophistication.

Petra didn't want to come to the shelter today, but I made it clear we needed to be on the same page. If we are going to take over the McCains' business operations, we are going to do it knowing what the wrong path reaps.

Traffic is light as we move through the village. The shelter is attached to a Catholic church, a grand and imposing structure. The bell tower rises, disappearing into the mist. Made of huge blocks of granite with delicate stained glass windows, the church is impressive.

Blue hops out and stretches, opening his mouth in a wide yawn then tilting himself forward, stretching his back legs as well. A giant creature of almost unnatural beauty, he matches his mistress perfectly. He moves to Sydney's side, and she rests a hand on his head as we walk toward the church.

In the back is a new structure, and it is here that the shelter resides. The priest who arrived last night to pick up the former prisoners was a short, pudgy man with gentle eyes. He answers the door now, looking more tired than he did at dawn.

"Thank you for taking the time to show us around," Sydney says. He nods, pulling at his cardigan sweater in a small sign of nerves.

"We are very appreciative of the donation."

"It's our pleasure to help an organization such as yours." Sydney reaches out and touches the man's arm. He meets her gaze. "Your work here is very close to my heart."

Her words make my own heart beat faster. This is why I joined Joyful Justice—to help exploited women get to places like this. To make sure they can be safe. To make sure they don't end up as sightless corpses on the beach because of some sick fuck.

I realize my fists are clenched and take in a deep breath to relax them. Sydney and the priest are moving down the hall. Petra touches my arm. "You are tense," she says.

"Tired," I answer.

"We can help many places like this," she says, her gaze scanning the hallway. There are closed doors on either side. We come out into a common area where young women watch TV, read in overstuffed chairs, and play cards.

It's as if a record skips when we enter. I feel suddenly huge and powerful and dangerous among these battered women. Frightened eyes take in my broad shoulders, my dark skin...my very maleness.

I shouldn't be here.

Sydney looks back at me, and I see the same conclusion in her eyes.

210

"I'll wait in the car," I say.

Petra moves with me, and Sydney gives a nod, turning her attention back to the priest, who is explaining the rehabilitation methods of the center.

Outside, in the fresh air, I take a deep breath and close my eyes. "You are a good man, Lenox Gold," Petra says, standing close to me. I glance at her—she is staring out into the almost empty parking lot. "You will do the right thing."

"But what is the right thing here?" I ask. "If we kill Michael and Murphy—"

"We will have done the world a favor." Petra cuts me off, her eyes landing on mine. "And you know it. Will you not take a little darkness into your own soul for the greater good?" Her question strikes me with the force of a blow, and I am stunned into further silence. "Sydney is not afraid of it. She is brave. Truly brave. That woman will do what it takes to make the world a better place."

"Killing isn't always the answer."

She holds my gaze. "Sometimes it is. If we let them live, they will keep doing what they have always done. But if we end their lives, then end Ian's, we can take over their business and change it the way Joyful Justice wants it changed."

I don't answer, still not sure what to do. Is Petra right, or is the fear in my gut?

A child's laughter from inside draws my attention. There are children here? The voice comes again, and I see a figure in the window. It's the younger Ukrainian girl, Viktoria. The McCain brothers promised her secretarial work...a visa, a life. She did not expect to be forced into prostitution.

"What if we could do more?" I say aloud, my thoughts floating out on my voice.

"We can do anything," Petra says, her tone sure.

"Girls like that," I say, gesturing with my chin toward Viktoria in the window.

Petra follows my gaze. "What about them?"

"Girls who just want a better life but don't want to work in the sex industry. Who want to be secretaries and waitresses. Anything in the West. What about them? What if we could help them too?"

"They must help themselves," Petra says, her voice edged with bitterness. I return my gaze to her. She is watching the girl in the window. "I was like that. I did not want to sell my body, but I did. And I freed myself. No one can free you, Lenox. No one but you."

"We freed those girls last night."

She shakes her head. "No, Lenox. We moved them from one situation to another. Now the real work begins. They must free themselves." Petra meets my gaze. "I will fight with you to open doors for girls like that. I will fight with you to make sure every woman who passes through our hands will step through the door with wide-open eyes. But I cannot promise you anyone else's freedom."

Her honesty strikes a chord in me, and I lean toward her—toward those hard lips, those hard eyes, that hard shell around such a human woman. My arm wraps around her waist, and I pull her tight to me, pressing my lips to hers. She melts into me with a soft moan.

So many contradictions: so strong and so supple, so wise and so dangerous.

"Is that a yes?" she says, breathless against me. "You'll work with me?"

Our foreheads press together, me bending down to her, Petra stretching on her toes to reach me.

"Yes," I answer.

"And we will kill Michael and Murphy?" she asks.

I kiss her again, and she bends to me as I bend to her. A partnership is born.

EK

Declan

SYDNEY IS in the garden with the priest. A low stone wall covers them to their waists. Just Blue's head pokes above it.

Sydney looks all concerned and noble.

Damn.

A woman's shelter. When I lost her last night at the dock, she must have taken that van full of women here...to this shelter...to be helped.

I lean against the building behind me and turn up my collar. Still doesn't make it okay she shot me. That she is a vigilante. Even if sometimes she does some good.

God, those girls are young...*and now free because of Sydney Rye.*

Sydney shakes hands with the priest, and after waving goodbye to a few young women enjoying the morning air, heads out the side gate onto the sidewalk.

I follow her, shadowing her on the other side of the street, light traffic between us. My hat is pulled down low, and the collar of my shirt hides my jaw line. Sydney is pale, tired looking. She was out late last night. The bitter taste of defeat is sour in my mouth.

She's a zealot, and I need to take her down.

She's saved all those women.

Fuck.

My hand wanders to my side, the old wound aching in this wet weather. I bet she has a lot of wounds that ache too.

A man crosses the street behind me toward Sydney, tall and lanky, wearing a hat low on his brow. There is something familiar about him. A streak of sun fights through the clouds and catches on a tuft of hair coming from under his hat. It's copper red.

Oh shit.

I'm running at him before I even have a chance to think. He reaches the other sidewalk, his attention riveted on Sydney. Blue turns back and, seeing him, let's out a bark of warning. Sydney spins on her heel, gray eyes flashing in the ray of light.

The redhead's arm comes up, and I smash into him from behind. We fall forward, landing hard onto the pavement, so that his wrist knocks against the curb, and a pistol spins out of his grip and across the sidewalk.

He struggles under me, all long arms and wiry strength. I grab at his wrist and yank it behind his back, getting my knee between his shoulder blades. My hat's come off, and a chill breeze cools my heated face as I find his other hand and pin it as well.

"Declan?" Sydney's voice is right above me.

I glance up, squinting against the white sky. *Shit.*

"Sydney, always a pleasure." I give her a charming smile.

She breaks into a laugh. "What the hell is going on?"

"I just saved your life."

She raises her eyebrows. "Thanks," she says, almost unsure. Sydney doesn't look well. Pale. Sickly, almost.

"You okay?" I ask.

"Better than that guy." She gestures toward the man on the ground. He is breathing hard but has stilled. "Who is he?"

"I'm an avenger!" the man yells.

"Sounds almost like you," I joke. Sydney gives me a wry smile.

"You will pay," the guy sputters. I take a closer look at his face. It's definitely Nathan Jenkins, Billy Ray Titus's right-hand man, last seen in Miami. *Shit. I need to tell Consuela about this...maybe I can get on her task force.* "Men won't take this anymore. We are rising up!"

Sydney rolls her eyes. "Seriously," she sighs. "If it's not one line of bullshit, it's another."

"I'll take care of him," I say, getting to my feet and bringing him with me.

"Here," Sydney reaches into her bag and pulls out a zip tie.

It's my turn to raise my brows at her. "Why do you have that?" I ask, even as I take it and loop it around Nathan's wrists. One is swollen from where it hit the curb, and he lets out a yelp of pain when I tighten the plastic.

"Want me to grab his gun for you?" Sydney asks.

"Don't touch it," I warn.

She takes a step back. "Nice seeing you and all, but I've got to go."

I narrow my eyes at her but just nod. Of course she isn't going to make a report. I'm actually saving Nathan Jenkins' life right now...so he is going to owe me.

Sydney gives me a tired smile. "Nice to see you looking so well. I owe you one," she says before turning and hurrying along the side of the church and disappearing around the corner. *Maybe it is better for Sydney to owe me than for me to imprison her.*

"You can't hold me," Jenkins says. "For I am not one man but many. The revolution has come!"

Oh Jesus. Another fucking revolutionary. *Like there is anything that wrong with the status quo.*

I pull him back and, unwrapping my scarf to cover my hand, pick up his gun, shoving it into my jacket pocket. Then I pull out my phone, and as I push Nathan Jenkins across the street toward my rental car, I call Consuela.

She picks up quickly. "Declan?"

"We need to talk," I say, a smile pulling at my lips.

Lenox

BROAD DAYLIGHT MAKES the safe house where we left the McCain brothers look rumpled, like a throw carelessly tossed over an old couch. The stone facade, wet from the almost-constant misting rain, gives off a chalky scent of mortar and age. Gray clouds swirl in the sky, the tall stands of wheat that surround the house wave lazily back and forth in the wind.

Petra climbs the steps first and unlocks the door, stepping into the dim space and holding the door for me to pass through.

My pupils contract, trying to pull the space into focus. *Something is wrong.* There should be a sense of life in here—the sound of breath.

We left the brothers tied up, gagged, and drugged. *They should not be awake yet.* Does a second dose not last as long?

My hand finds Petra's thin arm as she goes to close the door, stopping her progress. Those green eyes find mine, a question in them. My gaze communicates the concern, and her lips dip into a frown.

Leaving the door ajar, the pale light of a rainy day seeping into the hall, she pulls a gun from her purse. Small, feminine, with a mother of pearl handle, it sends my mind reeling back to the box that held the key to free Elsa.

Petra's betrayal, her dip into the dark side of our profession, rises unbidden, clenching my stomach and sending tendrils of doubt through my mind.

A soft sound, one neither Petra nor I made, yanks my attention back to the hallway, to the house, to the moment I'm standing in. *I am in danger.* But are my only enemies the men we left here...or is Petra still working with them?

Another creak sends my heart thumping and I tense, slowly reaching for my weapon. The blood rushing in my ears deafens me, and I sip in a long breath, endeavoring to calm down. Now is not the time for panic.

Petra moves past me, toward the living room, as I pull my gun from the holster under my jacket. Flicking off the safety, I raise it and follow Petra into the darkness.

Her movements are smooth and practiced, her black cashmere coat velvety in the dull light. She steps to the threshold of the living room and pauses, head swiveling toward where Michael should be tied to a chair. She gives a shake of her head. *He's gone.*

Petra scans the room—only dull shapes and blind spots to me. We are targets here, with the light on our backs. A sound in the wall, the scampering of clawed feet, sends shivers over my skin, drawing sweat down my back. *It's just a rodent.*

The brothers would probably run. Weaponless, wounded, the McCain brothers are better off coming for us later rather than lying in wait. This is their city.

Petra reaches out and turns on the overhead light, moving into the room. I follow, taking in the empty chair, the ropes hanging loose. *Michael must have woken up and worked off the rope.*

She moves slowly through the living room, bare except the few wooden chairs, toward the hall that leads to the bedroom we left Murphy tied up in. Pausing at the top of the hall, Petra takes a steadying breath, her arms still up, gun focused into the darkness. She inches forward and reaches out to hit the hall light.

It baths the narrow space in yellow, exposing nothing and no one. My shoulders relax. *It makes no sense for them to lie in wait.*

The hairs on the back of my neck prickle with sudden awareness, and I turn quickly, dropping low, my knee hitting the hard floor as my eyes focus on the living room behind me. Murphy is backlit by the open doorway, barefoot, holding one of our tranquilizer guns—the long barrel aimed for where my back was moments ago. *He must have followed us in the front door.*

I fire my weapon before he has a chance to react, the sound ricocheting through the old house—so loud, so wrong, in this dull, still setting.

The bullet hits Murphy in the center of his broad chest, widening his pale blue eyes as he stumbles back from the impact. He hits a chair, knocking it over, then falls with it, both crashing to the floor, the wooden chair splintering under his weight.

Labored breaths echo from Murphy as blood pools around him. I stay low, my ears desperate to hear past the pounding of my heart, the dying breaths of the man I just shot, and the blood rushing in my ears. *His brother is next.*

My eyes rake over the entrance hall where daylight still pools. I drag my eyes over the room one more time before turning slowly to check on Petra. She stands behind me, her weapon trained down the hall. *Watching my back.*

Neither of us speaks, both knowing Michael is here. We have one more foe to face...unless they called for reinforcements. The thought sinks leaden weight in my stomach, pinning me to the floor. *But there is no cell service or land line.*

Petra advances forward, the strands of hair that have escaped her twist floating around her. *Careless, beautiful girl. No such thing.*

I blink, centering my thoughts back onto the moment. Rising slowly, I send out my awareness, trying to sense into the rooms that line the hall. There are three. The door of the bedroom where we left Murphy bound is ajar.

As I step forward to follow Petra, the labored breathing behind me stops. I turn back. Murphy's eyes are still open, but he's gone very still. I swallow, staring into those unseeing orbs, a wave of nausea and guilt washing over me, a gentle lapping of the sea, not the rough surf of an angry ocean.

He deserved this fate. The world is better off without him.

Petra makes a noise, small, subtle...surprised. I whirl around. She stumbles, her black coat absorbing the light, making her skin look terribly pale as she hits the wall, her gun still up.

Petra fires, the bullet thunking into the frame of the bedroom door. *There is no one there.* Her hands shake, the gun loosening then falling from her grasp as she slips down the wall. The gun hits the floor first, and I fight my instinct to catch her, instead keeping my weapon up, trained on the empty doorway.

Michael must be in there.

I move forward slowly. When I am next to Petra, I glance down at her. A tranquilizer dart protrudes from her jacket. *But it shouldn't be able to penetrate that thick coat.*

Her breath is coming easily, steadily. Fear races down my spine. *She's faking it.*

Petra's hands lay limp, pale against the dark softness of her long coat. Her face is relaxed, all the lines smoothed out of it. I return my attention to the bedroom entryway but keep Petra in my peripheral vision.

A movement on the floor beyond the doorway catches my eye, and the sharp sting of a needle hits my leg. *He lay on the ground and shot me. Fuck.*

I put out a hand, thumping into the wall, my vision blurring. Michael steps into the hall, a satisfied smile on his face. The edge of my vision darkens. I hold onto the wall, but it's tipping sideways. I try to fire, but I've dropped my gun; my hands have gone numb.

Michael advances, slow and confident. *I'm going to sleep and never wake.*

My mother's voice whispers in my ear... "I love you, my sweet boy."

I failed her.

I slide down the wall, slumping against it in a pile of numb limbs. The weight of my eyelids bears down on me. Michael looms above, grinning, his face blurring from the tears pooling in my eyes.

The bang of a shot jolts me, and Michael stumbles back. Petra leaps after him, a blur of loose hair and flapping overcoat. *A caged animal released.*

My breath comes easily, my eyes drift almost shut. I can't fight it.

Petra's face, blood drops sprayed across her cheek, appears in front of me. She's grabbing my shoulder, lowering me to the ground.

"Sleep, sweet Lenox," she says. "I will take care of you."

My eyes shut, my brain descends into darkness. But one last thought...a warning bubbles up from the depths of my mind...

She will betray you.

CHAPTER TWENTY-FOUR

Sydney

I SHOULD HAVE GOTTEN *my period a week ago.*

Buying the pregnancy test reminds me of my youth...of pregnancy scares with boyfriends. Of the flitter in my heart at the idea of becoming a mother before I was ready.

But this—this lack of *ready*—is nothing I could've imagined.

Mulberry is the father. I have no idea how to reach him. *He will find me.*

The pharmacy is bright and cold, the air-conditioning blasting as I step through the sliding glass doors. *It's hot in Miami today.* Blue, Nila, and Frank follow me in, leashless as always. The woman behind the check-out counter widens her eyes but does not comment.

Dan

IT ONLY TAKES me a few moments to hack into the CVS camera. By then Sydney is moving down an aisle, her dogs in her wake. In blurry grayscale, their progress looks jerky, but I know if I was actually there in that CVS, I'd see how smooth Sydney's movements are...how her dogs almost glide behind her.

She stops and turns to a display. I squint my eyes. *What is she buying?*

She picks up a box and reads it. On another screen, I pull up a layout of the store. Family planning. *Is she buying condoms.* But for who?

Sydney puts the box down and picks up another. She looks down the aisle, checking in both directions. *No one coming.* She turns the box, and that's when I see it...a pregnancy test.

My heart starts to hammer and sweat breaks out on my palms. *Holy shit.*

Sydney turns to check out. *Who the hell is the possible father?*

EK

Sydney

I PAY with cash and accept the bag the cashier gives me. *It's so light.* Stepping back out into the warm night, I turn toward the hotel. *I couldn't be anywhere near Robert's house with this.* Up in my room, I drop the key on the bed and pull the box out of the bag.

No time like the present.

In the bathroom, I read the directions. *Hold the stick under my pee for five seconds.* I do as instructed. *If there is a plus sign in the first results window and a vertical line in the second, I'm pregnant.*

Liquid seeps across the first window, and a horizontal blue line appears. In the second window a vertical line materializes. *No plus sign.*

I put the stick down on the countertop and glance up at my reflection then quickly back down to the test...where a second line has emerged in the first window. *A cross.*

An image of my mother's face flashes before my eyes.

I'm pregnant.

I cover my mouth with a hand to stifle the sob welling up. My heart is thundering in my chest. *I might be sick again.* My eyes jump to my reflection. *Is this joy? Am I happy? Terrified.*

I have not felt fear like this since my brother died. I have not had this much to lose since then. *My God.* I'm pregnant.

$$EK$$

Turn the page to read an excerpt from
Savage Grace, Sydney Rye Mysteries Book 12, or purchase it now
and continue reading Sydney's next adventure:
emilykimelman.com/SvG

$$EK$$

Sign up for my newsletter and stay up to date on new releases, free
books, and giveaways:
emilykimelman.com/News

Join my Facebook group, *Emily Kimelman's Insatiable Readers,* to stay up
to date on sales and releases, have exclusive giveaways, and hang
out with your fellow book addicts: emilykimelman.com/EKIR.

SNEAK PEEK

SAVAGE GRACE, SYDNEY RYE MYSTERIES
BOOK 12

Sydney

I'M PREGNANT.

Gripping the pregnancy test in my hand, I can't stop staring at the blue cross in the window.

Tears start to roll, hot and slow, down my cheeks. I crouch, my knees cracking as I huddle in a low ball, emotion bowing me. My dog, Blue, whines and presses against my side, his warm tongue laving my cheek, his musky scent enveloping me. *A familiar comfort.*

Will my child love Blue as I do?

My phone vibrates on the bathroom counter, and I hiccup a sob. Squeezing my eyes shut, pressing more tears free, I hold my breath. Blood rushes in my ears, and my heart throbs in my chest...a tidal wave is washing me away. *I can't do this.*

The soft ping of a voicemail brings my eyes open. I'm staring at the cross again.

Blue shifts closer, leaning his warm weight against me. As tall as a Great Dane, with the elegant snout of a collie, the markings of a wolf, and mismatched eyes—one blue the other brown—Blue means the world to me.

My heart will have to make room for more.

But everyone I love dies.

Fear slices through me, adrenaline flooding my veins and bringing another soft whine from Blue. Standing quickly, the adrenaline demanding action, I glance at my phone.

Robert Maxim.

He can't know. My eyes trace to the trash can of the hotel bathroom. *Wrap up the test and put it in there.*

But my hand won't follow the advice. My fingers grip tighter, refusing to release the small wand of plastic. *The proof. The truth.*

Grabbing my phone off the counter, I step back into the hotel room. Blue stays close to my hip, his nose tapping my waist once, a gentle reminder he is there.

I shove the plastic wand into my bag, pushing it into a zipper interior pocket and closing it up. Locking it away.

Just throw it out.

I can't.

My hand strays to my stomach, and Blue's nose swipes against my fingers. Vision blurred with tears, I stand in the center of that hotel room, my mind reeling. Lightning sizzles across my vision, and thunder ricochets inside my mind.

Oh fuck me.

$$EK$$

Robert

SYDNEY IS NOT PICKING UP.

My hold on the phone tightens. I close my eyes and take in a slow, deep breath, relaxing my shoulders and consciously unclenching my hand. The news anchor on the television sounds gleeful as he predicts the devastation of the coming storm.

South Florida has never seen floods like this before.

Sydney picked a hell of a week to take some alone time. The mansion on Star Island—an enclave for the richest of the rich in Miami—is hollow without her. *Dammit.* I never needed company before.

My three marriages made this house feel overly full—full of clothing and shoes and purses and jewelry. Full of expectations and conversations. They all wanted so much from me.

I'm not a good husband. I don't love and cherish; I procure and protect. Each wife understood the deal before the wedding, yet inevitably found me lacking. Cold, inhuman, cruel even.

My pampered wives never knew cruelty. But they must have understood my capacity for it.

Sydney isn't my wife, but she knows me. *Really knows me.*

Blue's puppies, Nila and Frank, whom Sydney left with me because one giant dog is enough hassle for most hotels, shift at the sound of footsteps approaching my office. Nila's low growl wakes Frank, who rolls over and promptly passes out again. A guard dog he is not.

A light knock. Must be José, my chef. "Come in."

A Cuban immigrant with a head of hair Elvis would envy steps into my home office. "Can I get you anything?" he asks.

I have no appetite for food but a smile turns my lips. José cares about me—worries like a mother hen. "Some toast, please." José nods and turns to leave. "Brock told you the evacuation plans?"

"Yes," José nods. "I'll go with the rest of the staff. Is Sydney back yet?"

My sour mood floods back. "No, I can't get ahold of her."

"You'll reach her, sir."

I wave a hand of dismissal, staring at my computer screen. Glancing at my watch—a gold Rolex I bought back in '98 when I made my first million—I note the time. If I don't hear from her in ten, I'll hunt her down.

A man can only take so much.

Sydney

"A STORM IS COMING," Robert's voice is calm, but his words bolt terror through me. He knows. "Miami is under an evacuation order. Traffic will be hell. We'll take the helicopter. Where are you? I'll send someone to pick you up." I don't respond. "Funny—" He pauses, and I can hear the TV in the background. "They named the hurricane Joy." *My birth name.*

My mother's face flashes across my mind's eye—thin from her recent injuries, her eyes the same startling gray as mine, lit with a similar fervor.

Robert sighs. "I'm not trying to cut your solo time short, Sydney. I can't control the weather." He sounds disappointed in himself for the shortcoming, and that brings a smile to my lips.

All-powerful Robert Maxim can't control the weather. And he hasn't read my mind. My secret is zipped into a pocket of my purse. The storm is not a metaphor but an actual hurricane bearing down on Florida.

"I'm at the Jubilee Hotel," My throat is still raw from the crying I did earlier, and my voice comes out gritty. "I'm surprised you didn't know that; you're usually such a stalker control freak."

Robert huffs out a laugh. "I'm working on those tendencies."

I sit on the edge of the bed, and Blue leans against my leg. "Thanks for calling." I clear my throat, emotion roughening my voice. "For looking out for me."

I've never thanked him. Probably because he's tried to kill me almost as many times as he's saved me. But still... in his own way Robert Maxim cares. We've taken a long and twisted road marred by potholes, fallen trees, and loose electric wires but the journey has cemented a close friendship. We understand each other.

"You're welcome." There is a note of surprise in his voice. He didn't expect my gratitude. I'm not good at thank you's, or goodbyes... or any of that normal, healthy emotional stuff. "Brock will be there soon." Robert references his head of home security.

My next call is Dan. As the phone rings cross the thousands of miles between us I play with one of Blue's velvety years.

"Hey," Dan's voice is thick with sleep. "Everything okay?"

No! "Sure, sorry if I woke you." I glance at the clock on the side table. It's 2 p.m. here, which means it's 4 a.m. where Dan is, on an island in the middle of the Pacific. It serves as the headquarters for Joyful Justice —the vigilante organization we founded together.

"No worries." He's sounding more awake now. Dan is a computer hacker/genius and often keeps strange hours. If he gets sucked into a project, Dan stays up for days at a time.

"I wanted to check in and see if you had a line on Mulberry..." My voice drifts off into nothingness. Mulberry is another founding member of Joyful Justice, and the father of my child. *Holy shit.*

Mulberry is avoiding me for some valid reasons—after almost dying while searching for me in ISIS-controlled territory, Mulberry lost part of his leg and a lot of his memories. He didn't remember me or any of the trauma we'd experienced together. Mulberry reunited with his ex-wife, and I let him. I didn't fight for him. I should have told him the truth. That I loved him... and he loved me.

Instead, I tried to let him have a safe and "normal" life. A laugh gurgles in my chest at how ridiculous that sounds even as a thought in my head, let alone as a sentence spoken out loud. When Mulberry's memories came flooding back, so did a tidal wave of anger...at me. So, yes, he has valid reasons to avoid my calls, but now I've got a life-altering bomb to drop on him.

"He's still in the wind," Dan says. "He knows I'm looking for him. Took out a bunch of cash and either isn't using a phone or has a burner."

I chew on my lip, staring at Blue. His eyes are closed, his dark lashes fanned over his white fur, as he luxuriates in the ear petting. "Okay, thanks."

"Don't worry," Dan says. I hear him shifting in bed, his voice lowering to calm and comfort me. "He'll turn up."

The last time Mulberry and I saw each other. When... my gaze shifts from Blue to my stomach... Mulberry told me he wanted to be a part of Joyful Justice again. But then he ghosted us. And that is difficult to do. "I need to talk to him. Please Dan, find him."

"I'll keep looking." Dan promises.

"Thank you." We hang up, and I watch Blue for another beat before picking myself up. Brock will be here soon. Eventually, I will tell Dan and the rest of the Joyful Justice council that I'm pregnant. But for now I've got a city to escape, and a secret to keep.

Continue reading *Savage Grace*:
emilykimelman.com/SvG

Sign up for my newsletter and stay up to date on new releases, free books, and giveaways:
emilykimelman.com/News

Join my Facebook group, *Emily Kimelman's Insatiable Readers,* **to stay up to date on sales and releases, have exclusive giveaways, and hang out with your fellow book addicts:** emilykimelman.com/EKIR.

AUTHOR'S NOTE

Dear Reader,

Thank you so much for continuing the adventure with Sydney Rye! I know that's a hell of an ending. You might hate me a little right now—maybe a lot. But the thing is, I don't have much of a say on how these things go. I'm along for the ride as much as all of you.

When I started this series, I only knew a couple of things for sure—Sydney would be a killer and, at some point, become a mother. When James died in the first book, I cried like a baby. I didn't see it coming at all, but it gave Sydney the conviction to kill and began the process for how she evolves through the entire series. And I have no idea what's going to happen with the next book. I'll find out when I start writing it.

But explaining my writing process is not the real reason I'm including this note. It's actually to talk about Ketamine. Maybe some of you raved your problems away with it in the 90's, but for those of you who don't know about Ketamine, it's a powerful drug that is now being used to treat depression and other mental health issues. Research is still being done about how and why it helps, but a couple of people very close to me have recently been treated with Ketamine and found it relieved their debilitating depression. It's kind of a miracle, actually. It is even being administered in some Emergency Rooms for suicidal thoughts with great results.

Like I said, I don't have a say in how Sydney Rye's story goes, but we all have a say in our own stories. So, if you or someone you love is suffering from depression or other mood disorders, please look into Ketamine. There are clinics all over the United States and a lot of compelling research that it helps people.

It doesn't work for everyone, but that doesn't mean it's not worth trying. Even just *trying* to fight depression can help defeat it.

Be brave,

Emily

P.S Let people know what you thought about *Betray the Lie* on your favorite ebook retailer.

ABOUT THE AUTHOR

I write because I love to read...but I have specific tastes. I love to spend time in fictional worlds where justice is exacted with a vengeance. Give me raw stories with a protagonist who feels like a friend, heroic pets, plots that come together with a BANG, and long series so the adventure can continue. If you got this far in my book then I'm assuming you feel the same...

Sign up for my newsletter and
never miss a new release or sale:
emilykimelman.com/News

Join my Facebook group, *Emily Kimelman's Insatiable Readers,* to stay up to date on sales and releases, have exclusive giveaways, and hang out with your fellow book addicts: emilykimelman.com/EKIR.

If you've read my work and want to get in touch please do! I loves hearing from readers.
www.emilykimelman.com
emily@emilykimelman.com

facebook.com/EmilyKimelman
instagram.com/emilykimelman

EMILY'S BOOKSHELF

Visit www.emilykimelman.com to purchase your next adventure.

EMILY KIMELMAN

MYSTERIES & THRILLERS

Sydney Rye Mysteries

Unleashed

Death in the Dark

Insatiable

Strings of Glass

Devil's Breath

Inviting Fire

Shadow Harvest

Girl with the Gun

In Sheep's Clothing

Flock of Wolves

Betray the Lie

Savage Grace

Blind Vigilance

Fatal Breach

Undefeated

Relentless

Brutal Mercy

Starstruck Thrillers

A Spy Is Born

EMILY REED

URBAN FANTASY

Kiss Chronicles

Lost Secret

Dark Secret

Stolen Secret

Buried Secret

Date TBA

Lost Wolf Legends

Butterfly Bones

Date TBA

Made in the USA
Monee, IL
24 September 2024

66555301R00142